"OUR LAST SHILLING"

"OUR LAST SHILLING"

TONY SQUIRE

Contents

I dedicate this book to all who have served in the armed forces, whether in a combat or support arm, each person being part of a well oiled machine, each dependent on one another. When you were needed you were ready. Let no man put asunder.

Cover Information

Cover design by Tony Squire.

Cover photographs are courtesy of the Australian War Memorial, Canberra.

Front Cover (Top):

Accession Number: A02684.

Maker: Unknown.

Place Made: Ottoman Empire, Palestine.

Australian War Memorial Description: 'Thunder of a light horse charge'. This photograph has been described as one of the charge of the 4th Light Horse Brigade at Beersheba on the 31st of October 1917, taken by a Turk whose camera was captured later in the day. An enquiry undertaken with the object of establishing its authenticity revealed that it was probably taken when this Brigade staged near Belah, in or about February 1918 a representation of the charge for a cinematographer. Above is the original caption for this photograph. The photograph has been the subject of controversy, insofar as a number of claims have been made in relation to its origins. Once the prospect of the photograph being taken by a Turkish soldier was disproved, it was thought that the photograph had been taken by 2169 Pte Eric George Elliott of the 4th Light Horse Machine Gun Company. Pte Elliott was said to be operating as a range finder when the charge past him on 31st October. However, it is unlikely that this is a photograph of the actual charge. The real charge took place over bare ground on a slight downwards slope, and the horses were partially obscured by the dust they kicked up. Both riders and horses, unlike those in this image, were carrying all their kit and equipment. As the original caption suggests, it was probably taken when two regiments of the 4th Brigade, Australian Light Horse, re-enacted the charge for the official photographer Frank Hurley, at Belah on 7 February 1918. Hurley's diary records filming such a re-enactment, although none of his footage taken on the day remains. It is probable that another person photographed the event.

Copyright: Item copyright : Copyright expired: Public Domain.

Front Cover (Bottom):

Accession Number: E00833.

Maker: James Francis (Frank) Hurley.

Place Made: Europe: Belgium, Flanders, West-Vlaanderen, Broodseinde.

Australian War Memorial Description: Supporting troops of the 1st Australian Division walking on a duckboard track near Hooge, in the Ypres Sector. They form a silhouette against the sky as they pass towards the front line to relieve their comrades, whose attack the day before won Broodseinde Ridge and deepened the Australian advance.

Foreword

As I mentioned in my first two novels in the ANZAC Chronicles, and will continue to do so, I still find it perplexing why the school curriculum teaches so little about the Great War and the ANZACs. We seem to know almost nothing about the numerous regiments formed during the war or that approximately eight to ten per cent of the country's population at the time, volunteered to fight. Yes, they volunteered - there was no conscription in Australia.

When it comes to the battles they fought, most people are familiar with Gallipoli, the Somme, and the charge of the Light Horse at Beersheba. But how many can say that they know about the battles of Gaza, Lagnicourt, Bullecourt, Polygon Wood, and many more? This is why my novels focus on two Queensland regiments, the 9th Battalion and the 2nd Light Horse Regiment. You may or may not have heard of them; they didn't participate in all the famous battles, but they were involved in many. Through my fictional characters, Archie, Percy and Rueben Taylor, my books aim to bring the Great War to life in full and terrifying detail, for war is not a game, it is a battle of personal survival.

In the first two novels of the series, "...UNTIL YOU ARE SAFE" and "TO OUR LAST MAN", we follow the Taylor boys from their enlistment in 1914 to Gallipoli, then to the parting of ways in 1916 as Percy and the 2nd Light Horse remain in the Middle East, while Archie and Rueben, with the 9th Battalion, head to the Western Front. This third instalment concentrates on the battles of 1917.

As mentioned in the first two books in the series, my main characters are fictional, but their units and the events described are real. For my research, I relied on two remarkable books: "History of the 2nd Light Horse Regiment A.I.F. - 1914 - 1919" by Lieutenant Colonel G.H. Bourne, DSO, and "From ANZAC to the Hindenburg Line - The History of the 9th Battalion A.I.F." by Norman.K. Harvey, BA, AACI. These invaluable accounts, written by those who were there, provide incredible insights into the regiments' formation, trials and eventual return.

In my novels, I strive to mention actual soldiers from these units whenever possible, often featuring my fictional characters alongside real individuals on specific missions. While my characters accompany these men, the glory remains solely theirs, as it should. The battles, dates, and locations in my novels are authentic, and I believe my descriptions convey how challenging a soldier's life was at the turn of the twentieth century, relying mostly on foot travel, or for the Light Horse, their mounts.

I hope I have done justice to their stories and look forward to shedding more light on them in one final novel of the series.

1

"To our last man and our last shilling"

After a year marked by harrowing and terrifying battles, the 9th Battalion remained out of the line for almost two months, finding a rare moment of respite. This pause, however, was not a time for rest; it was a period of intense preparation and transformation. Corps and Divisional Headquarters staff descended upon the men, imparting vital lessons in trench mortars, Lewis Guns, bombing, signalling, and observation - each tactic revised and rewritten based on up to date and hard won experiences of fighting soldiers, like these men, who had faced the enemy firsthand. Those officers and NCOs selected for this crucial training were tasked with passing on their newfound knowledge to their battalions, companies, and platoons.

Reinforcements also began to trickle in from Australia, but this time the volunteers were coming via England, and not Egypt. The newcomers found themselves at Perham Down Camp on Salisbury Plain, where they received invaluable training, before they, and the battalions' newly recovered wounded, were sent to join up with the 9th Battalion on the western front. Upon arrival in France the new recruits were treated to severe final training, for a two week period, at the infamous "Bull Ring" training area at Etaples, preparing them for what lay ahead.

The weather had been bitterly unkind and miserable since the previous October; constantly cold and wet, sapping their spirits. The locals informed the troops that this had been the harshest and coldest winter that they had experienced in many years. The 14th of January 1917 ended the wet spell with a hard frost which swept in, freezing the muddy earth beneath their feet, lasting for three days, only to be exacerbated on the 17th by a very heavy snow fall which blanketed the land, plunging temperatures even lower. It was bitter cold, and the ground was encased in six inches of snow. The mud froze, and on the front lines it was reported that the ground was so solid that eighteen pounder shells ricocheted without penetrating the surface, the earth being frozen to a depth of three feet. Shell holes too were a solid mass of ice, standing as mere ice sculptures, remnants of past violence.

But, despite it being so cold, the change in the weather conditions, encompassed by the fact that they were not in the trenches, cheered the men greatly, improving both their spirits and their health. After leaving the muddy trenches of Flers, most of the battalion were ill in some way or another, and had continued to wear their woollen hats, scarves and gloves, in order to keep warm. Many also wore long woollen underwear, woollen singlets, flannel shirts, corduroy knee breeches, putties, and long gum boots up to the thigh. This, along with their tunic, sheep skin vest and great coat, plus battle equipment and ammunition, left the troops wondering how they were able to move around at all.

In the end the Commanding Officer, Major Neligan, had ordered the men to discard these and kept them active and warm through organised games, exercises, marches and drills. You would have expected the men to rebel against such activities, but no, they relished and enjoyed them, the result being their combined rapid recovery of mind, body and spirit.

Despite all of the activities, the battalion was still regularly on the move; but not towards the fighting.

For the first week of January they had remained at Bazentin-le-Grand before being transported by train to Dernancourt, where they spent another week. Apart from a boxing competition, which added a competitive spirit to the proceedings, something unusual occurred; the battalion was ordered by the Division Commander to observe a three day rest and relaxation period.

"What *is* this army coming to?" joked Captain Ponsonby.

This wasn't the end, as the "rest and relaxation fairy", as Clancy put it, just kept on giving. Bresle was the battalion's next location, and here they spent ten days playing battalion sports on the snow covered fields and, thanks to the money raised by the people of Queensland, a belated Christmas Dinner was held almost four weeks to the day when their time on the front line had prevented them from celebrating. As it transpired, it was fortunate that there was an ample supply of food and beer, as just before the troops were about to partake in their Christmas feast, a batch of hungry new recruits arrived, resulting in the food offerings having to be stretched further than expected.

Nobody minded the intrusion as new men from Australia were always welcome. These young men, dubbed the "Fair Dinkums" by the veterans, had travelled halfway across the world to join them, and though they were inexperienced, they were volunteers to a man and were quickly embraced, met with hearty slaps on the back and a few friendly jabs as they were shown to the mess tent, where a belated Christmas dinner was about to be served.

"Look boyos, another batch of Fair Dinkums," noted Taff as he beckoned them to sit down at the table.

There was no ceremony about it - here, new men were absorbed into the battalion as naturally as if they had been there all along.

As the "Fair Dinkums" settled in, they couldn't help but eye the spread laid before them. It was a feast in every sense - roast goose, potatoes, pudding, *and* even beer. The veterans explained how this was a rare treat. Christmas had come and gone, but their celebration, even though late, was just as good, if not better. The war had no regard for calendars, after all, and the men had learned to make do with what they had, whether that meant a day of quiet in the trenches or a meal that reminded them of home.

The new lads, having spent weeks at sea with little more than ship's rations, were stunned by the generosity. One of them marvelled at the spread before them.

"This... this is better than anything we had on the ship," he said, his voice tinged with awe, "we were expecting Bully beef, so this is a nice surprise".

"Yeah mate, today *is* your lucky day eh," Clancy said, pouring the soldier a beer, "Christmas is wherever and whatever we make it".

As the men tucked into the meal, the veterans offered their new mates tips and advice, little gestures to make them feel at ease. It was more than just a meal; it was acceptance into the battalion family.

On the 24th of January 1917 the battalion was on the move again, this time to Fricourt in northern France. The roads were frozen and slippery and many an ANZAC ended up on his backside, much to the whoops and laughter from their mates; one notable casualty being CSM McBride, who simply scrambled back to his feet, slipping and sliding every which way, smiled and nodded, then carried on marching.

"Hey Clance is that it? No witty remarks?" Roo shouted after him.

Clancy made no reply and slowly raised a two finger salute to his mate, causing a ripple of laughter throughout the ranks of marching men.

"Charming!" replied Roo, whilst tutting and rolling his eyes.

As the men marched, their footsteps caused the surface of the road to become sloppy, which combined with the slippery mud and slush, pitted with shell holes filled to the level of the road with mud, they could only stagger and slide into them knee and thigh deep. The roadside was littered with ammunition limbers and wagons, shattered and broken. Dead mules and horses lay half covered with slush, and the stench of rotting flesh was sickening. The sight was a depressing one, and many an ANZAC cursed the war with every carcass that they passed. These animals had died in harness as thousands of men did, but it was not of their own choosing or will.

The camp at Fricourt had fallen into a state of disarray under the never ending grip of the freezing European winter. The thawing snow had turned the ground into a quagmire, and duckboards crisscrossed the muddy expanse, providing the only means for the men to navigate the treacherous terrain without sinking into the mud. But, this was merely a prelude to their next discomfort. On the 2nd of February, they arrived at Bazentin-le-Petit, yet another uncomfortable camp that offered little respite. Fortunately, their stay there was short lived, and soon the battalion moved on to Albert, where they would find a more stable footing for the next three weeks.

Enemy aircraft were rife all over the allied lines, carrying out strafing and bombing raids at every opportune moment, with Lewis Guns being placed, ready for action, in the event of such attacks.

Roo had a theory about how to down an aircraft based on his experience when hunting for deer and rabbits back home. Clancy was a bit dubious about the whole idea.

"These aren't wild animals mate. They don't stand still do they?"

"Yeah? When have *you* seen a rabbit or deer stand still? I always used to find that if you aim just ahead of the direction of travel you get them every time," replied Roo, "and I bet if a plane was coming straight at you, you could get the pilot no problem".

"Well, maybe we'll get a chance to try it out eh?" said Clancy.

There were concerts and picture shows during their stay at Albert. Charlie Chaplin was the biggest draw for the men, who sought a distance from the war with his innocent comedy routines.

The battalion, however, soon came down to earth with a thud when they began to train and rehearse for an attack which, they were told, was only days away.

The middle of February brought with it a welcome thaw and an end to the frost which had greeted them at the commencement of each day, dampening their uniforms and equipment, as well as the essential firewood with which to build cooking fires *and* keep warm.

"Bloody hell boys," said Clancy, "I reckon we've lived outside for nearly two and a half years now...off and on".

"Yeah, I think my body has forgotten what a bed feels like," added Taff.

"Mattresses stuffed with lovely soft feathers," added Roo as he dreamed of home.

"Feathers? Ours were always straw. You must be one of Freddy's posh mates or something," Clancy quipped.

"Why be uncomfortable when you don't have to be? That's all I'm saying," replied Roo.

"Did I hear someone using my name in vain...again?" asked Captain Ponsonby.

Clancy said nothing, but Roo and Taff pointed directly at him.

"Hmmm, why does that not surprise me?" laughed Ponsonby.

"Bloody dobbers!" said Clancy, smiling like a child who had been caught in the act of doing something wrong.

With the thaw came a thick fog which blanketed the surrounding countryside for most of the month. But, despite the foggy conditions the battalion pressed on with their attack training, practising assaults on trenches similar to those which they would encounter at their objective in the coming days. Much of the information about these trenches was gleaned from the aerial photographs taken by the Royal Flying Corps. For the new men this training was a Godsend and no doubt would see them right in their first taste of battle.

Taff's army bed was apparently calling when the battalion returned to the camp at Bazentin-le-Petit on the 21st of February, but they were annoyed to find it in a very dirty and muddy condition. Any disappointment was soon pushed to the rear as the 3rd Brigade was soon back in the front line, with the 9th Battalion positioned near Eaucourt L'Abbaye, having relieved the 11th Battalion. Here they faced a small enemy salient known as 'The Maze', which was formed by two trenches which met at an angle; 'Bayonet Trench' from the east and 'Gird Trench' from the north west. The point of the angle faced the middle of the 9th's sector of the front line.

As 'B' Company took up their positions Archie scanned the area of no man's land, which he estimated as being one hundred and fifty yards wide.

"At least we're out of bombing range," he said.

"Not the big guns though by the looks of the ground here," replied Captain Ponsonby, as he noted the many craters which scarred the ground to their front, before handing his binoculars to Archie, "take a look five hundred yards forward. That's 'Bank Trench'...the prize...possibly...but it's yet to be confirmed".

"Bank Trench?!" exclaimed Clancy, "they've got some strange place names round here".

"Well I intend to make a deposit...of this," announced Taff as he held up his bayonet.

"I think *bayonet* trench is a good place for *that* mate," said Stowie.

"Better then Gird," said Roo.

"Isn't that a vegetable?" asked Ten Bob.

"Or a gut ache?!" replied Stowie.

Another five hundred yards to their right, along Bayonet Trench, was a sunken road called 'Yellow Cut', and *it* ran to the rear of the enemy. Whilst, five hundred yards to the left of 'The

Maze', along 'Gird Trench', was a similar sunken road known as 'Blue Cut'.

"Yes chaps there certainly are some imaginative names in this section of the front line, but I suspect that a beer connoisseur perhaps christened the rest," said Ponsonby.

Clancy's ears seemed to grow larger at the mention of beer.

"Beer? Now you've got my attention".

"I'm confused with it all now," added Ten Bob as he scratched his head.

"Why are you always scratching? Have you got lice or something?" asked Clancy.

The rest of the group looked around at their surroundings, then Ten Bob shrugged his shoulders, shook his head, and nonchalantly replied.

"Well...yeah...have you not noticed where we are?"

Ponsonby coughed, rolled his eyes and managed a cheeky grin.

"Goodness gracious chaps. Let me explain. We have an 'Oat Lane', 'Rye Trench', plus 'Malt' and 'Wheat' trenches. All ingredients for the amber nectar, as dear Clancy would put it," announced the Captain.

"There's trenches everywhere here, is this why this place is called 'The Maze' skipper?" asked Roo.

"Give my good friend a prize...indeed it is dear Rueben," replied Ponsonby, "Gird and Blue are crossed by 'Bank Trench', and seven hundred yards beyond by 'Oat Lane'. Then about four hundred yards further on we have 'Rye Trench', with the village of Le Barque behind that. At the north west of the village we have 'Malt Trench', while Rye becomes Malt as it moves on to the right, and finally where Rye crosses Blue, about fourteen hundred yards beyond 'The Maze', it becomes Wheat".

"Bugger me...*I'm* confused now," said Taff.

Clancy now interjected.

"Boys, forget all of this rubbish. Think back to what we have been rehearsing in Albert these past few weeks".

"Yeah, that was a bit of a mess, much like a..." said Ten Bob as the penny finally dropped, "a maze".

"Yes mate, from the photos from the flyboys they built a replica of this area," announced Clancy.

"...so...we already know this place like the backs of our hands," replied Ten Bob, feeling quite proud of himself and relieved at the same time.

"Halle-bloody-lulah!" exclaimed Clancy as he slapped Ten Bob across the back of his head.

At the beginning of the month some attacks and artillery feints had been made on 'The Maze' and the trenches near Gueudecourt, and troops from the 1st Division had made a preliminary raid on 'The Maze' on the 10th of February. The raiders had found the enemy resistance stronger than anticipated, resulting in the postponement of the big attack.

Before the battalion had arrived, the area had been bombarded by allied artillery, hence the moonscape which now confronted them.

Using their trench periscope the men surveyed the ground to their front. The landscape was a mangled mess of wire, debris, and deep craters, blackened from countless explosions.

"I don't know how anyone could have survived that lot...look at it," said Archie, swapping places with Taff.

Taff scanned the area and tried to count the shell holes, but gave up. As he sat back down in the trench other soldiers took turns looking through the periscope.

"I don't see how anyone could be out there, there are so many craters, and the wire entanglements and sandbags have all been blown to hell," he said.

Ironically Taff had apparently foreseen his own immediate future as the CSM and Lieutenant Sargent arrived fresh from Company Headquarters.

"Taff me old mate, you must have a crystal ball or something," said Clancy.

Taff looked up at the two men as Stowie slapped him across the shoulder and laughed.

"So, that's why you walk so funny mate".

"Huh?" said Taff, as he suddenly understood the joke, "oh bugger off you dosey Yank bastard".

"Come on fellas this is serious stuff," interrupted the Lieutenant.

"Oh, righto sir...sorry...what is it?" asked Taff.

"Gather up your section, we have a job for you," replied the officer.

On the night of the 23rd and early hours of the 24th of February, Taff and his section were tasked to make their way towards, and recce, the German lines. A thaw now swept through the landscape, bringing with it a renewed downpour.

Initially the section had to make a quick and silent dash, in the darkness, across a small area of open ground before dropping in to the apparently abandoned German forward trench; which they managed without incident. The night felt tense as Taff and his section crept through the trench, their steps muffled by the churned up earth beneath their boots and the rain which was pouring steadily. 'The Maze' was aptly named, a labyrinth of dugouts and narrow passages, barely wide enough for two men to walk abreast. Every now and then, a far off boom of artillery broke the silence, followed by the brief, ghostly illumination of an enemy flare in the distance, casting long shadows across the jagged landscape.

The trench itself was a claustrophobic mess of broken boards and collapsed walls, courtesy of the relentless bombardment by the Royal Artillery. It smelled of damp soil and the lingering sting of cordite. Taff kept his hand firmly on his rifle, the cold metal a strange comfort as his eyes scanned the path ahead in the darkness. The others moved behind him in a silent, tense procession. No one spoke, their breathing barely audible, drowned out by the odd rumble of artillery fire as the enemy carried out the occasional sortie on not only the 10th Battalion's part of the line, but on its own lines.

The section moved slowly, their nerves on edge. The world above them was alien, the barbed wire swayed in the light breeze, its sharp points glinting in the faint light. The posts holding it up were broken and twisted, like the bones of some long dead creature, giving the place an even more desolate feel. The remnants of what once might have been a forest or farmland was now a wasteland, a barren moonscape where nothing moved but the wind. The trench wound on like an endless snake, drawing Taff and his section deeper toward the enemy. No man's land was non-existent here, just a continuous line of trenches leading into the German positions, now eerily quiet. The walls of the trench were jagged, broken in places where the almost constant artillery fire had collapsed the earth. The only structures left standing were the mangled stumps of posts, twisted and bent, and the remains of the wire that once stretched overhead, was now a tangled mess at their feet.

Taff continued on with his men, his breath shallow in the cold night air. The silence was unsettling. Even the distant booms of artillery seemed to have paused, as if the world was holding its breath. Flares were still being launched sporadically in the distance, briefly lighting the sky in pale, sickly flashes, but here, in 'The Maze', it felt like they were the only souls left alive.

As they neared the forward trench line, the oppressive silence grew heavier. The men behind him moved carefully, their boots barely making a sound in the soft earth. Every so often, they'd pause at a junction, Taff motioning for them to wait while he peered around a corner, his heart thudding in his chest. But there was nothing; just more empty trenches, gaping like hollow scars in the landscape. The German lines ahead too seemed abandoned, but no one was ready to trust it.

"That's bloody strange," Taff thought to himself, "there's not a sound or sign of anyone here".

The veteran Corporal was worried. Too many times had the enemy pulled back, waiting to ambush those foolish enough to think they had fled. The enemy lines were somewhere beyond, shrouded in the dark, and the stillness felt like the calm before a storm.

Taff whispered to his men to make their way back to their lines, but to keep an eye out just in case it was a trick. Again they had to clamber out of the German forward trench and make their way across the narrow strip of ground towards their start point, where Taff halted the section and held his rifle above his head to form a T shape, the signal he had pre-arranged with the commander of that section of the trench, thus preventing any needless noise which would carry across the quiet night and alert the enemy of their presence.

As the last man lowered himself quietly into the trench Taff confirmed that all were accounted for and congratulated them on a job well done.

Entering the OC's dugout, Clancy and Captain Ponsonby noticed a worried expression on his face.

"Pick your chin up off the floor mate, you got back in one piece didn't yer?" said Clancy with a smile.

"That we did. But something isn't quite right," replied Taff.

"How so?" enquired Ponsonby.

"Well boyo...er...sir...it was strange see. There were flares fly-ing here, there and everywhere, and even the occasional shell," replied Taff, "but there was not a one to be found".

"What? No one at all?" asked a surprised Ponsonby.

"No sir. Not a soul," said Taff, "reminds me of our exit from ANZAC it does".

"I agree. That *is* rather unusual," replied the Captain as he donned his steel helmet, "come on Taff, you and I are going to report your intelligence to the CO and see what he makes of it...oh...and good work Corporal, I'm glad you and your chaps are all safely returned".

"Safe?! Ha!" Clancy added, smiling.

The CO was taken aback by the news and wondered whether the enemy had retreated or were planning something. His decision in the end was to send out a another patrol for a more detailed recce, but this time in daylight just as the sun was beginning to set, in order to give a clearer view.

At 1700 hours that evening a patrol, commanded by Archie, and consisting of Taff, Stowie, Lance Corporal Griffiths and Privates Charlton, and King, set out. With luck, the day had turned out to be a foggy one, so there was no chance of the patrol being spotted; plus they had the added protection of a newly dug maze of saps which ran from the Aussie to the German lines. Again there was an eerie silence which unnerved the men. Archie, not willing to take any chances, held up his hand to halt his men just as they reached a zig zag bend in the trench. The bends were not only notorious for trip wires but were also a risk of running blindly in to an enemy machine gun nest. As the patrol members stood, hunched, observing in all directions, Archie reached in to his pouches and pulled out a shaving mirror and a pair of pliers, which he used for cutting barbed wire. Placing the mirror in to the mouth of the pliers he slowly moved it forwards so that he could see clearly around the bend, and along the trench.

"Ripper!" Archie quietly exclaimed when he saw that the trench was indeed empty.

Turning to his men he whispered instructions that they were to split into two parties, one going left and the other right. Taff was to lead one of the groups.

"Listen fellas, we need to check and clear every dugout, but I don't want to bring any attention to us, so don't chuck bombs in, just throw something solid," Archie advised, "if its occupied they'll panic and run out straight away".

Each man nodded their understanding, and then the two groups went their separate ways. As suspected each dugout was empty, except for a black cat which suddenly sprang from one of the shelters causing Taff and his small group to jump.

"Bloody hell!" yelped Taff as he leapt backwards, pointing his bayonet at the terrified feline, "I hate bloody cats!"

After twenty minutes both groups were satisfied that the trenches had been deserted, and rendezvoused at the junction.

"How did you go Taff?" asked Archie.

"Same as last night sarge; there's no one yer," the Welshman replied.

For some reason, unknown to the ANZACs, only two nights prior, there had only been twenty men from each enemy regiment occupying the front line trenches, and they had fully withdrawn on the morning of the 23rd, so that by the time their absence had been confirmed they had been gone for thirty six hours. The Germans had begun their withdrawal to the Hindenburg Line, and, for the Australians, what they would later call the Outpost Villages Battles were about to commence.

"Our reputation has obviously preceded us eh boys?" joked Stowie.

"I dunno mate, this is really weird," replied Archie.

Weird or not, Brigade Headquarters saw this news as an opportunity, with orders being issued at 2038 hours, only ninety minutes after the patrol's return, for the 9th Battalion to occupy 'The Maze' forthwith. Patrols from 'A' and 'B' Companies were immediately dispatched. Naturally the CSM tagged along.

Clancy was quite impressed with the German trenches, which had been the objectives of the proposed attack by the battalion, for they were dry and there were some very well constructed dugouts, some of which were packed with large supplies of grenades and flares.

"Hey Roo, these square heads sure have it good eh?" Clancy noted.

"Well, they *have* been here for a while so have had the time to make things comfortable for themselves," replied Roo.

"Yeah, well, it's our turn to be warm and dry now eh?" said Clancy.

The company patrols quickly established defensive positions, and a runner was sent back to Battalion with a message that "all is clear", resulting in the advance of 'A' and 'B' Companies, with 'A' Company occupying 'Bayonet Trench' and 'B' 'Gird Trench'. By 2230 hours a trench two hundred yards beyond the enemy front line, the proposed second objective, had also been occupied.

It had been a good day for the 9th; a two hundred yard advance without any casualties, or a shot being fired.

"I can go for this sort of advance any day of the week," said a relieved Clancy.

"I agree, but it is a little concerning is it not?" replied Captain Ponsonby.

Clancy slapped his mate on the back.

"Oh come on skipper don't put the moz on it, good things do happen *sometimes* you know".

Ponsonby nodded.

"Yes, I suppose you're right dear boy".

"And, before you ask, the boys have had an ammo resupply, and there is more on the way. Gotta love this maze eh, makes a good supply line," said Clancy.

The night didn't go without *some* excitement, with 'Bank Trench', five hundred yards forward of 'The Maze', finally occupied at 0130 hours, following a minor skirmish with some enemy snipers, who were quickly driven out.

Enemy artillery and the shell ravaged terrain caused delays with all patrols. Flares were still lighting up the sky regularly, which did actually aid the patrols, who had been feeling their way along the trenches in the darkness. One fighting patrol even had a contact with the enemy at a point eight hundred yards beyond 'The Maze', but was driven back. Two further patrols later found no signs of the enemy.

Things were getting stranger by the minute.

The remainder of the battalion was now occupying all abandoned German trenches, and the 10th and 7th Battalions had moved into position of the 9th's left and right flanks, respectively.

Drizzle was the men's worst nightmare at this time as it slowly soaked in to their woollen uniforms. Those sleeping in the dugouts were dry for the moment, but would soon take their turn on sentry, or in the work parties who were linking up the old lines with newly created saps, as well as constructing bomb stops; earthen or sandbagged barricades erected across trenches to block them from would be bombing or raiding parties. As they dug and built, they encountered as yet undiscovered dugouts, and went about the routine of clearing them. As Taff lifted the hessian door of one such dugout and tossed in a rock, he heard a sudden muffled yelp.

"Hande hoch!...schnell!...rouse!" he shouted.

"Ein moment," came the reply, "nicht scheezen bitte".

"Did he just say what I think he did?" asked a surprised Stowie.

"Yeah. He wants us to wait a moment...cheeky sod!" replied Taff.

"Come on you buggers!" shouted Stowie.

As Taff and Stowie nervously pointed their rifles into the dugout, two old men dressed in German uniform, minus their boots, came limping out in to the trench. One of them managed a few English words as he pointed to their feet.

"Trench foot...schwartz...nicht gut".

"Too right mate...hey Arch...take a look at these bludgers," shouted Taff.

Archie had been positioning sentries but, job done, moved on down the trench to Taff, Stowie and the two German soldiers. Stowie, mean time, was conducting a search of the dugout.

"Did you just say bludger Taff?" asked Archie with a smile, "I think you're turning into a *real* Aussie mate".

Taff grinned contentedly at the realisation.

"I *am* boyo aren't I? Well that's got to be good then hasn't it? Anyways, take a look at these two's feet".

Archie glanced at the men and their feet.

"Bloody hell, that doesn't look too good Pop," Archie replied as he looked one of the men in the eye, "what are you blokes still doing here?"

"Old men...very sick," replied one of the soldiers.

Stowie heard the German's reply as he emerged from the dugout.

"Not too old to let these off though eh?" he said, holding up a crate full of flares, "I reckon these two were left here to make us think that their regiments were still in place".

The two men grinned, seemingly proud of themselves.

"Well, you did a good job fellas," said Archie, "but I think you both need to see the doc...STRETCHER BEARERS!"

After much tutting and shaking of heads, the stretcher bearers carried the old men off to the Regimental Aid Post.

By 0600 hours a dense fog had descended over 'The Maze', enveloping the area like a thick soup.

"This reminds me of the foggy mornings back home in the winter," said Roo, "it always turned into a sunny day though when it was like that".

"There's no fear of that happening here in this jumped up, never come down place!" groaned Clancy.

"Yeah, it'll probably rain," added Taff.

Roo rolled his eyes.

"Blimey, you two blokes sure have got a downer on you today...come on, cheer up, it'll be spring in a couple of days".

"Spring?! Back home spring was warm. This bloody place is just cold and damp. Knowing our luck it probably *will* rain," replied Clancy.

"Or snow," said Taff.

Roo shrugged his shoulders.

"I give up".

Just then Captain Ponsonby and Archie arrived, along with six company men.

"Did someone say give up?" asked Ponsonby, "hopefully that will just be old Fritz over there".

"Yeah, if we can find him mate," replied Clancy.

"Well chaps, I have *just* the solution".

'B' Company had been ordered to send out a patrol to examine the ground to their front. The fog was still as thick as ever, which was deemed an advantage, but there were other battalion patrols out there...somewhere...so they had to be mindful of them and be extra vigilant. The enemy were definitely out there as there was still the occasional shot.

"It's probably more of those *old* bludgers," said Clancy.

"True. But at least we'll know," replied the Captain.

The plan was for Archie to lead his patrol of six men, plus himself, to examine the trenches ahead of them.

"Do you mind if I tag along Arch? I could do with a break from this sad lot," said Roo, looking over at his mates.

Archie turned to the Company Commander.

"What do *you* reckon skip?"

"I suppose two heads *are* better than one," replied Ponsonby, "but *do* take care...all of you".

It was decided that the quickest and most direct route was to go over the top and across no man's land. As the fog was still thick it also seemed a relatively safe option. The password Waltzing Matilda was decided upon as the Germans had a difficult task in pronouncing the letter 'W'.

"Righto boys, off we trot," said Archie in an upper class accent.

The mud was still not their friend as the eight men nervously clambered over the parapet one by one. There were a couple who could not get out of the mud, their mates offering a hand and pulling them up, but they quickly regrouped, managing to scrape the mud off their weapons before they moved off.

"Listen boys, keep your wits about you and don't fire unless you are sure. Remember, there are friendlies out to our front," whispered Archie, "'Bank Trench' is our objective, so let's get there with no fuss eh".

The patrol formed in to a diamond shape so as not to lose touch with each other. The area was severely cratered, so movement through the fog was slow and undulating to say the least.

Just short of their objective, shots rang out and several moans from wounded men were heard very clearly. Archie immediately threw up his hand signalling the men to halt, then waving the patrol closer towards him and whispering.

"I think those voices are Aussies boys, so we are going to try and find them and help them if we can".

Reaching the edge of 'Bank Trench' they discovered another battalion patrol, from 'D' Company, crouching low within the trench. Their officer, Lieutenant Adams, was dead. Instead of wearing his steel helmet he had decided to wear his slouch hat, perhaps as a bit of bravado; who knows? For his trouble he had been shot in the head by a sniper. As Archie's patrol began dropping into the trench a sudden burst of enemy machine gun fire wounded all but Roo, who had dropped down first. Most had been hit in the stomach, whilst Archie had been shot in the right leg. Luckily none of the wounds were life threatening, as the shots had come from a considerable distance. Any closer and each man would have literally been cut in half. Nonetheless, Archie was annoyed.

"Bugger! Bugger! Bugger!" he shouted, "the first time I've been wounded, and look where we are!!"

As Roo bandaged his cousin's wound, curiosity got the better of him.

"What did it feel like Arch?"

"What?" Getting shot?" replied Archie, "it was like being kicked by a horse, but also it bloody well burns".

Roo checked the other men, who all seemed able to move. He then conversed with the 'D' Company men who informed him that they were holding until 'D' Company had advanced on their position.

Although wounded, Archie was still ruminating on their predicament and called Roo over.

"Mate, do you reckon you can find your way back to company lines and tell them that the battalion needs to advance here now?"

"Of course I can. I *am* part Dingo you know, and besides, I found the station all those years ago didn't I?" replied Roo.

Archie smiled.

"Yes you did didn't you...and only eight years old too," said Archie, "I've always admired you for that; now bugger off and get us some help".

As Roo vanished into the fog, Archie checked his men and ensured that they were in position to meet any assault which might come.

"Check your weapons boys and make sure your magazine is fully charged".

Roo crawled away over the pock marked terrain, sheltering in huge craters, the result of heavy shelling, and managed to get clear of any danger. In the mean time Archie and the two patrols waited for what seemed like forever. One of the soldiers turned to Archie.

"What's keeping them sarge?" he asked, his hands bright red from clutching the wound to his stomach.

"Don't worry mate, Roo will get there, you can count on it" Archie replied, grasping the man's shoulder.

The enemy, however, had other ideas as a single shot suddenly rang out. Some of the Aussies were startled, as one of their number, who had been sheltering at the bottom of the trench, suddenly keeled over, dead.

Shots were now ringing out from their front and sides, and it appeared that the enemy were attempting to surround them. Archie fumbled around in his satchel and pulled out three Mills Bombs, then signalled to his men to take cover, as he pulled the pins and tossed each grenade in a different direction. The bombs obviously reached their targets as several screams of pain came screeching across the battlefield. Pointing to some of his men, Archie calmly called out some snap orders.

"Righto, you four blokes, when I give the order I want you to stick your rifles over the parapet...not your heads...and fire off five rounds each...but not too fast. Have you got it?"

The men nodded as Archie spoke again, this time to everyone.

"Quickly all of you, we are leaving here right now. The fog should shield us as we head back to our own lines. Ready?" said Archie, as the soldiers nodded in relief, "GO! Riflemen...FIRE!!"

The four men fired into the fog as ordered, as Archie turned his attention to the wounded. The trench was deep, and climbing out, especially with injuries, was not an easy undertaking. Two of the unhurt men rushed to help a wounded mate, his leg badly shot through by the rogue machine gun earlier. One man crouched low, bracing himself as a step, while the other boosted the injured soldier up, gripping his arms tightly and hauling him over the edge of the trench. Another pair of soldiers did the same nearby, hoisting a man with a bleeding shoulder, carefully navigating the slick, muddy sides of the trench. Every movement had to be quick yet careful; too much noise or hesitation could cost lives.

Once the wounded were out, the four riflemen scrambled after them, their hands slipping in the mud as they pulled themselves up, panting, following their mates out of the trench and to their rear. The fog thickened, swallowing the sounds of gunfire behind them. As they joined the rest of the group, the party covered their withdrawal with a further volley of .303 rounds and bombs. The race back was now on as the troops, with the wounded on their shoulders or supported between two men, began to make their way across the treacherous waterlogged craters of no man's land, hoping the fog would be enough to shield them from the enemy's sights.

Suddenly, screams echoed from another crater not far off. Archie turned, signalling to two of his men to come with him. Archie grimaced in pain as the three men moved as fast as they could to where they found a huge shell hole, deep and wide, with a young Aussie soldier trapped up to his shoulders in the mud, his face pale with terror. Archie cursed under his breath.

"Bloody hell, we've got to get him out!" one of the soldiers muttered.

Archie quickly came up with an idea.

"Get your rifles, one man in the middle to stretch 'em out, make a chain and let him grab on to it."

The Aussies sprang into action, but it was no use. The chain of rifles couldn't be extended far enough, and every time they tried to reach the soldier, the more the man would struggle, causing him to sink deeper into the mud, the slimy mess swallowing him bit by bit.

"Help me! For God's sake, shoot me!" the soldier pleaded, his voice breaking, but Archie and his men couldn't do it. They couldn't pull the trigger on one of their own, no matter how desperate the situation. So they stayed with him, watching him go down, shaking their heads in disbelief as the man slowly disappeared into the mud; and he died.

Archie's jaw clenched.

"Poor bastard and I don't reckon he was the only one. Thousands of 'em, stuck and gone like that. Bloody thousands".

The two patrols made it back to their lines with no losses, and as their mates helped them down into the trench, the stretcher bearers began their work of treating and evacuating the wounded men.

Roo was there waiting as he imparted the news that 'D' Company had just advanced, whilst 'B' was preparing to follow.

Archie smiled, as he lowered himself to the ground for a rest.

"About bloody time," he said as his mates came to shake his hand and wish him well.

"They finally pinged you eh Arch?" laughed Stowie, "hurts doesn't it?"

"My bloody oath it does mate," Archie replied, his face betraying the pain that he was in.

"Well, I suppose we'll see you when we see you," said Stowie, "don't hurry back, and kiss some of those nurses for me".

Archie laughed.

"Yeah...right," as he beckoned Stowie and Taff closer, "listen fellas, look after yourselves, and keep an eye on Roo for me eh?"

"I think Roo will be the one looking after *us* mate; but yeah we will," replied Stowie.

"Hey you blokes my ears are burning here," announced Roo as he grasped Archie's hand, "take your time coming back. I'll let Perce and the oldies know what happened".

Archie reached up and pulled Roo in close for a hug.

"Thanks mate," he replied, a tear welling in his eye.

"Come on boys...re-union's over...on the stretcher sarge and we'll get you to the RAP," said Private Boyle, one of the stretcher bearers, a recipient of the Distinguished Conduct

Medal for his courageous efforts in bringing in the wounded from no man's land while under fire, along with *his* mates...unsung heroes one and all.

Whilst 'B' Company had been getting ready, 'D' Company had rapidly moved forward with the 7th Battalion on their right flank, and had easily driven off the opposition at 'Bank Trench'. The fog was still very thick, but on they went, collecting another lost patrol, which was led by Lieutenant Shrewsbury, moving in to extended line between Yellow and Blue Cuts. At approximately 1220 hours they were moving down a long, gentle slope between 'Bank Trench' and Le Barque village. The ground was very open and, as they confidently advanced, the fog quickly lifted, evaporating as the afternoon changed to a fine sunny one, revealing much. A few hundred yards to their front they could clearly see their German foe in their trenches. Unfortunately for them the view was reciprocal, as the enemy immediately let loose on them with machine guns and heavy artillery.

The 10th Battalion were with them on their left, but the 7th had been held up further to the rear, so were nowhere to be seen. The battalion and company groups halted and dived for cover in the shell craters to await a lull in the opposing fire.

'B' Company, along with 'C' Company, who were now in 'The Maze', were ordered by the CO to advance and assist the forces who were pinned down ahead. 'C' Company, however, were unable to move as the enemy machine guns had the exact range of their trench, and were now ripping like mad dogs in to the sandbagged parapet. If they were to move now, casualties would be high.

In the mean time Captain Ponsonby's 'B' Company were now advancing cautiously forward, with Roo guiding them towards 'Bank Trench'. Advancing across a cratered and muddy landscape was often a nightmarish ordeal that tested the physical and mental endurance of the men. The once pristine terrain had been transformed into a surreal, hellish wasteland, scarred by constant artillery bombardment and the relentless churn of war. The craters, remnants of shell explosions, pockmarked the ground, and each step was perilous with the uneven and slippery terrain. The men found some of the obstacles unavoidable, wading through knee deep mud, their boots being sucked in to the slimy mud with every laborious step that they took, the weight of equipment and soaked uniforms adding to the physical strain, turning what should have been a straightforward advance into an exhausting and gruelling ordeal. But it wasn't just the mud and the craters, for the ground was also strewn with debris from shattered trenches and the detritus of war, with tangled masses of barbed wire, intended as a defensive barrier, now lying twisted and ensnared in the mud, creating yet another obstacle course that impeded their progress. But they carried on regardless, as they had always done.

The fog had not lifted in this particular section of ground, so visibility was limited, the battlefield obscured. The air too, was heavy with the stench of damp earth and the acrid scent of explosives, and the constant booming of artillery provided a disorienting backdrop to the already chaotic scene. As of yet 'B' Company had not been seen by the Germans, so were advancing unhindered. The NCOs, including Taff, Stowie and Sergeant Mac were quietly encouraging the men as they moved. At first Roo had lost his bearings, but the tell tale sound of .303 fire to their front acted as a beacon towards 'D' Company. As he halted in an attempt to quickly scan the forward ground Roo caught sight of a communication wire. Deciding that it had most likely been laid by 'D' Company signallers, he deduced that if he followed it, it should lead them to 'D' Company.

Grasping the cable with his left hand and running it across the top of his rifle barrel, Roo continued forward with 'B' Company in tow, until they finally located 'D' Company, still sheltering in their craters. After a quick few pleasantries the two companies settled in to await the arrival of 'C' Company who, once the suppressive fire on their trench had subsided, rapidly moved forward to link up with 'B' and 'D' Companies.

Captain Knightly took overall command of the three companies, taking the decision to advance through the shower of artillery and machine gun fire towards 'Oat Lane'.

Being huddled in a muddy trench whilst being subjected to an artillery bombardment was one thing, but advancing *through* it was another. As the companies edged forward the atmosphere was tense, the fog was slowly beginning to evaporate, and the rumble of distant artillery and rattle of machine guns was a constant reminder to the troops of the peril they were now walking towards. Then it came, a deafening roar as the shells hurtled through the air, whining and whistling as some missiles mercifully overshot the lines of Aussie soldiers, exploding in the muddy earth to their rear. But the enemy gunners soon obtained their range as round after round fell amongst the soldiers, the bone shaking impact causing the ground beneath them to tremble with each explosion, the acrid smell of gunpowder hanging in the air, the blasts sending plumes of dirt and debris in all directions, and this, coupled with the deadly brrrrr and rat tat tat of machine gun fire, created a surreal and disorienting atmosphere. As each man looked left and right the constant barrage made it impossible to communicate with their fellow soldiers, the overwhelming noise, making it difficult to distinguish between the thunderous roar of exploding shells and the screams of those caught in the mayhem. Men were falling sporadically all over the line, some hit by bullets, the brutality of the impact tearing through flesh and bone, and simply crumpling to the ground, whilst others with limbs contorted, were thrown violently by the impact. The artillery was doing its worst today too as men vanished into thin air following direct hits, others being torn into pieces, their limbs scattering in all directions. The war machine was having a field day on the 9th Battalion, leaving behind a trail of devastation, but still they kept moving forward.

By the time they had 'Oat Lane' in their sights, at 1530 hours, the combination of bullets, shells, shrapnel and other debris had caused many casualties. Now the men were out for vengeance.

The roar of artillery now faded as the Germans, not wanting to hit their own men, ceased firing, and the sound of explosions was replaced by the frenzied pounding of boots as Captain Ponsonby led his Company across the last stretch of open ground. Clancy, Stowie, Roo, and Ten Bob were among the battered remnants of the three companies, faces streaked with dirt and rage. Taff and Sergeant Mac were nowhere to be seen and, for the moment the fog of war concealed this, with each man now concentrating on the enemy soldiers to their front. The German trench lay ahead; barely fifty yards away, and within its walls, the enemy began to falter, their scattered fire growing thin as the Aussies surged closer.

A wild shout erupted from Roo, echoed by the others, and the Australians broke into a sprint, closing the distance with murder in their eyes. The Germans, realising their impending doom, scrambled to flee, but it was too late. A few managed to clamber out of the trench, running desperately across the torn landscape, but rifle shots cracked behind them, and several dropped mid stride, their bodies tumbling to the ground as the Aussies picked them off with deadly precision.

The first wave of Australians hurled themselves into the trench, boots sinking into the mud. Captain Ponsonby was the first to drop in, firing his revolver twice before he smashed it across a German's face, sending him crumpling to the ground. Clancy followed, bayonet fixed, driving it into the chest of a fleeing soldier, the scream cut short as he twisted the blade free, blood spurting across his uniform. Stowie, his magazine now empty, swung the butt of his rifle with all his might, caving in a helmeted skull with a sickening crunch. The once clean earthen walls of the trench were now painted with gore, the tight space a killing ground.

Ten Bob lobbed a Mills Bomb ahead of him into a dugout, the blast sending dirt and body parts flying, the shockwave rattling the bones of everyone nearby. Whilst Tomo fired into the dugout just to make sure. Shouts in English and German echoed through the trench, but the defence had collapsed, overwhelmed by the sheer violence of the assault.

The battle was one of pure bedlam as the soldiers fought like mad men. Amongst them Roo was making use of his bayonet and rifle as he shot, stabbed and slashed his way through the trench, impaling terrified German soldiers, often yanking his blade free just in time to parry another's thrust. The trench was a madhouse, screams, and shouts mingling with the constant crash of bombs and the crackle of gunfire.

Captain Ponsonby, bloodied but still standing, gave a wild grin to Clancy as they pushed deeper into 'Oat Lane', both men now fuelled by pure adrenaline. The Germans ahead were scattering, with some tossing their rifles aside as they tried to escape the fury of the Australians. No mercy was given and there was no thought or time for such pleasantries as surrender. Stowie and Ten Bob were unyielding, slashing and smashing through the retreating enemy, every swing of their rifles and every thrust of their bayonets adding to the carnage.

A handful of Germans managed to break free of the trench, sprinting into the open, slipping and sliding, some falling on their faces then managing to scramble to their feet. Ponsonby, cool under fire, raised his revolver and fired at the fleeing soldiers, whilst behind him, Clancy and Roo shouldered their rifles, taking careful aim. A few more shots rang out, and several Germans staggered, collapsing in the distance. The ones who made it further were still running, shadows vanishing into the smoke that drifted across the battlefield.

The trench was slick with blood, bodies piled high in corners, but the Aussies barely noticed. Their breath came in ragged gasps, but they had fought like men possessed, their rage for their fallen comrades fuelling the slaughter. The trench, once a defensive line, was now nothing more than a charnel house, filled with death and destruction.

Finally, as the last German fell, gutted by Roo's bayonet, silence descended over 'Oat Lane'. The surviving Australians stood among the carnage, panting, their hands trembling from the sheer ferocity and physicality of the fight. Captain Ponsonby wiped his revolver on the tunic of a fallen German, his eyes scanning the death and devastation around him, as a macabre feeling of satisfaction engulfed him.

"Bloody hell," Stowie muttered, leaning on his rifle.

Ten Bob, his bayonet dripping with blood, gave a grim nod.

'Oat Lane' was theirs, taken by fierce determination and savagery, but at a cost written in the bodies scattered across the mud.

But it was not over, as during the regroup and cleanup phase two machine guns and two enemy soldiers were discovered in a dugout. The men, from the 5th Grenadier Regiment had witnessed the bloodthirsty Australians at work and decided that escape was the better part of valour, as they unexpectedly pushed past their captors and scrambled out of the trench, running for their lives, in a mad attempt to reach their own lines. They didn't bank on young Lieutenant Sargent who was having none of it and, to the amazement of the troops, gave chase, the men whistling and cheering him on.

"Halt! Halt!" he called out, whilst gaining ground on the desperate German soldiers.

As he got to within ten yards of the fugitives the two men dropped to their knees and threw their hands in the air, whilst the Aussie troops cheered and whooped in amazement and delight.

"Nicht scheezen...bitte," one of the Germans blurted out, pleading for his life.

The Lieutenant aimed his revolver at the men. His eyes were wide with anger, and his chest was pumping as he tried to regain his breath, but he quickly calmed himself as he saw the worried expressions on the men's faces. With a jerk of his head he signalled for the men to stand up and walk to the rear, but one of the men instinctively reached to pick up his rifle.

"LEAVE IT!" shouted Tomo, "come on, this way!"

As Lieutenant Sargent and his prisoners reached the Company he was congratulated by Roo and Stowie.

"That was a bloody good run sir...good on yer," said Roo.

Tomo smiled and nodded.

"Thank you Sergeant T; yes I never knew I had it in me".

"You did good mate," said Stowie as he looked around the faces of the remaining men, "hey fellas, you haven't seen Taff have yer?"

"Not since we moved off mate. But he'll turn up; he always does," said Roo, reassuringly.

Stowie wasn't convinced, as with the amount of shells and bullets that had been flying around, anything could have happened.

"Well I'm going back to take a look," Stowie announced.

Roo looked towards Lieutenant Sargent, who nodded, then turned to Stowie.

"Alright Greg, but don't be too long about it," said Roo.

"Greg?!" exclaimed Stowie, "you *must* be serious".

"I am mate...just be careful eh?"

Royal Flying Corps observers, as well as German prisoners, had reported that 'Malt Trench' was heavily defended. By 1700 hours the cold winter night had already closed in, so it was decided to send out a number of patrols to recce it.

Roo led one of the patrols, accompanied by Ten Bob, the two men grimly aware they were the last still standing from *their* original group. Stowie and Taff had not yet returned, and Roo's gut churned with worry. But, there was no time to dwell. There was a job to be done, and thoughts of their missing friends had to be banished to the back of his mind. As one patrol ventured up 'Blue Cut', and Roo's along 'Ginger Cut', a sunken road which branched off from 'Yellow Cut' on the right, between 'Oat Lane' and' Wheat Trench', they prayed that it would be an easy stroll, there was anticipation in the air, every step on the uneven ground echoing in their ears, as they moved cautiously through the trench...but fate had other plans.

A crack rang out, and Roo instantly felt the hot whistle of a bullet skim past his ear. Snipers, hidden among the rubble and debris, tracked the Australians' movements, rifles trained from concealed positions, shooting at them for much of the way. The hand of fate or fortune was on their side though this day as the Germans were having a bad day with regard to accuracy, with bullets striking the ground around them, splintering wooden supports and kicking up plumes of dust, but not finding their mark. Still, the feeling of uneasiness was high, every missed shot a reminder of how close they were to death. Ten Bob, a different man to when he had first joined the battalion in Egypt, gave a low snigger.

"They shoot worse than my little sister, and she's only six".

Roo, surprised by the remark, turned to his mate.

"Your six year old sister has a *gun*?"

"*Yeah..?*" replied Ten Bob, equally surprised by the question. Roo laughed.

"Remind me not to come round to *your* house for tea. Sounds more dangerous than here".

The snipers may have been off their game, but another danger lurked, with many would be assassins hiding, ready to pounce. As the patrol continued on, a shot rang out from a nearby dugout, followed by the sound of a rifle being cocked. Without hesitation, Roo and Ten Bob, and the rest of the men, dropped low and rolled to the side, just as another volley of shots erupted from the dark hole in the earth. They barely had time to register the movement before a shadow lunged at them from the dugout, a bayonet glinting in the dim light. Roo reacted fast, his rifle swung in a brutal arc. The German soldier grunted as the butt of Roo's rifle connected with his jaw, sending him crashing back into the dugout, blood, saliva and teeth spraying from the man's mouth. Ten Bob, quick to follow, lobbed a bomb into the entrance, the explosion rocking the trench, sending dust and dirt into the air, and silencing any further movement from within. The Aussies moved on, not wasting time to check whether the enemy soldiers were dead or alive.

But the battle wasn't over yet. As they advanced, two Germans rushed out of another hole, rifles at the ready, their faces contorted with desperation. Immediately, Roo dropped to one knee, squeezing the trigger. His shot took the first German in the chest, sending him sprawling backward, dead before he hit the ground. Ten Bob fired right after, his bullet catching the second man mid stride, sending him crashing into the trench wall. The soldier was still alive so Ten Bob lurched forward and finished him off with his bayonet , the man twitching for a moment before his soul left him.

A momentary silence fell, broken only by the ever present artillery and rhythmic cracks of rifles to their front and rear. Roo wiped the sweat from his brow, his pulse pounding in his ears. He glanced at Ten Bob, who gave a nod.

"Cheeky buggers!" Ten Bob muttered darkly, "hopefully that's the last of them".

The small band of ANZACs pressed on, muscles taut, rifles at the ready. There could be more enemy concealed in the shadows, but for now, they had survived, dealing summarily with the German soldiers they had encountered.

The Australian patrols had been successful in staving off all attacks, and now held large sections of 'Malt Trench', blocking any attack corridors with wire and sand bags hastily dragged down from the parapet.

At around 2300 hours Brigade Headquarters ordered the 9th Battalion to occupy 'Rye Trench' and connect up with the 12th Battalion on their left. This they managed without incident.

"We'll soon have the ingredients for a beer," joked Clancy.

Ponsonby scratched his head.

"I don't really know if these *are* the ingredients or not you know old chap. I was merely jesting with you."

"Jesting or not *I* could do with one," remarked Roo, resting, having returned from his patrol, "hey Clance, you haven't seen Stowie or Taff on yer travels have you, *or* Sergeant Mac for that matter? It's been nearly ten hours now".

"No mate. But a lot of blokes got knocked by the big guns on the way in, so I don't know what to think," replied the CSM as he caught a glimpse of a familiar figure moving slowly along the dark trench.

It was Stowie. But something wasn't right. The solid framed Texan, renowned for his fierce demeanour in battle seemed distant. As Stowie came in to the light of the flickering cooking fire his mates could see that his eyes were red, and tears were welling up. His tunic was stained crimson and in his arms he carried what appeared to be a full sandbag, cradling it like you would a baby; but the sack was dripping with blood.

"Heyyy…here he is…Stowie me old mate," said Clancy with an uneasy smile.

Stowie was in a world of his own, glassy eyed and stumbling about like someone who had had a few too many, eventually dropping to the floor of the trench, where he carefully laid down his sandbag.

His voice trembled as he spoke; tears rolling down his cheeks. Even Clancy's chin quivered at the sight of Stowie's obvious distress.

"I found Taff," Stowie explained.

Roo felt a sense of relief, but also worry.

"Where is he? Is he wounded mate?" Roo asked.

"It took me all afternoon to find all the pieces...but here he is...in the sack..." Stowie announced as he sobbed uncontrollably whilst pointing at the blood soaked sandbag, "he must have been blown to bits...had to find all of him...you know...for a proper funeral".

Clancy and Roo were devastated, as was Ten Bob. Taff had been one of the originals, along with Archie, Ponsonby and young Jacko, and now *he* was gone. Another name to be etched on stone somewhere, and for what, the actions of a lone gunman three years earlier, and some senseless political pacts?

Captain Ponsonby and Lieutenant Sargent were not aware of Taff's fate when they arrived at the terrible scene.

"What's up chaps?" Ponsonby enquired.

"It's Taff," replied Stowie pointing at the blood sodden sack.

"Taff?" said Ponsonby as he picked up the sandbag, "golly *this* is heavy, what's in...it...my God...poor Taff".

The stunned captain gently lowered the sandbag on to the ground. Taff was *his* friend too yet, despite all of the death he had seen over the years, he did not know what to do.

"What would mother do?" he thought to himself.

Then it came to him as he knelt beside Stowie and threw his arms around his sobbing friend. His embrace was genuine. All present were family. They had endured, laughed and cried together, and now was a time to cry...and so, they did.

Over the next twenty four hours Wheat and Rye trenches were finally captured; 'Wheat Trench' by two platoons from 'D'

Company, whilst later, bombers from the 9th Battalion and men from the 12th Battalion seized 'Malt Trench'. All three of the captured trenches were on the outskirts of Le Barque.

The 9th Battalion men were exhausted, as no doubt every man who had fought along this front was. They had had no sleep or food for four days now, apart from what they had taken with them at the start of the attack. Finally, at about 2200 hours, the 9th were relieved from the front line having expended hundreds of Mills Bombs and countless rounds of ammunition.

As they marched to the rear the men pondered the monetary cost of the war to date.

"I reckon our government must have a money tree or something," Clancy remarked.

"What do you mean?" asked Roo.

"Well, bullets aint cheap are they?" replied Clancy.

Captain Ponsonby was in earshot and quickly added his thoughts.

"Well they did say that Australia would fight to our last man and our last shilling did they not?"

Government finances aside, many ANZACs had been lost over those four days, their mates managing to slip away to stand vigil and say a silent prayer as the fallen, including Taff, were laid to rest, their duty done, never to see Australia's shores again. Some, like their mate and mentor Sergeant MacDonald were gone forever, listed simply as missing in action, their likely fate having been vaporised by a direct hit from an artillery shell; no grave, just their names inscribed on some monument somewhere in the corner of a foreign field.

Each of Taff's mates would pen a letter to his parents who had arrived in Australia from Wales, where the prospects for their son were better than working down a coal mine for a pittance. The Great War had put an end to that. Rhys Williams, Taff, from the Welsh town that was unpronounceable, was no more.

2

No alarms of bugles, no high flags

Since the previous September the enemy had been constructing fortified defences along a line of some one hundred miles distant. The Siegfried Line, as the Germans called it, was the German front line between Arras and Soissons, which formed a salient. A salient, sometimes called a bulge, is a section of the battlefield that juts into enemy territory. This position is dangerous because the enemy surrounds it on several sides, leaving the soldiers inside exposed. The enemy's front line curving around the salient forms a "re-entrant," an inward pointing angle. If the salient is too deep, the enemy can cut off its base, trapping the troops inside without reinforcements or supplies. However, if the soldiers *in* the salient managed to break out through the tip, they *could* strike at the enemy's rear, potentially catching them off guard from behind.

The allied forces knew it as the Hindenburg Line. It consisted of two parallel lines of trenches which were protected by an extremely thick belt of wire entanglements, with a reserve line behind. The line seemed impenetrable. In early 1917 the Germans had swapped the muddy and damaged trenches of the Somme for this line of good, dry trenches, with the added advantage that it shortened their front, and could be held by fewer troops...but for what purpose? The lines' existence had become known to the allies in February, but they had no idea that the Germans were going to withdraw *to* it. The British 5th Army had intercepted a German wireless message indicating their possible retirement, and patrols too had noticed a marked absence of flares and noise on the enemy front line, but Division Headquarters, for some reason, had not been made aware. Corps Headquarters was, however, privy to the 5th Army's wireless interception, but even *they* had not passed the information down the chain of command. Thus, much like the final days at ANZAC Cove, the enemy withdrew under the noses of the allied forces, aided by the fog, without arousing any suspicion.

After receiving reports that the ANZACs were in 'The Maze', the Germans had bombarded their old trenches that night, the 23rd of February, to stop the hounds in their tracks before they got the scent. On the 24th German patrols had discovered 'The Maze' to be empty owing to the fact that the Australians were *actually* advancing. Not what they had anticipated; and it was *these* patrols that had put up the brief fight, before withdrawing to the safety of the Hindenburg Line.

On withdrawal from 'The Maze', the 9th was at first stationed just a short distance from its last held forward position, but the next day they were relieved by the 2nd Battalion and made their way back to Bendigo Camp at Bazentin-le-Grand.

After a day of washing the mud off their uniforms and bodies, it appeared, to those in charge at least, that they were well rested; thus for the following week they became the "let's get tired" parties, as Clancy had referred to fatigue duties at Gallipoli.

"Who the hell thinks of these names anyway?" remarked Clancy, "I mean...*fatigues*...struth!"

"Yeah, it's certainly nothing like any party I've ever been to that's for sure," Roo added.

"Well, I suppose the result befits the name old chaps," added Captain Ponsonby, smiling.

"Not for you though eh...you bludger...what do *you* reckon Tomo?" Clancy asked.

Lieutenant Sargent was taken aback, and felt a little guilty at his perceived laziness.

"I don't mind helping, Sergeant Major," he replied.

"What? And put the snipers out of business?" laughed Ponsonby.

Clancy and Roo joined in the laughter whilst Lieutenant Sargent seemed stumped.

Clancy slapped the officer on the back.

"Haven't you *heard* the story...er...joke?"

"No. What story?" asked Tomo.

"Well, when we were on the front line at ANZAC, Taff, God bless him, was looking through his field glasses along our other units' trenches," Clancy explained, "anyway, in this one trench he said he could see eight men and that one of them was an officer. When I asked him how he could tell that at that distance, he told me that only *seven* of them were working".

Ponsonby chuckled to himself.

"So, Tommy, dear boy, if you don't want to be a prime target you must *always* appear active".

Clancy scoffed, stifling a laugh.

"*Appear* being the right word in you blokes' case eh?"

Another move to Shelter Wood, near Contalmaison, was on the cards, and here they remained for the next two weeks, training in even more new methods. The Great War became a steep learning curve for the armies of the British Empire, and no doubt the Germans too, with outdated frontal assaults becoming few and far between. As they had been doing anyway, the new methods of attack and reconnaissance in small groups were becoming the latest military doctrine. Also, from mid February, specialist Lewis Gunners, bombers and rifle grenadiers, were now distributed at platoon level, rather than being attached to battalion or company headquarters. These men, and their various weaponry, would join smaller groups of men and be employed to attack nests of the enemy, rather than waste lives on senseless battalion level assaults.

On the 23rd of March the battalion moved to Bresle, a strategic region located on the border between the sea and the forest of Normandy and Picardy, famed for glassmaking since Roman times. Here they continued their training, much to the relief of the soldiers, as the camp at Shelter Wood had not been very sanitary when they first arrived.

Twelve days later the battalion was on the move again, this time to Montauban, a historical town, situated about thirty miles north of Toulouse, on the banks of the Tarn River, famed for being largely constructed using the attractive pink stone found in the region. Shanks's Pony was their method of travel and despite the fact that it was the middle of spring, the march there was extremely cold and wet. Everyone's spirits were low, and dampened, literally, by the experience, until the battalion cooks moved along the lines of marching men, with hot tea. This act by the hard working kitchen staff definitely raised morale.

"Hey cookie, you should stick some rum in this tea," Stowie suggested.

"Taste it corporal; you might be surprised," replied one of the cooks.

Stowie inhaled the aroma from his cup and took a sip.

"You bloody beauty!"

"Mum's the word mate," replied the cook, holding his index finger to the side of his nose.

The Germans had completed their withdrawal to the Hindenburg Line by the start of April, but the British and French were close on their heels.

By early April, the shattered remnants of the villages of Boursies, Demicourt and Hermies were the only places on the ANZAC front which had still to be taken, standing as frail barriers between the southern division of the 1st ANZAC Corps and the iron walls of the Hindenburg Line. But plans were already being made for an attack by the 1st Division, with the 3rd Brigade being allocated the capture of Boursies. The Battle of Arras was about to begin.

The 9th Battalion moved up to the front line at Lagnicourt as day descended into night on the 6th of April. Again the day had been cold and wet, and movement through the slimy mud was a slow and arduous task. The Fifth Army's lines were dangerously stretched. The Division was holding a very wide front, forced to cover a staggering twelve thousand yards, with the 9th Battalion being responsible for approximately three thousand yards of it. This was an invitation to disaster for the Germans lying in wait. The line itself was made up of outposts, which were between fifty and a hundred yards apart, with support troops held in the sunken roads.

The first few days were pretty quiet, give or take a few barrages of machine gun and shell fire here and there, until the 12th Battalion attacked and seized Boursies on the 9th of April. The attack had been a bloody affair beginning after a brief but intense five minute bombardment that shattered the quiet of the previous night. At 0400 hours, the battalion had pushed rapidly forward toward a windmill heavily defended by German guns, but typical of the unusual European weather, heavy snow began to fall, blanketing the landscape and hampering the advance of the Australians and all of the Allied troops who now had to trudge with difficulty through deep drifts in no man's land. The darkness still lingered, and visibility across the battlefield was poor, but with the wind at their backs, the soldiers moved forward, the squall of sleet and snow whipping into the faces of the German defenders. The ferocity of the bombardment and the swirling snow had caught many of the Germans off guard so much so that the advance of the 12th Battalion had been undetected until they were halfway to the target, at which point the Germans unleashed a devastating barrage of gunfire, cutting down men in the front lines. The attackers, however, had pressed on with a reckless charge that broke the enemy's defences, forcing them to flee, leaving the windmill bloodstained but in Aussie hands. Some Germans were captured half dressed, stumbling out of their dugouts in the first two lines of trenches. Others, attempting to flee, were stuck in the knee deep slush and mud of the communication trenches, some without even their boots. It was a swift and unexpected blow that shattered their defences. But, the Germans were not done, for as soon as the Aussies had secured the position, German artillery began hammering the newly captured trenches, pounding the earth with unrelenting ferocity. But the worst was yet to come. At 2200 hours, waves of German soldiers launched a fierce counter attack, threatening to overwhelm the Australians. The line buckled under the pressure, teetering on the edge of collapse, but a few soldiers rallied their comrades, pulling reinforcements into the fight, managing to claw back the lost ground in a desperate struggle. After hours of brutal fighting, by dawn on the 9th of April, the exhausted and bloodied battalion had successfully captured the village, but at a tremendous cost; two hundred and fifty six soldiers lost, with over a hundred from the lead company alone. As a result of this sterling work by the men of the 12th Battalion, the 9th were ordered to advance a further eight hundred yards; thus their outpost line was pushed out to that distance.

In their new position the 9th prepared themselves for an assault on Queant. The usual pep talks were being given by officers and NCOs, whilst the CSMs and Quartermaster staff ensured that ammunition and equipment were re-supplied and ample stocks of bullets were on hand in the support trenches for the ammo parties.

On the 11th, the men were still in the same position. At 0600 hours Stowie was peering through a loophole when he noticed some movement about four hundred yards ahead. Looking through his field glasses he spotted what appeared to be a Hun; possibly an observer. He was all alone, himself looking through a pair of field glasses, with his head and shoulders above the parapet. Stowie was still reeling from the loss of Taff and was always on the lookout for enemy soldiers to exact some revenge on.

"What a foolish fella," he thought to himself.

Stowie's loophole was well hidden, a plate of steel or iron, about three eighths of an inch thick, set into the parapet, with a hole just big enough to put his rifle through. There was a big bush of giant nettles growing around the loophole, which added to its invisibility. Stowie slowly pulled back the bolt on his rifle and pushed it forward again, loading a .303 round in to the chamber. He then took careful but quick aim, breathing in and out slowly, holding his breath, then he pulled the trigger. In less than a second the bullet met its target, as the soldier spread his arms out and fell backwards, throwing his field glasses in to the air as he fell.

"Got yer, yer bastard," Stowie uttered in a low voice, the single shot alerting battalion men along the line.

When Stowie saw the man fall a strange thrill shot through him, it was a different feeling to that which he had experienced when he shot his first Turk at Gallipoli, for there was no guilty feeling today, just one of satisfaction. For one instant he felt elated, but the feeling soon passed and he was his normal self again, looking for more targets, but none came, as the battalion's left flank suddenly erupted into a storm of machine gun and small arms fire.

"What the blazes?" shouted Roo as he grabbed a periscope and began observing the commotion, "Look what you've done now".

Stowie shrugged in surprise.

"Nothing to do with me mate".

Stowie was right. The death of the enemy observer was nothing to do with what was now occurring, for, as planned, the 4th Australian Division was attacking the Hindenburg Line. The battle of Bullecourt was on.

Shouts of "STAND TO!" rippled along the battalion lines, and bayonets were clicked on to rifles, as the men prepared for whatever might come at them.

"Gis a squiz Roo," said Clancy.

As he looked through the periscope he couldn't believe his eyes. The Division had attacked as a body of men *only*.

"I thought there were supposed to be tanks with them; and where was the artillery?"

The tanks had failed to arrive in time for the assault, some suffering mechanical difficulties, others simply lost, and it was *they* which were to be the artillery barrage; but it was not to be. The tenacity of the Aussies, however, ruled the day and the 4th Division succeeded in breaking the Hindenburg Line. Yet, whether due to bad planning or the brutal speed of the attack, supplies soon dried up, forcing the Division to fall back, resulting in the 9th Battalion's attack on Queant being cancelled.

Stowie seethed with rage, his mind consumed by vengeance for his fallen mates, Taff and Big Mac.

The following day, however, brought a taste of retribution for him when an enemy patrol unexpectedly popped up about twenty yards to the front of his outpost. The post's Lewis Gun was in the very capable hands of Private "Ten Bob" Kropp, now a seasoned veteran, but this fact made no impression on Corporal Stowe, whose fury had no patience for restraint, as he elbowed Kropp out of the way, grabbed the machine gun from his hands and let rip.

There was no thought of short bursts as Stowie gritted his teeth and the roaring gun drilled into the enemy soldiers, emptying a full magazine and bowling over the unsuspecting patrol. The deafening crack of bullets tearing through flesh was almost drowned out by the cries of the enemy soldiers as they crumpled in a heap, caught completely off guard by the onslaught. Blood sprayed and limbs twisted as bodies fell, but to his disgust and surprise, only two of the enemy were dead, whilst the remainder, some wounded, shaking with terror, instantly threw up their hands. Stowie spat on to the ground and cursed to himself as he begrudgingly beckoned the Germans to the out-post and accepted their surrender.

"Search 'em and sit 'em down over there," Stowie growled, his eyes blazing, as he scowled defiantly at the men, booting each one up the backside as they filed past him with their heads down.

"I thought you were going to kill them all mate," said Ten Bob, feeling somewhat relieved.

"Mate, I might be mad as hell, but a murderer I aint," replied Stowie, a calmer expression on his face, "besides, I want to know why old Fritz withdrew, yet now he's sending out recce patrols. Something aint right".

The next day, the 13th, a post of twelve 9th Battalion men was ordered to advance six hundred yards towards Queant, most likely as a result of the previous day's enemy incursion.

On the 14th the battalion was relieved by the 12th Battalion, trudging back toward the sunken roads near Morchies. Al-though the relief was officially completed by midnight, the muddy quagmire beneath their boots stretched the march into an agonising crawl. Men slipped, cursed under their breath, and grumbled about the impossible terrain and, as the hours dragged on, the muddy ground meant that it took an age for most of the men to finally reach the rendezvous point.

"Bloody hell, Stowie," muttered Ten Bob, his voice barely above a whisper as he steadied himself on a half buried tree root, "it feels like we're marching through a flamin' swamp".

Stowie gave a low grunt, wiping mud from his brow with the back of his hand.

"A swamp would be drier," he muttered, "keep moving, mate. Can't be far now".

Nearby, Roo stumbled in the dark, catching himself just before he hit the ground.

"This better be worth it," he whispered hoarsely, "if I see another bloody ditch, I'll throw myself in and sleep there!"

Clancy, shuffling along beside him, gave a quiet chuckle.

"We'll be lucky if we even find the rendezvous point before dawn," he whispered back.

The men struggled on, teeth gritted against exhaustion, their whispered complaints swallowed by the night. When they finally reached the rendezvous point, hours had slipped away, and most of them collapsed into the mud where they stood, too tired to even grumble anymore.

On the 15th of April Stowie's question about the enemy's intentions was finally answered. Because the British and Empire forces were pressing closer to the Hindenburg Line, they had swiftly launched a major offensive around Arras. This aggressive push had left their defences overstretched and vulnerable in key areas, including Lagnicourt. Recognising this weakness, the Germans seized the opportunity to strike back, launching a counterattack, at 0400 hours, in the Lagnicourt sector, with twenty three battalions. In an expertly conceived stealthy manoeuvre, they managed to slip through a gap between the flanking positions of the 12th and 17th Battalions, catching the defenders off guard. However, their objective wasn't to hold the territory for long, but to disrupt the Allies by occupying Lagnicourt for a single day, and capturing or destroying as much equipment and supplies as possible.

The companies of the 9th had been deployed to support the 12th, whose Battalion Headquarters was located in the back of a sunken road, one thousand yards to the rear of Lagnicourt, close to a cross roads. The front line in this sector was approximately one thousand yards in front of the village. About a mile and a half behind the 12th Battalion's headquarters, was Vaulx-Vrau-Court, and another thousand yards to its left, was the Lagnicourt Valley, and in that valley were some Aussie field artillery pieces and their crews. The Noreuil Valley, a mile further left contained even more Australian artillery.

The lightning speed and overwhelming numbers of German infantry rapidly surrounded the 12th Battalion outposts and supporting picquets, and although they put up a determined fight they were forced to withdraw.

The enemy then quickly overran the village, seizing several artillery batteries from the 1st Australian Division, and as the enemy onslaught surged forward, fighting erupted in the Lagnicourt Valley at around 0530 hours. The Gunners there were in an impossible situation and, knowing that all was lost, stripped their guns of their breech blocks and withdrew with them, the artillery pieces falling into the possession of the enemy.

"We'll be back later!" shouted one defiant gunner.

For almost two brutal hours, pandemonium engulfed the battlefield. The German assault had burst like an unremitting tide, overwhelming the 1st Division's forward artillery batteries and swallowing Lagnicourt in a deadly storm of bullets and steel. The village trembled under the weight of the onslaught as the Germans continued their advance past Headquarters 12th Battalion in the direction of Vaulx-Vrau-Court. But the Australians refused to break, and, against the overwhelming numbers, they stood defiant. At this moment in time every man was required to do his bit, with Lieutenant Colonel Elliot, the 12th Battalion's CO, calling out cooks, signallers, batmen and all Headquarters staff and placing them at the side of the sunken road to the front of the headquarters. From this position they laid down a devastating fire on the enemy who, by now, had managed to penetrate almost two miles behind the Aussie front line.

Ten minutes earlier a 12th Battalion man had arrived at the bivvie area of 'B' and 'D' Companies, which were on the road between Morchies and Maricourt Wood. Apart from sentries the men had only just settled down for a few winks. Clancy was doing his rounds when the man rushed in and dropped in to their trench. His news was startling to say the least.

Clancy grabbed the man's webbing strap as he rose to his feet.

"What's the rush mate?"

The soldier took a few breaths and, with a gulp, blurted out his message.

"The Germans have broken through in their thousands!"

"Eh? I haven't heard anything," replied a stunned Clancy.

"No, they snuck in...no artillery...no nothing".

"Bloody hell! Sneaky bastards...STAND TO! STAND TO!" Clancy shouted, "get up unless you want to be killed in your beds".

"Beds?!" asked a surprised Stowie, his eye brows raised.

"You know what I bloody mean!" replied Clancy.

Like his men, Captain Ponsonby had just managed to drift off in to the land of nod when he felt someone hit him on the leg with a stick and yell out.

"THE BOSCHE HAS BROKEN THROUGH!"

Ponsonby was wide awake immediately, he and Lieutenant Sargent dashing down to the 'D' Company commander, Captain Boylan.

"Have you heard? The Hun have broken through our lines," Ponsonby asked.

"Yes mate," replied Boylan, "I reckon we need to fix bayonets and line the road to the front of the bivvie area to meet the buggers when they get here".

Ponsonby nodded his agreement and turned to Lieutenant Sargent.

"Tommy, go and pass the word to the CSM would you old boy?"

"Consider it done sir," the Lieutenant replied as he turned and ran towards the company lines.

At first the troops thought the officers were having them on due to the fact that the enemy had advanced without a sound. Not even a shot. But once the shooting broke out minutes later, no one required further convincing.

The speed of the German advance soon became apparent when the Gunners, who had been overwhelmed earlier, came running towards them.

A message from Lieutenant Colonel Elliot also arrived with orders for the 9th Battalion companies to advance.

"I bloody *knew* something wasn't right!" exclaimed Stowie.

Ponsonby led their respective companies forward in artillery formation; small clusters of men moving in calculated waves, in the hope of minimising casualties should the inevitable barrage of shells rain down. The air was tense, heavy with anticipation, every man knowing that the quiet was only a cruel calm before the storm.

Both OCs deployed scouting parties to their front. Roo, as usual, led 'B' Company's party, his eyes constantly scanning the horizon. As his section crested the top of Lagnicourt Valley, the sight before them was staggering. They could see very plainly that it was indeed a target rich environment, with the enemy as far as the eye could see, an unbroken sea of grey clad figures stretching out across the battlefield like a living carpet, filling the ground like a vast colony of ants.

As he observed through his binoculars, his hands steady despite the growing unease, Roo made out what appeared to be the 12th Battalion's headquarters; but something was off. Had it been overrun? The sight was unclear, but the danger was very real.

"Bugger!" Roo muttered under his breath before turning to his men, his voice now more urgent, "we'd better let the skipper know".

The scouting party edged slowly to their rear, carefully, each man keeping low, their eyes never leaving the distant enemy; their hearts pounding. The muffled crunch of their boots on the dirt and the rasp of strained breaths filled the silence. The enemy was closing fast.

When Roo's report reached Captain Boylan, his fury was instant. His face hardened as he turned to Captain Ponsonby.

"Freddy, I'm taking my company in now to counter attack," Boylan snapped, his voice a mixture of urgency and rage.

"Right, 'B' will come with you in support," Ponsonby replied, his tone calm but firm, "I'll get a message to battalion for more men".

As they moved out, the landscape seemed to pulse with tension, every distant sound amplified by the stillness before battle. By the time the two companies reached 12th Battalion's headquarters at 0620 hours, there was a noticeable sense of relief; the headquarters *hadn't* fallen. However, the Germans *were* advancing towards it, the ground almost trembling beneath their boots, distant sounds of enemy artillery growing louder, the first sounds of an advancing storm.

Colonel Elliot was grateful for the arrival of the two companies and immediately deployed them along the road with his rag tag band of support staff, quickly forming a defensive line, rifles snapping into place, hearts pounding in unison. As they crouched in position, eyes locked on the enemy advancing from the dawn haze, the far off thunder of shells began to merge with the sharp, distinct chatter of German machine guns.

Adrenalin was now flowing fast and furious through each man's body, but they remained calm and steadfast as they had always done.

NCOs and officers alike now walked the line of men dispensing encouraging words.

"I don't know about you blokes but I haven't had my brekkie yet and I'm bloody starving, so let's get this done," Clancy joked.

"Yeah mate, these Bosche aren't very considerate are they?" Roo added.

"Well alright then...let's eat *these* bastards for breakfast then boys!" shouted Clancy, much to the delight of all in earshot.

At two hundred yards, they came, the horizon erupting with grey uniforms charging forward, their war cries barely heard over the rising roar of battle. Then, the swelled defensive line began its work as over three hundred Aussie rifles, and the odd Lewis Gun, opened fire, the once tranquil French countryside seeming to explode as the rifles rang out in unison. The sharp crack of each shot cut through the air, and the distinctive rattle and rat tat tat of Lewis Guns joined the fray, their rhythmic bursts spraying lead into the mass of bodies. The sound was deafening, a wall of noise as rifles spat fire, bullets whistling through the air, tearing into the enemy with brutal efficiency.

Men screamed. The German front ranks crumpled under the firestorm, bodies collapsing. Arms flung wide as they were thrown to the ground. The dirt erupted in small geysers of blood and soil as the bullets found their marks. Limbs twisted in unnatural angles, soldiers fell in heaps, their comrades stepping over the bodies, edging forward into the deadly hail. Some clutched at their throats, choking on blood, while others staggered forward with fatal determination, only to be cut down in a blaze of gunfire.

The smell of gunpowder hung heavy in the air, mingling with the sharp, metallic tang of blood, and the acrid smoke from the rifles and machine guns mixed with the dust kicked up by explosions, turning the battlefield into a choking, blinding fog. Yet even through the smoke, this fog of war, the Aussie riflemen could make out flashes of pale faces, contorted in pain, wide eyes staring blankly as life drained away, the ground beneath the advancing Germans rapidly becoming a crimson morass, slick with the blood of the fallen.

Despite the devastation wreaked upon them, the Germans pressed on, their shouts now drowned by the din of battle. But the Aussies held firm, each man independently firing at will, the soldiers almost trance like, firing, lifting up their bolts, pulling them back, pushing them forward again and squeezing the trigger, their individual rounds adding to the constant volleys from their defensive line, cutting through the enemy ranks, men collapsing like wheat before a scythe.

The screams of the wounded and dying filled the gaps between the rifle shots, the horror of the scene overwhelming the senses. But there was no time to think. No time to stop. The Aussies reloaded, fired, reloaded again, their rifles becoming extensions of their bodies, their world narrowing to the small strip of land between them and the charging enemy.

The Germans were barely two hundred yards away, but they would get no closer. Not today.

"I hope we can hold them mate," said Clancy to Ponsonby.

Looking to the rear Ponsonby suddenly smiled.

"What's up with you mate, have you got wind or something?" Clancy quipped.

"No, look," said Ponsonby, pointing.

The remainder of the 9th Battalion and two companies of the 20th Battalion were moving forward at the double. As they reached the forward line Ponsonby shouted to his men to advance towards the enemy. It was just after 0700 hours, and the

Australian battalions were now mounting a fierce counterattack.

As the battalion and a half of ANZACs surged forward to join forces with the other battalions on their flanks, the battlefield erupted with the sharp, rattling crack of heavy machine gun fire from Lagnicourt. The first bursts tore through the advancing line, downing twenty men from the 9th Battalion, their bodies hitting the dirt hard. Blood soaked through their uniforms. They were wounded, but not seriously, with some even managing to clamber to their feet and rejoin their mates. That was it for the Aussies. Whereas others may have fled, the enemy machine gun assault had lit a fire in their hearts and they advanced like a triumphant Roman Legion, their bayonets flashing in the light of the rising sun like the fangs of a beast ready to tear into its prey, the sun casting their silhouettes long over the muddy ground.

The Germans had obviously not counted on this determined wall of steel, and panic began to set in as they watched the Aussies closing the gap with terrifying speed, their machine gun fire losing its effectiveness as fear took over. What was once a well co-ordinated assault crumbled before the dogged advance of the ANZACs. The Germans began to falter, their ranks breaking apart as soldiers turned and fled. Boots pounded on the blood soaked earth, their retreat now a desperate flight for survival. But escape was no longer an option, as the British were now placing a barrage between the Germans and their rearward escape route.

With a shrill whistle, the shells screamed overhead, their high pitched wails piercing the air like messengers of death. The first explosions tore into the fleeing Germans, detonating with a concussive force that lifted men off their feet, ripping through their ranks in clouds of dirt, shrapnel, and blood. Bodies were torn apart in the blasts, limbs and chunks of flesh thrown skyward as the shells ripped open the earth, turning their escape route into a slaughterhouse.

The barrage was unyielding; pounding the Germans as they ran, shell after shell slamming into the ground with brutal precision, cutting off any chance of retreat. Explosions sent fountains of dirt, twisted metal, and gore flying in all directions. Men were vaporised where they stood, while others were thrown like rag dolls, their screams lost in the deafening roar of the artillery, the ground beneath their feet becoming a quagmire of blood, churned earth, and broken bodies.

What moments ago had been an organised retreat was now a scene of utter carnage. Germans crawled on hands and knees, dragging themselves through the mud, their once pristine uniforms now stained with blood and filth. Some tried to shelter in shell holes, only to be swallowed by the next blast, whilst others staggered forward, disorientated and shell shocked, their faces masks of terror as the walls of smoke and fire closed in on them.

The ANZACs, who had halted just short of the barrage now watched from their positions, bayonets still at the ready, as the enemy was obliterated before their eyes. The barrage was doing their work for them now, cutting down the Germans in waves, leaving nothing but shattered bodies in its wake. Within minutes, a confident enemy attack force had been reduced to a writhing mass of the dead and dying. The few Germans still standing were barely recognisable, their uniforms tattered, their faces gaunt with horror. Some still clutched their rifles, but their hands shook uncontrollably, their spirits crushed by the sheer devastation that had befallen them.

The ANZACs didn't need to cheer; the sombre satisfaction of the battlefield was enough. This was the price the enemy had paid for underestimating them, and the Australians marched on, their path cleared by the wrath of the Royal Artillery and their Australian counterparts.

The Australian infantrymen soon passed by the enemy front line and began leaving Lagnicourt, which was on their right. Seeing a great opportunity, Lieutenant Wittkopp, with a band of men from the 9th and 12th, entered Lagnicourt and bagged a haul of prisoners.

Meanwhile the artillery barrage was still on the far side of the village, pounding away, but causing a temporary halt of the advancing Aussies, their advance stalled under the threat of friendly fire landing too close. Dirt kicked up from a shell hit nearby, sending everyone crouching instinctively. Captain Ponsonby wiped the sweat from his brow, squinting at the mayhem ahead.

"Damn it, we're like pheasants ready for the taking here!" he muttered under his breath.

He turned to the battalion signallers, who had been following behind the advancing line, laying communications wire as they went.

"How are you doing with comms chaps, are we up and running yet?"

One of the signallers nodded, frantically adjusting the wires.

"Cable's good, sir! We're connected!"

"Good show chaps, now let's get this artillery range lengthened shall we?" Ponsonby replied as he held out his hand for the hand set.

After a tense moment of static and muffled voices, he spoke calmly, but clearly into the receiver:

"This is Captain Ponsonby, 9th Battalion...location Lagnicourt village. We need to advance. Shift barrage forward two hundred yards from current fall of shot...immediate effect!"

The response came quickly, the crackle of the line barely masking the urgency on the other end. Ponsonby nodded to himself and handed the receiver back. He then turned to his men.

"Artillery's moving up...prepare to advance...we've got ground to take!" Ponsonby shouted, rallying his men with a wave of his hand.

As the creeping barrage moved on, the Aussies pushed forward again, determined to break the enemy lines and finish what the enemy had started.

In this modern war, all arms interoperability was beginning to come in to its own. As the battalion moved forward through the haze and dust, their eyes caught sight of a Royal Flying Corps Airco DH4 bi-plane soaring low over the enemy lines, giving the Germans some bursts with its Vickers machine gun, much to the delight of the troops. The aircraft's engine growled above them, louder than the distant boom of artillery.

Clancy shaded his eyes, looking up at the plane.

"Would yer look at that? He's certainly giving *them* what for eh?" he said with a grin, nudging Roo, who was grabbing a quick gulp of water from his canteen.

"Well, he's got guts, flying that low," Roo replied, his voice tinged with admiration.

But not all of the men were convinced.

"What's he playing at?" Stowie muttered, watching as the DH4 veered away from the German trenches, only to loop back for another run, "he's not just having a crack at them with his gun...look at the way he's circling".

Ten Bob frowned, peering through a pair of field glasses.

"I reckon he's trying to tell us something, he's flying low enough to scare the skin off a snake".

Ponsonby, who was crouched behind a mound of dirt, joined in.

"Actually he's spotting for the artillery chaps".

A shell exploded in the distance, close to the German lines. Then another...even closer. The men ducked instinctively as a third came down, this time right where the aircraft had been only moments before.

"Bloody hell," Clancy said, grinning, "you're right, that bloke's telling the big guns where to aim".

Stowie scratched his head.

"But how is he doing that?"

"Oh, some sort of Morse code thingy. All done over the wireless these days," replied Ponsonby.

Stowie was impressed.

"It's a shame there's no way to speak directly to the pilots".

"I'm sure that will come soon enough," said Ponsonby.

As they spoke, the aircraft circled again, dipping its wings towards the Aussies this time. As he flew overhead the pilot leaned out, waving and pointing toward a line of bushes ahead of the battalion.

"I think he's trying to show us something," said Roo.

Captain Ponsonby raised his field glasses to his eyes, straining hard. Then he saw it, concealed in the bushes; a machine gun nest, camouflaged so well that it was nearly invisible.

"He's right! Sneaky blighters, I didn't even see that!"

Clancy clicked his fingers and whispered to the men.

"Quick, get the rifle grenades ready, and we'll give them a proper send off".

In swift succession the rifle grenades flew over the bushes, and moments later, explosions tore through the enemy position. Cheers erupted from the men as the bi-plane roared overhead once more, banking side to side as if waving to the soldiers below, and then disappearing into the distance.

Clancy slapped Roo on the back.

"What do yer reckon? Those flying corps boys just saved our bacon eh?"

"Yeah mate," Roo replied, grinning, "let's hope they can stick around for a bit longer".

At 0730 hours the barrage finally lifted to reveal huge numbers of enemy dead strewn around the battlefield and the village. The men had seen death and destruction on a huge scale before, but this was different.

"Bloody hell!" Roo thought to himself, as he made the sign of the cross.

Captain Ponsonby clambered to his feet and beckoned the men to do the same; signalling for the advance to continue.

"Here we go again," Roo muttered.

"Do you have *other* plans dear boy?" said Ponsonby.

Roo turned to his Captain and smiled.

"No...I was just thinking out loud mate".

Again the line of the new artillery barrage managed to trap many German soldiers between *it* and the ANZACs. The sight of hundreds of Aussies menacingly waving their bayonets and calling out their usual obscenities as they marched, was enough for the fenced in Germans, who began to hold up their hands and surrender in droves.

Clancy and a few men were quick to round up the fugitives and send them to the rear.

"Roo...Stowie...sort out these square heads will yer boys?"

The two mates nominated a small squad and swiftly rounded up the surrendering Germans; relieving them of their weapons and any souvenirs they could acquire.

"Got a Luger mate?" Ten Bob asked a young German officer.

The officer gave him a blank look.

"Ich verstehe nicht".

"Eh?" replied Ten Bob, expecting some help from Stowie, "what did he say?"

"Probably the same as you mate," replied Stowie, who roughly grabbed the German officer, liberated him of his pistol, and tossed it towards Ten Bob.

The small party rounded up one hundred and forty seven prisoners, two machine guns and two converted Lewis Guns.

"Hey look at this Roo," said Ten Bob as he admired the Lewis Gun.

"Yep, they sure are full of ingenuity these blokes eh?" replied Roo, mulling things over in his head, "or, they're getting short of their own weapons".

"With any luck eh?" said Ten Bob.

Other ANZAC units were now streaming forward, and the prisoners were passed rearwards through them; rich pickings for others.

"By the time these blokes get to the rear the only thing they'll have left is their dignity," said Stowie.

"It could be worse," replied Roo.

As the artillery barrage petered out, the hundreds of advancing Aussies now had a clear view ahead and could see hordes of the enemy running back to the Hindenburg Line.

By 0830 hours the Australian front line had been retaken and their positions were where they had been twenty four hours earlier. As the men re-occupied their trenches, outposts were established, sandbags were replaced along the parapet and the all important billy tea was brewed.

"You can always rely on Rueben to have the billy boiling...any biccies?" joked Captain Ponsonby.

"Cheeky bugger..." replied Roo, as he instinctively ducked as an artillery shell flew overhead.

To their front was a gap in the enemy wire entanglements, through which it was suspected that the Germans were retreating. This was now the target of the artillery, as shells whined above them, slamming in to the wire and fleeing soldiers. The barrage roared on for ninety minutes, after which no man's land was finally empty of the enemy.

The German offensive had been designed to counter any attack by the ANZACs and was purposely made before they had had time to sufficiently dig in. After their many disappointments the previous year the German high command had decided to show the allies that they were still a force to be reckoned with, and knew how to both attack and conquer.

This they did with crack re-enforcements from the 3rd Guard Division. Their intelligence sources had told them that there was Australian artillery in the Noreuil Valley; however, until they had discovered them during their advance, they had not been aware of the Batteries in the Lagnicourt Valley. Five of the Aussie guns had been destroyed, whilst the remainder returned the favour throughout the next day. Realistically the attack was meant to be a large scale raid, their intention being to capture and hold seven villages, and carry out as much destruction as possible in the ANZAC lines.

This large scale attack, and eventual rout, had extended left and right of the Brigade line and had been perpetrated by over sixteen thousand troops...and defeated by four thousand. The ANZAC artillery had fired its greatest number of rounds in one action to date...forty three thousand shells to be exact. The struggle had been desperate and unforgiving, but by the time the dust settled, the Australians had retaken the village, the streets littered with the bodies of friend and foe alike.

Victory had come at a terrible cost, with over one thousand Australian casualties, most from the 1st Division; the 9th Battalion suffering seven dead and twenty eight wounded. But the Germans had paid an even higher price; more than two thousand three hundred of their own lay dead on the battlefield, their ranks shattered. The Australians had not only held their ground but had bloodied the enemy in the process.

For the next thirty hours or so the 9th occupied the front line just outside Lagnicourt Village along the road to the south east, leading to Louverval. The once picturesque village, which had stood for centuries, was now little more than a shell; roofs blown apart, walls crumbled, and streets scarred with shell holes. As they dug in, the men looked back at the ruins with a mixture of sorrow and disbelief.

"Hard to imagine it ever being a village," Clancy said, staring at the jagged remains of what had once been stone cottages, "where do you reckon the villagers will go now?"

"Buggered if I know mate. They were lucky to get out, I suppose," Roo replied, sweat rolling from his brow as he worked to shore up their position, "their homes, everything they've known, it's all gone. I can't imagine what we'd do if this happened back home".

"They'll rebuild," Tomo said firmly, though his gaze lingered on the destruction, "after the war, I mean. It'll take time, but people always find a way".

Stowie shook his head, leaning on his rifle for a moment.

"A village like that, standing for hundreds of years...now look at it. Nothing but rubble. I can't see how anyone would *want* to come back".

"I don't suppose they have a choice really," Clancy added, "I mean, where else would they go? It's not just the buildings, it's their land. Their lives".

Roo thought for a moment.

"It's sad really isn't it?" he said, "we come here to rescue these people from the Germans and we end up destroying their town in order to do it".

A heavy silence fell over them, as the far off sounds of war echoed all around them.

Clancy glanced back at the road that led out toward Louverval.

"Still, can't help but wonder how long it'll take. Years maybe? But when this is all over, they'll want their homes back; same as we would".

"Perhaps," Roo nodded, "but it won't be the same village. Too much blood in the soil now".

The men fell quiet again, turning their attention back to improving their defensive position. But the thought of the shattered village stayed with them; another casualty of the war, like so many before and yet to come.

The next day they were relieved by the 5th Battalion, moving back to positions in the sunken roads between Mochies and Beaumetz-Lez-Cambrai. A defensive line was now being constructed in order to counter any further break through attempts by the enemy, so the 9th remained in the rear, providing working parties for these new defences.

At the end of their shifts the working parties stumbled back into their positions, boots caked in mud and faces smudged with sweat. Clancy, Roo, Stowie, and Ten Bob were dragging their shovels, grumbling about the hard day's work when Roo spotted a familiar figure squatting beside the fire, carefully tending to a billy of tea.

"Archie!" Roo called out with a grin as he began running towards his cousin.

Archie looked up, his face lighting up at the sight of his mates, as he hugged Roo.

"G'day boys...tea anyone?"

Clancy glanced at the billy, a cheeky smile stretching across his face as he reached out and shook Archie's hand.

"Archie, mate, I know you've been in hospital, but surely they didn't teach you to brew *that* in there?"

Stowie leaned in, pretending to inspect the billy.

"Yeah, mate, you sure that's tea? Smells more like something we'd use to clean the dunnies".

"Or maybe it is the dunny?" added Clancy.

Archie chuckled, stirring the pot.

"Yeah, yeah, laugh all you want boys, but if you don't want any, then that's all the more for me".

Stowie stretched out on the ground, tipping his hat back.

"I reckon if it doesn't kill us, it'll at least put some hair on Ten Bob's chin".

Everyone laughed, except Ten Bob, who ran his hand over his stubbornly patchy chin.

"Oh, bugger off; I've got whiskers...look," Ten Bob complained as he beckoned his mates to inspect his face.

Clancy ran his palm along the young soldier's jaw and laughed.

"Mate, my granny's got more whiskers than you".

Roo nudged Archie.

"How's the old leg Arch?"

Archie tapped his thigh.

"It's mended, but the doc reckons I'll have a bit of a limp from now on".

"So you'll be even slower than usual then?" said Ten Bob with a smirk.

Clancy glared at Ten Bob then patted Archie on the shoulder.

"Well, it's good to have you back mate, limp and all. How was the hospital?"

Archie's smile faded slightly as he poured the tea, his eyes distant for a moment.

"I saw some things there, boys. Blokes with wounds you wouldn't believe. It certainly makes you think".

A brief silence settled over them as the weight of Archie's words sunk in.

"Well, it can't be any worse than what we see on the battlefield every day," said Stowie clearing his throat, whilst looking at Archie's tea, "and after seeing all that, I guess even your *brew* might seem half decent".

Archie threw his head back with a laugh, flicking some hot tea in Stowie's direction.

"You'll drink it and like it, mate!"

The mates gathered around the fire, passing their tin mugs, their laughter chasing away the day's weariness. Despite everything, Archie was back, and that was enough for now.

3

We lived, felt dawn, saw sunset glow

The risk of a new German offensive was now so great that orders had been received from higher authorities for the troops to sleep in their uniforms.

"Now that's an order from someone kipping in a chateau if *ever* I heard one!" exclaimed Clancy.

"They must think we are all wearing pyjamas and having a bedtime story or something?" added Stowie, whose comment encouraged the men to start singing 'Kiss Me Goodnight Sergeant Major'.

"Hey Clance, will you be my mum?" laughed Roo, as Clancy smiled and swiped the air above Roo's head.

In reality the troops in the field had always slept fully clothed and booted in order to be ready immediately if attacked. Taking your boots off in the line was a risk that you had to take during daylight, but even then they could be lost in an artillery strike or sudden attack.

At mid day on the 19th of April shouts of "Stand to! Stand to!" echoed along the line. A report had been received that the Germans were advancing along a line against the left front. The battalion watched and waited for half an hour but no attack came. The 20th brought a similar story, but again, nothing, that is until a single shell crashed in to 'C' Company causing eleven casualties. This intermittent bombardment continued for the next few days, with the 9th suffering another eight casualties on the 22nd.

On the 24th of April the Battalion was relieved by the Manchester Regiment with much friendly banter being exchanged and shouts of "Ey up chum" from the Aussies. Baupame was their next stop, a strategic town since Roman times, not only because of its farming and more recent light industry, but because of its position as a crossing point between Artois and the Flanders plain on one side, and the Somme valley and the Paris Basin on the other, with many roads passing through the town.

The Battalion remained here for the next week, providing working parties at the rail head, working six hours on and twelve hours off, unloading stores and ammunition. The men had become more accustomed to digging out new positions, so this was a bit of a novelty for them.

"Crikey look at all this stuff," said Ten Bob, marvelling at the apparently endless rows of crates.

"Yeah, I reckon Australia will be broke by the time this is all over," Stowie noted.

"What was it that Freddy said a while back about fighting to our last man and our last shilling?" asked Clancy.

Stowie scoffed.

"Our last shilling I can cope with".

Resting outside their billets at the end of their shift, Clancy and Archie were curious when a car, caked in dust, and containing two French officers and a civilian pulled up. The two soldiers watched with interest as the three men carried out a quick survey of the yard, then began to pace out the area.

"I wonder what those jokers are up to Arch?" said Clancy.

The men had a brief discussion, then one of them headed back to the car, returning with a shovel.

"Perhaps they're pirates searching for buried treasure," replied Archie.

The man with the shovel began to dig, and within minutes the three men became quite animated. One of them reached into the newly dug hole and pulled out a large sturdy bag which jangled like a child's money box.

Clancy and Archie's interest was sparked as they simultaneously leaned forward in their chairs, watching intently as the men pulled several bundles of banknotes from the bag. The men were so pleased with themselves that they each danced a little jig then, as quickly as they had arrived, they were gone.

Clancy and Archie looked at each other in disbelief.

"Well I'll be buggered!" exclaimed Clancy.

Many weeks prior, on the 8th of April 1917, the 2nd Light Horse Regiment had made camp on the edge of sand dunes at Khan Yunis, the staging ground for the second battle of Gaza. The terrain there was markedly tougher and harder than the sandier desert conditions to which they had grown accustomed, necessitating the issue of picks, shovels, and carriers for their saddles.

"Blimey, this ground is like bloody iron. I think I miss the softer sands, if you can believe that," said Percy trying desperately to break the earth with his shovel.

"Yeah mate, I've already snapped two shovels, at least the sand gave way a *bit*," replied Chugger as he held out his shovel for all to see.

"This flaming heat during the day doesn't help either. It's stifling. I feel like a roast chook out here," laughed Davo.

"Aye, and then its bloody freezing at night. You can't get a good kip, one minute you're sweating, the next you're shivering," Boggy added.

As Percy rested for a moment and leant on his shovel he could hear the young boot black boy making his rounds of the dismounted troops.

"Shoe shine, shoe shine. Only a penny. Bloody good price cobbers".

The young lad, known as Farook by the soldiers, had latched on to Percy and the boys over the past few weeks. They felt sorry for him and often allowed him to clean their boots, even if they didn't need doing.

"Ey up, here comes trouble," said Boggy as he noticed Farook heading in their direction.

Farook was aged about eight years old. He spoke very good English with an accent that alternated from Egyptian to that of a Cockney and, although his clothes were quite ragged he always kept himself clean. Farook halted in front of the group of Aussies and looked around at them all, a broad smile beaming across his face, and in a sort of Australian accent he greeted them warmly.

"G'day you old bastards, how's it goin'?"

Immediately Chugger rose to his feet and gave the boy a sharp but gentle slap across the back of the head.

The boy flinched. A puzzled expression on his face.

"What have I told you about bad language? And who taught you that anyway?" growled Chugger.

Farook pointed at Boggy.

Boggy laughed.

"You bloody little dobber. No coins from *me* today".

"See...look...more bad words. You slap him? Yes?" said Farook.

Chugger thought for a moment, then cast a glare towards Boggy.

"Yeah. Maybe later...and it won't be a pretty sight neither".

"If my mum heard you talking like that, Farook, she'd clip you round the ear," added Percy.

"Yeah, well I reckon *you're* due for a few clips when you get home then mate," said Chugger.

Percy laughed and nodded.

"Yeah, you're probably right".

"I *have* no mama, or papa," said Farook in a sudden outburst, "just my donkey. His name is Bow Bells, but I just call him Bow".

Farook's words brought a sudden interest to the men.

"Bow Bells? I've heard of that before," said Percy as he looked at the boy, "come and sit down mate and let's have a chat".

Percy patted the ground next to him and beckoned the boy over.

"Roll up your sleeve mate," said Percy.

The boy, although surprised at the request, obeyed, and rolled up his sleeve to reveal that the skin on his arms, untouched by the scorching sun, was pale; not like a local at all.

Percy's four mates all peered at the boy's arm as if they were trying to focus their vision on a tiny object.

"I bloody knew it!" Percy exclaimed.

"Knew what?" asked a puzzled Boggy.

"Young Farook here isn't an Arab at all. Just look at his skin *and* his accent," said Percy as he turned to the boy, "where were you born Farook?"

"Cairo," replied Farook.

"Hah...see, he's a bloody Gyppo," said Chugger.

"I not a bloody Gyppo!" the boy insisted, as he kept an eye out for the quick back hand of Chugger, "my mama was Hala from Cairo and my papa was an English soldier".

The British Army had garrisoned Egypt since the end of the last century, and Farook explained that his mother and father had married against Hala's family's wishes, and after his father had been killed at Krithia two years ago his mother's family had murdered her and sold *him* to a local boot black.

The men couldn't believe what they were hearing.

"They killed your mum and *sold* you? That is disgraceful!" exclaimed Davo.

"My master, very bad man. He beat me every day. But I lucky," said Farook, nodding.

"Lucky? How do you work that one out?" asked Percy.

"Smaller boys...my master break their legs so they can be crippled beggars. Earn much more money".

"Bloody hell. Sounds like Fagin out of 'Oliver Twist'...what a bastard!" replied Boggy.

Farook told them how one day he had finally plucked up the courage to run away and follow the Australians, stealing his shoe shine kit and Bow, the donkey. He remembered how his father had told him that he was a Cockney as he had been born within the sound of the Bow Bells, which rang out from the Church of St Mary-le-Bow in London; a story which Percy's father had also told him, years before.

"If my master find me, he kill me".

"Well, you are safe with us now young mate...isn't he boys?" said Percy, looking round his friends.

Each man nodded their agreement and shook the boy's hand.

"Let no man put asunder eh?" said Boggy.

Percy thought for a moment.

"You remind me a lot of my cousin Roo running away to find home. He was only eight then".

The boy suddenly became excited.

"I am eight too Mister Percy".

Percy smiled.

"Is your name really Farook?"

"No. I am Alfie, Alfie McGuire," the boy replied.

"Then Alfie you shall be from now on," said Chugger, patting Alfie on the head.

As the regiment tried to dig in, there was some good news in that the mail had caught up with them and one of the postal orderlies was doing their rounds of the line.

During their rest periods each man was comforted with news from home, and as they sat round their cooking fires, letters in their hands, the air was still, the only sounds the occasional crackle of the fire and the rustle of paper as they read. Percy leaned back, glancing over at Chugger, who had just folded up his letter.

Chugger stood tall at six feet one, with a build that came from long days spent cutting sugar cane and driving the plantation trains before the war. His muscular frame and rugged features gave him a commanding presence among the men of the Australian Light Horse. Always quick with a joke or a cheeky remark, he seemed every bit the extrovert, outspoken and full of life. But beneath the humour, Chugger was more reserved, a traditional man who kept his deeper thoughts to himself. His personal life was his own to treasure. Unmarried and without a girlfriend, he never spoke much about romance, though his mates often teased him about it. Despite his bravado, there was a quiet, almost shy, side to him that only a few ever glimpsed.

"Who's that from, Chugs? Your lady friend back home?" Percy asked with a sly grin, fishing for information from the man he had known for three years, yet didn't *actually* know much about.

Chugger snorted, shaking his head.

"Nah, mate. No woman waiting on me".

"Really?" Percy raised an eyebrow, "In all the years you've never mentioned anything about it. I thought you were just keeping it quiet".

"Quiet? Me?" Chugger laughed, flashing his usual grin. "The truth is, there *is* no girl. Most of my pay goes to my sister. She needs it more than I do. We sort of brought each other up you know, since mum and dad died when we were kids. She's managing, but I can tell she's worried. Makes this place feel just that little bit more further away, you know?"

The group fell silent for a moment, surprised by the rare glimpse into Chugger's private life.

Boggy jumped in attempting to raise the mood.

"Well, what about you, Davo? You're a bit of a dark horse too mate. Got any sheilas fighting over your ugly mug?"

The group erupted in laughter, but Chugger sat back, content to let the conversation drift away from him. He wasn't one for talking about himself, especially when it came to matters like this.

Outspoken as he was, some things, like his quiet responsibility for his sister, weren't for sharing.

Percy put his arm around Chugger's shoulders.

"Don't worry mate, I'm sure we'll be home soon enough eh?"

Chugger nodded and sighed a little sigh.

"I've got a letter from *my* mum. She's worried sick but tries to hide it," said Johnno.

Percy glanced over to Johnno.

"Yeah, Lil's the same. She says they're keeping the station running, but I reckon she's hiding how tough it really is. It feels strange knowing they're struggling while we're out here," said Percy, "hopefully my pay allotment is a help, and Archie and Roo's".

"From what you tell us I reckon they'll be right mate," said Chugger.

Percy nodded.

"Thanks mate. No use worrying about what you can't change. Besides they are a bunch of real goers eh? Mind you I do miss seeing Frank growing up too".

A short silence fell on the men as they pondered.

"*My* mum says she's knitting socks and scarves for the winter," said Davo attempting to lighten the mood.

"Write back and tell her to knit faster will yer mate," laughed Boggy.

"I've had letters from Archie and Roo as well," said Percy.

This news made everyone's ears prick up.

"Ripper mate. How are they doing?" asked Chugger.

"When this was written they were in a rest area" Percy replied, "sounds like they had a terrible year last year. The Germans are well dug in and the artillery is really bad; but they're doing their best, and...oh...bloody hell!"

Percy paused, shook his head and wiped a tear from his eye.

Quiet surrounded the men. Chugger thought for a moment. There was obviously bad news, but did he really want to hear it? Boggy broke the silence.

"What is it Perce?"

"Young Jackson has been killed. In December at some place called 'Factory Corner'...artillery barrage...poor bastard," Percy announced.

There was silence again as each man contemplated the dreadful news.

Johnno looked around his mates, who were now all feeling quite despondent.

"Funny how a letter can lift or dampen the spirits, especially in this hellhole of a place".

Percy nodded.

"That it does. The good news keeps us going, doesn't it...and the bad news...well, we've just got to get through each day".

"And each night. Hard ground, hot days, cold nights...what a bastard?!" said Chugger.

"Let's just hope we don't have to camp on ground this hard again. My back can't take much more of it," said Boggy, holding up his broken shovel "now, who's got a spare shovel? Mine's bloody buggered".

The troops also began experimenting with, and were eager to get their hands on, the newly issued Hotchkiss Automatic Rifle, a light machine gun that promised to pack a punch. Gas operated and air cooled, it could reach targets up to four thousand two hundred yards away. At twenty seven pounds, it wasn't exactly light, but with its thirty round feed strip, it offered firepower that could turn the tide in a fight. Later models allowed for belt fed ammunition, making it even more versatile. Manufactured in Britain to fire the standard .303 round, the Hotchkiss Mark I found its way into the hands of the Australian Light Horse, the New Zealand Mounted Rifles, the Imperial Camel Corps, and the Duke of Lancaster's Own Yeomanry during the Sinai and Palestine campaigns. For the men, it was more than just another weapon, it was a welcome addition to their kit, one they knew would serve them well in the campaigns to come.

As on the Western Front, it was expected that gas may become a frequent visitor to the desert battlefield; so much instruction on chemical warfare was provided by divisional training staff.

On the 12th of April, 1917, the 2nd Light Horse Regiment arrived to relieve the Warwickshire Yeomanry at the outpost line towards Abasan-el-Kebir, a small village, built of stone, dating back to ancient Roman times, but now part of the Ottoman Empire since 1596.

On arrival the regiment quickly began setting up defensive positions.

"Major Stodart says this place has got some history, dating back to the Romans," said Percy.

Davo gazed at the old stone buildings.

"It's funny isn't it?"

"What is?" asked Johnno.

"That we're fighting over a village that's been here for centuries. Makes you wonder what those Romans would think of us now. Same land, different armies," said Davo, "and you never know, that Roman who stabbed Jesus when he was on the cross could have stood here".

"Or even Jesus himself," replied Johnno as he surveyed the area straining his imagination.

"No time for wondering, mate, we need to set up our possies. If the Turks are about I don't think they are going to give us a warm welcome," said Percy.

The 2nd Regiment's stay was to end two days later when they were relieved by the Dorsets, marching out on the evening of the 16th with the ANZAC Division to Shellal, on the Wadi Ghuzze. Here they watered before manning an outpost line of five miles, stretching from El Nagili to El Dammath, El Imara and Goz-el-Gelieb. The regiment was so overstretched, that the vast distance left them barely able to man the observation posts.

The men weren't at all impressed with their new positions.

"Five miles? How are we supposed to cover *that* much ground?!" exclaimed Boggy, "Bloody Generals!"

"Yeah mate it's a lot of territory for just our regiment, and we've barely enough men for the observation posts," added Davo.

"Look boys we've got a good line of sight from here, and besides our Generals are bloody good," said Percy.

Johnno coughed a "yeah right" under his breath, which drew Percy's attention.

"If you can do any better with what we've got then please let me know".

There was silence.

Percy smiled.

"I thought so...Chugger!"

"Sarge?" replied Chugger.

"Sort out a rota, and boys keep a good eye out. I don't trust these bloody Abduls one bit," said Percy.

"Have you got a bad feeling Perce?" asked a concerned Chugger.

Percy shrugged.

"We'll see what the night brings eh?"

As the half moon cast long shadows over the weathered and stony ground, the men of 'C' Squadron settled into their positions.

The night was eerily quiet save for the occasional rustle of a desert breeze, but there *were* enemy patrols about. As Percy peered into the darkness, his eyes strained to catch any sign of movement. The stillness was unnerving, every sound amplified in the silence. He glanced at his fellow troopers, their silhouettes outlined by the dim light of the moon. Each man was visibly tense; they all knew from experience that the enemy was near, lurking somewhere in the night.

Suddenly, the quiet was shattered by the faint clatter of hooves and the low murmur of voices. Percy's heart pounded as he quietly alerted his mates via hand signals passed along the line, the men of 'C' Squadron tensing, silently readying their rifles. The enemy patrol, oblivious to the hidden Australians, drew closer, their figures emerging from the shadows. Percy raised his hand, signalling the men to hold their fire. The patrol, a small detachment of Turkish cavalry, moved cautiously, their outlines clear against the pale earth illuminated by the moonlight. As soon as the opportunity arose, Percy's hand dropped.

"FIRE!" he shouted, startling the men and horses to their front.

A volley of shots rang out, echoing across the desert. The Turks, caught off guard, scrambled for their rifles whilst trying to control their frightened horses, and returned fire haphazardly. 'C' Squadron maintained their discipline, picking their targets and firing with precision. The skirmish was brief but deadly, the air filled with the crack of rifles and the sharp smell of gunpowder.

As quickly as it had started, the exchange was over. The enemy, realising they were outmatched, retreated into the night, their figures disappearing into the darkness. Percy and the boys watched them depart, maintaining their positions, eyes scanning for any signs of a counterattack.

Chugger rubbed his eyes and spat on the ground.

"You bastards!" he shouted in to the darkness.

"What's up with you mate?" asked Percy.

"I'm buggered mate," replied Chugger, "every time it's my turn to sleep some bloody Jacko turns up and ruins it".

"Perhaps we should leave out a do not disturb sign just for you mate," laughed Boggy.

Chugger nodded.

"Yeah...too bloody right mate".

The rest of the night passed without incident, the enemy patrol seen off by the defiant stand of 'C' Squadron. But the dawn's first light revealed the toll of the night's engagement. Six Turks and two of their horses lay dead about twenty yards to their front. Percy looked around at his weary but determined mates.

"Good work, lads," he called out to the troops, "hey Chugger, any closer and they'd have been in your sleeping bag lying next to you".

Chugger peered over the pile of sand bags which formed a makeshift parapet.

"Bloody hell they *are* close aren't they?" he replied, eyeing the horses up and down, "horse steak for brekkie anyone?"

Percy nodded.

"Take a few of the blokes with you and see if there are any maps and useful stuff on the Jackos too while you're there".

Gaza, a city of ancient conflicts, had always been a prize worth fighting for. Over millennia, it had seen Egyptians, Assyrians, Greeks, and Romans march through its streets. It had fallen to Caliph Omar in 635 AD, Saladin in 1187, and Napoleon in 1799. Now, it was once again a contested ground, a focal point in the struggle between empires.

In the preceding months, the Egyptian Expeditionary Force (EEF) had achieved several victories, reclaiming the Sinai Peninsula and advancing into southern Palestine. However, the First Battle of Gaza had served as a prelude to the difficulties which lay ahead. The near victory had left the EEF determined but wary of their enemy's stubborn fighting ability.

On the morning of the 17th of April 1917, the windswept sands of southern Palestine witnessed the start of a crucial moment in the Sinai and Palestine Campaign of the Great War. The EEF, still recovering from their narrow defeat at the First Battle of Gaza, faced a daunting challenge. The ancient city of Gaza, now a battleground once more, was fiercely defended by an Ottoman garrison that had significantly strengthened its positions since the last battle. Their defences, fortified with artillery and machine guns, stretched from Gaza to Beersheba. They were well prepared, their trenches deep, barbed wire entanglements thickened, and spirits high, bolstered by reinforcements that had transformed their positions into formidable strongholds. They awaited the British with confidence.

The EEF knew that breaking through these fortifications would be no easy feat, yet under orders from their command, they launched an assault with three infantry divisions supported by two mounted divisions. Despite a plan for a swift and decisive strike, the advancing soldiers faced overwhelming odds. Turkish artillery rained death upon them, and entrenched infantry cut down wave after wave of British attackers. The EEF suffered staggering losses, with casualty rates soaring to fifty percent or more in some units, gaining only a few blood soaked yards of territory.

The Desert Column, comprising the Imperial Mounted Division and ANZAC Mounted Division, played a crucial role in supporting the main infantry assault on Gaza.

Deployed on the right flank of the eastern force, the Imperial Mounted Division initiated its advance towards the Atawineh and Hairpin redoubts at 0630 hours, an hour before the infantry attack began. The division attacked dismounted, moving on a wide front spanning two miles. The 4th Light Horse Brigade extended the line from the Imperial Camel Brigade towards Wadi el Baha, south east of Gaza. Meanwhile, the 3rd Light Horse Brigade and the 5th Mounted Brigade continued the advance towards Atawineh, whilst the 6th Mounted Brigade remained in reserve.

The 4th Light Horse Brigade made notable progress, capturing a position overlooking the Gaza to Beersheba road near Kh Sihan. The 3rd Light Horse Brigade approached Atawineh closely, capturing seventy prisoners, but came under heavy enfilading fire from Sausage Ridge to the southeast of Wadi el Baha, which forced them to halt by 0915 hours.

The 5th Mounted Brigade faced intense resistance at Sausage Ridge. Supported by the Wellington Mounted Rifles Regiment from the New Zealand Mounted Rifle Brigade, they managed to advance with the aid of artillery fire from the Ayrshire Battery, yet despite capturing the southern end of Sausage Ridge, they were unable to progress further towards Hairpin redoubt due to fierce Turkish fire. The Canterbury Mounted Rifles Regiment reinforced them later.

Around noon, the New Zealand Mounted Rifle Brigade moved forward, despite facing heavy casualties from Turkish artillery and aerial bombardment. They established machine gun positions within striking distance of Hairpin redoubt, with Turkish troops only four hundred yards away. However, further advances were halted as Turkish counterattacks intensified later in the day.

The ANZAC Mounted Division was tasked with covering the right flank of the Imperial Mounted Division and exploiting any gaps in the enemy line. They commenced their operations towards Hareira, with the 1st Light Horse Brigade leading a dismounted attack. By noon, they occupied Baiket-el-Sana, but faced a vigorous Turkish counterattack from Hareira later in the afternoon. The Leicester Battery and their machine guns successfully repelled this counterattack, stabilizing their position.

The 2nd Light Horse Brigade, positioned south of Wadi Imleih, defended against Turkish cavalry attacks, supported by machine gun detachments. They repulsed an assault by Turkish cavalry and Bedouin forces, eventually holding their ground until nightfall.

Throughout the day, both divisions of the Desert Column endured heavy casualties from enemy artillery and machine gun fire, as well as persistent counterattacks. Despite these challenges, they effectively supported the infantry's main assault on Gaza, preventing significant ground loss until the battle concluded at dusk.

Having been relieved on the 18th of April by the Yeomanry, the 2nd Light Horse Regiment rested for fourteen hours at Shellal, before moving out with the brigade at 2000 hours to Khirbet Erk, which was one and a half miles south west of Baiket-el-Sana, a commanding ridge north of Wadi Imleh, about one mile south of the Turkish line.

The column pressed on through the rugged terrain, the lighthorsemen shifting in their saddles as their mounts picked their way over ridges and through uneven valleys. The ride was rough going, the pace was slow, the ground unforgiving, as they passed crumbling stone ruins, dry riverbeds and wadis that looked like they hadn't seen a drop of water in years. Close behind, young Alfie, the boot black boy, clung tightly to his donkey, Bow, the little animal gamely keeping up, though the rough going jostled them both. Alfie's wide eyes took in the barren landscape, while Bow's hooves kicked up dust with every step, the two of them determined not to be left behind.

They arrived under the cover of darkness on the 19th and, along with the 3rd Light Horse Regiment were held in tactical reserve to the 1st Light Horse, who had been deployed as advance guard on the ridge. No doubt an enemy break through was expected and the brigade was determined to be ready for all eventualities.

The second battle of Gaza was now on along a front line of twenty two miles, stretching from the Mediterranean coast to Tel-el-Sheria and Hareira. Lessons had been learned from previous battles, and the whole force of mounted troops had been deployed, dismounted, to the fight, on the right flank. The ANZAC Brigade had the New Zealand Mounted Rifle Brigade on its left and the 2nd Brigade on the right.

At 1300 hours the 2nd Light Horse Regiment relieved the 1st Light Horse Regiment on Baiket-el-Sana, whilst the 3rd Light Horse Regiment were to prolong the 2nd's right and join up with the 2nd Brigade. To the troops it was becoming apparent that their role would be a bayonet charge just after sunset.

Up until being relieved, the 1st Light Horse had experienced a reasonably quiet tour of duty, with just the occasional enemy gunshot here and there. As the sun beat down ceaselessly, casting harsh shadows across the parched landscape of sand and scrub, the 2nd Light Horse's day was just about to get worse. Having trotted up to the line, dismounting swiftly, and sending their horses to the rear, the Turks began to advance before they had time for a debrief or to settle in, launching a sudden and ferocious assault. Across the shimmering expanse, the Turkish soldiers advanced in disciplined ranks, their bayonets glinting ominously in the midday sun, as they called out their usual praises to their God. Within seconds gunfire erupted from both sides, the sharp crack of rifles ripping through the air. Bullets tore into the sand, kicking up puffs of dust, while others found flesh, sending men crashing to the ground, bloodied and broken, the lucky ones diving for cover behind sparse rocky outcrops and low standing vegetation. Commands were shouted hoarsely above the din, struggling to be heard over the ferocious noise of battle. The air stank of cordite and sweat, and still the Turks kept coming, men falling only to be replaced by the next rank as they closed the distance.

Major Chambers, whilst laying out squadron positions, shouted orders to his men, directing their defence with the swift precision of an experienced commander. But in the midst of the turmoil, a sudden crack shattered the air and he staggered, a look of disbelief crossing his face as blood stained his uniform, as he collapsed wounded, pistol in hand, on the ground.

His men, shaken and angered by the loss of their leader, now fought harder and more determined than ever, rifles and machine guns crackling and rattling as they returned fire, holding their ground with stubborn courage.

As the gunfire reached a fever pitch, the ANZACs crouched low, their eyes scanning the battlefield for targets. The ground to their front was a nightmare - Turkish bodies crumpled and strewn across the dust, while Australian soldiers fired continuously from behind sparse cover. The cracking and thumping of rifles mingled with the stuttering rattle of the Hotchkiss machine gun, which Chugger had taken charge of, his fingers dancing across the trigger as Davo fed strip after strip of ammunition into the hungry weapon. Each burst ripped through the Turkish ranks, sending men toppling like dominoes.

"Keep it up fellas!" Percy shouted over the gunfire, his voice hoarse but steady as he squeezed off a shot, watching as a Turkish soldier spun and collapsed, his bayonet clattering to the ground.

Boggy, not far off, was a blur of movement, his rifle kicking against his shoulder as he fired with deadly accuracy.

"Come on, you bastards!" he growled, his face streaked with dirt and sweat, aiming at a group of Turks charging with bayonets, their cries of "Allah Akbar!" cut short as his bullets found their mark, dropping them where they stood.

But the enemy kept coming, their numbers seemingly endless as more surged forward, some falling in heaps as the Australians cut them down, others making it dangerously close. The ground vibrated as the Hotchkiss spat fire again, mowing down an entire line of charging soldiers, their bodies crumpling grotesquely, blood spraying the sand a crimson red.

"Reload!" Chugger shouted, Davo frantically yanking out the empty feed strip, his hands shaking as he replaced it with another.

Suddenly, a Turkish soldier lunged from the smoke, bayonet raised, aiming straight for Davo who, with a roaring cry, grabbed his rifle and swung it up just in time, blocking the strike, then drove the butt of his weapon into the man's face with a sickening crunch. The Turk staggered back, blood pouring from his shattered nose, but before he could recover, Davo rammed his bayonet into the man's chest, twisting it with a grunt of effort. The Turk's eyes went wide with shock as he fell to the ground like a rag doll, blood pooling around him.

Nearby, Percy fought off two attackers at once, parrying one bayonet with his rifle while toppling the second Turk with a vicious kick to the gut. The man doubled over, but Percy didn't hesitate, bringing the butt of his rifle down hard on the back of the man's head with a sickening thud and crack, his brain spilling out on to the sand.

"More coming!" Johnno yelled, recharging his magazine with frantic hands.

Sure enough, another wave of Turkish soldiers crested the ridge, bayonets glinting as they charged headlong into the fray.

Chugger grinned, sweat dripping from his brow as he lined up the Hotchkiss once more.

"Have some of this Abdul!" he shouted, squeezing the trigger and unleashing another torrent of death.

The Turkish line staggered under the barrage, bodies torn apart by the merciless hail of lead. Blood sprayed the air, limbs shattered, and men fell screaming, clutching at their wounds as they writhed in the sand.

Percy surveyed the scene of carnage as he wiped the blood from his face with a trembling hand, his breath coming in ragged gasps.

"I think we're holding them," he muttered, though he wasn't sure for how long.

As the last of the Turkish soldiers retreated, leaving their wounded and dead behind, the Australians let off a few more rounds for good measure.

"And don't come back neither!" Chugger shouted as he sent a final burst of death from his Hotchkiss.

As the battlefield finally fell silent, smoke curled from the hundreds of ANZAC rifle barrels like ghostly tendrils from a forgotten graveyard. Chugger looked over to Percy, both men faces blackened, exhausted, but alive.

"Looks like they've gone mate".

"For now," Percy replied, "they'll be back".

As the noise of the fighting died away the battlefield was filled with the cries of the wounded and dying, the sharp tang of gun smoke hanging heavy in the air, as the angels of the army, the stretcher bearers, darted among the fallen, whisking the wounded from both sides away to makeshift aid stations hastily set up in the rear. Major Chambers was in a serious condition and, sadly, later died at the field hospital at Tel-el-Jemmi.

As the brazen attack had unfolded, the 3rd Light Horse had not been in position as expected, on the 2nd's right, but for good reason; so the CO had borrowed a squadron of the 1st Light Horse temporarily to fill the gap. It transpired that as the South Australian 3rd Light Horse Regiment were moving into position they had observed an enemy cavalry brigade assembled on the 2nd Light Horse's immediate right, but out of sight of the 2nd. The Turks were shelling the 2nd's led horses *and* Wadi Imleh, whilst his infantry were threatening Sana. The cavalry brigade was also a dangerous and looming threat to the regiment's horses. The CO of the 3rd, therefore, had taken the bold and sensible decision to halt and observe the enemy cavalry, informing Brigade Headquarters of his reasons. Had he dismounted as planned, his flank, horses, and those of the 2nd

would have fallen prey to the Turks; luckily this did not happen and the surprise infantry assault had achieved nothing for the Turks. The enemy infantry was repulsed at Sana, partly thanks to the ANZACs new automatic rifles, and the position was held. The left, however, was a different story.

A staff officer had sent the regiment's horses right into the firing line, in broad daylight, resulting in many casualties from shell fire. No word had been received to withdraw, so the CO of the 2nd at once ordered the horses back to the rear. A little later an actual withdrawal order *was* received, but this time, under regimental supervision, the horses were led up in the dark. By this time the regiment had held for seven hours and evacuated in good order, joining up with the brigade at midnight and moving to a position just north west of We Li Sheikh Nuran, arriving at 1000 hours on the 20th.

The men, although always occupied, had time to consider the actions of the previous day.

"Can you believe that staff officer sent our horses right into the firing line?" said Percy, feeling perplexed.

"It's right what they say about officers...brain out, hat in...well some of them anyway," added Chugger.

"It's a good job our CO had the sense to pull them back," said Davo, there's no room for stupid mistakes out here...one wrong decision and it costs lives".

"And horses," added Percy.

"*And* my poor old feet if we end up on bloody foot," said Chugger

At midday the troopers mounted their horses, and formed up in three ranks, as the column prepared to move out. It was then that the thought of being on foot was the least of their problems. Percy and Chugger, exchanged quick glances, each checking their equipment and looking in all directions for any signs of danger.

Percy felt uneasy, sensing something...but what?

His question was soon answered.

The column had barely begun its advance when a faint humming sound droned like a wasps nest in the distance. Percy paused, his ears straining to identify the source. The humming grew louder, unmistakably the approach of enemy aircraft. Heartbeats quickening as the dreaded realisation set in.

Suddenly, three sleek looking bi-planes swooped low from the sunlit sky, their menacing silhouettes casting shadows over the dusty terrain, their engines' roar drowning out all other sound as they began their deadly work, ruthlessly strafing the road with machine gun fire, and unleashing a torrent of bombs on the men and horses below.

"SCATTER...NOW!" was the cry that echoed throughout the lines of troops.

There was no panic, just order, of sorts, as the lighthorsemen instinctively scattered, seeking cover amidst the chaos.

Young Alfie too, aboard Bow, followed the lead of the soldiers spurring his donkey off the road and as far away from the gunfire as he could.

Chugger's horse reared, neighing in terror as explosions tore through the column. Dust and smoke billowed, obscuring the scene as men shouted orders and cries of pain mingled with the thunderous blasts. The aircraft strafed the ground with brutal precision, leaving devastation in their wake.

In the midst of the attack, Percy and Chugger, now separated by the melee, struggled to maintain control of their horses, as the ground shook under the terrifying assault, riderless horses whinnying and bolting in terror. Some soldiers managed to get a few shots off as the aircraft flew over the long lines of men and horses; but to no avail.

As swiftly as they had come, the enemy aircraft veered away, disappearing into the vast expanse of the sky. Silence descended, broken only by the groans of the wounded and the mournful whimpers of injured horses. Percy and Chugger, faces sombre, surveyed the aftermath, two men were dead and seven wounded, not to mention the loss of forty one horses.

Chugger watched in anger and shouted to the sky as the aircraft flew calmly away, their days work done.

"Are you happy now you bastards?!"

As he wiped his brow he heard Alfie shouting then turned to see the young lad, seated on his donkey, trotting towards him.

"Mister Chugger, mister Chugger!" he called out as his donkey drew up next to the soldier, "how are you? Are you well?"

"Yeah mate, I'm good," Chugger replied, feeling surprised to see the boy, "how are you going?"

"I am good also. Those flying machines are proper bastards, yes?" Alfie replied.

"Yes mate they are," said Chugger, resisting the urge to slap the back of Alfie's head, "now let's go and find our mates shall we?"

Being far from any sizeable civilisation the decision was made to bury the two dead men near to where they had fallen, the positions of their graves carefully marked on a map for possible later recovery. Grave markers were hastily constructed from wooden ammo crates and the names of the men etched into the wood.

Chugger was annoyed at the sight of the wooden markers.

"It's a bloody disgrace that we daren't mark their graves with a cross...bastard Arabs!"

Sadly, leaving any signs of the infidel Christian religion would result in desecration by the intolerant Bedouins who had lived there for generations.

"Isn't their God the same as ours but just with a different name?" asked Johnno.

"Yeah mate, but their God, it appears, doesn't believe in peace and love," Boggy responded.

"But isn't that what religion is all about...men living together as one?" replied Johnno.

"Not here mate. They only tolerate us because we are fighting their battles for them...the mongrels!" said Chugger as he spat on the ground, "as soon as this is all over they'll go back to their old ways of killing each other because they are the wrong sort of Muslim".

"Wrong sort of Muslim?" replied a surprised Johnno.

"Yep...the sooner we are home the better I reckon," said a scornful Chugger.

Boggy added to the conversation.

"Christianity has been just as bad in the past you know".

"Yeah, but *we* grew up mate, *and* our religion was here before these Muslims," replied Percy.

"Well *I* don't think much of *any* religion," said Boggy.

"What? Not at all?" replied Johnno.

"I'll tell you what I believe. I believe that yes there was a Jesus and a Mohammed and whoever else, but their books, like the Bible, were written by men, not God, to keep us lower classes in order through fear," Boggy explained, "I think there really is a divine being who loves us all, just not what religion teaches us. I'll tell you a story of the disgusting things that Christianity does to innocent people. Years ago in my town back in England there was a fella who took his own life. I don't know why, but he just did. Anyway when the day came for his funeral the vicar wouldn't let the coffin pass through the church gates, it had to be lifted over the fence".

"That's disgusting," replied Johnno.

"Too right, and to add even more insult, his headstone was placed the wrong way round so that you had to go round the back to read it. Where is the dignity, let alone love and compassion, in that I ask you?" Boggy growled, grinding his teeth in anger, "and that is why you'll never find me in a church or at a religious service".

"Don't you pray mate," enquired Davo.

"Yeah I pray, but to the God of love and understanding, not the version that rich men have created".

"You know Pete I think you have something there mate...good on yer," said Percy, as he gripped Boggy's shoulder.

There was much toing and froing over the next few days, digging in here, and patrolling there. The 22nd of April brought with it a severe heat wave, made worse by the lack of water. But, despite this, the regiment constructed a defensive position at Hill 310, along Wadi Ghuzzi, and west to Ghabi. The left of the line was held by the infantry, and was dug a lot closer to the enemy. On the 27th of April the 2nd Light Horse again took up the Shellal Hisea section of the front line, on which they dug in and laid out concertina wire, whilst also managing to send out scouting parties.

Whilst all of this was going on, the second ANZAC Day passed without a thought, although a few silent prayers were muttered here and there.

4

"Once more into the breach"

At the beginning of 1917, General Joffre had been replaced by General Nivelle. He had been instrumental in repelling the Germans at Verdun, believing in quick and dashing methods. He had originally decided on a large scale offensive in the French sector, with the British assisting with a subsidiary attack. The German withdrawal to the Hindenburg Line interfered with his plan, however, despite this, in mid April he launched a huge attack at the Chemin-des-Dames, near Laon, a crest line between the Aisne and Ailette valleys, its location and underground quarries making it a veritable fortress. It had acquired the name in the 18th century, as it was the route taken by the two daughters of Louis XV, who were known as the Ladies of France. At the time, it was the most direct route between Paris and the Château de la Bove, near Vauclair, on the far side of the Ailette.

In order to weaken the German defences, General Nivelle, a professional artilleryman, had preceded the attack with a six day bombardment by over five thousand three hundred guns. This heavy barrage had a negative effect and gave the Germans plenty of warning that a major French assault was on the way. When the seven French army corps had attacked on the 16th of April, they had underestimated how prepared the Germans were; the enemy having dug deep shelters into the old stone quarries beneath the ridge. Here they had taken cover from the French shells. Their positions had also given them the advantage of higher ground, allowing them to control the southern slope where the French were advancing.

Despite heavy German counter fire and bad weather, French infantry, including colonial Senegalese troops, managed to reach the top of the ridge on the first day. But once they were on the plateau, their progress was halted by the continuous fire of the Germans' new MG08/15 machine guns. The French suffered forty thousand casualties on the first day alone, and, over the next twelve days, losses mounted, and by the end of the offensive, the French had suffered one hundred and eighty seven thousand casualties, while the Germans lost one hundred and sixty three thousand.

Although the Germans had taken losses, the scale of French casualties for such little gain was seen as a catastrophe, and the slow evacuation of the wounded only added to the perception of failure. Within the weeks to come Nivelle would be forced to resign, and the French Army plagued by mutinies across several infantry divisions. In the mean time he and Haig thus decided upon constant small offensives whose purpose was to wear down German resistance.

Bullecourt was now back on the attack menu.

Towards the end of April, the Hindenburg Line endured an almost never ending barrage of shells. Day and night, the rumble of guns near and far never ceased, a low, rolling storm that rattled teeth and bones and turned the sky into a shifting grey haze. The 9th Battalion had been warned to be prepared to move at a moment's notice, though the men wondered how anyone could expect them to move having alerted the enemy, with this constant artillery barrage, that they would soon have visitors.

"Nothing like letting them know we're coming with all of this shelling, eh?" Ten Bob remarked, wiping dirt from his face as he crouched near Roo's billy of tea that was refusing to stay on the boil.

The crash of an artillery round hitting its target shook the earth again, sending a thin shower of dust and dirt down from the trench walls. Roo, sitting nearby, cursed under his breath as he tried to strike a match to re-light the fire under his billy can.

"I think tea is a bit of a lost cause in this racket," Roo muttered, glancing up as another distant thunder clap from a big gun made the ground vibrate beneath them, "the fire either goes out or it spills before you get a sip".

"I reckon there's more than just tea in that billy now mate," said Clancy.

Stowie, shrugged as he tended to a pot of all in stew that, with every impact, had been sloshing over the edge.

"Better the tea than us, mate I suppose, but it sure is getting harder to feed and water ourselves at the moment eh?"

"I wouldn't mind if the ground stopped bloody shaking for five minutes though," Archie grumbled, as he crouched low, holding the brim of his steel helmet, whilst trying to shove some damp bread into his mouth between the tremors. His voice was barely heard above the roar of another volley overhead, the sharp whistling of shells drowning out any thought of quiet conversation.

Clancy stood, leaning against the trench wall with his arms crossed, keeping a wary and watchful eye on the horizon. The sky was bruised with smoke, and the crash of friendly artillery hammering into the German lines seemed to come in waves, as if the very air was being punched.

"We should be used to it by now I suppose?" he said, though the bags under his eyes betrayed the suggestion.

No one slept easy with shells falling day and night, and the few minutes of rest they could snatch between bombardments were always uneasy, bodies jolting awake with each tremor that shook the ground.

"Yeah mate, I've given up on sleep altogether. A fella can't even close his eyes around here," Stowie muttered, still nursing his stew whilst pulling his tunic tighter against the chill of the damp trench air, "it's like riding a horse...feels like the ground's always got a mind to buck us off".

As another batch of shells howled overhead, Archie gave a short laugh.

"You think it's bad now? Wait until we're moving again and the mongrels are shooting at us".

"Something to look forward to eh?" said Clancy with a wry smile.

The earth shuddered again as another shell found its mark somewhere along the Hindenburg Line. The men barely flinched this time, though the steady shower of dirt and small debris clattered off helmets and billy cans. Even their conversation seemed resigned to the endless cannonade; their voices raised just enough to be heard over the ever present background noise of the Germans being pummelled.

On the 2nd of May the 1st Division carried out an assembly test to check the response times of each battalion. The 9th Battalion sprang into action as soon as the alarm was raised and, within thirty minutes, not just the infantry but the entire battalion - support troops and all - were formed up and ready to move out.

For the infantry, who lived with nothing more than the essentials packed tightly into their kits, quick responses had become second nature. Only the items they were actively using ever left their packs, which meant they were always prepared to grab their equipment and go. But it wasn't just about personal readiness. Many of the infantrymen, after securing their rifles and shouldering their packs, immediately pitched in to help the support troops pack up the stores and equipment.

'B' Company, having secured their own equipment within minutes of the alarm, were already hauling ammunition crates to the waiting carts.

"Come on lads, let's get this done quick smart!" Roo urged, his voice rising above the clattering of boxes and shouted commands.

"Give us a hand with these water cans, will yer?" one of the storemen called out, and without hesitation, a few infantrymen rushed over, lifting the heavy containers and stacking them neatly for transport.

There was no division between the infantry and support troops when it came to being ready on time. The battalion operated like a well oiled machine, everyone knowing that getting the stores packed and the equipment loaded was just as important as grabbing a rifle.

"Can't be lugging it all yourself, mate," Ten Bob grinned as he passed a crate of rations to a storeman who nodded gratefully, "we all want to move out on time, don't we?"

Even with the weight of their own kit on their shoulders, the infantry never hesitated to assist, for they knew that when the order came to advance, every item packed away, every piece of equipment properly secured, meant the difference between a smooth move and chaos.

By the time thirty minutes had passed, the 9th was formed up in three ranks, every man accounted for, from the riflemen in the front to the storemen, cooks and stretcher bearers in the rear. It wasn't just the fighting men who were ready; the entire battalion was set to move; and not a minute wasted.

The Commanding Officer gave a nod of approval. The test had gone off without an issue, thanks in no small part to the men who worked together with the precision of the veterans that they were.

On the 3rd of May, the Second Battle of Bullecourt erupted with a colossal enemy bombardment that sent shivers through the earth for miles around. There was definitely no playing in the fields among the daisies, the sounds of laughter, *or* the enjoyment of spring's embrace, for the air vibrated with the deafening roar of German artillery, and the ground trembled beneath a constant fusillade of shells that turned the landscape into a hellish wasteland. Fields that had once been crisscrossed with trenches and barbed wire now lay shattered, pockmarked with deep craters, smoking remnants of what had been lines of defence, whilst the trees, or what little remained of them, were splintered and charred; their skeletal frames looming out of the dust and smoke. The air was eerily still - no birds sang here. The once vibrant landscape had fallen silent, as if even nature had abandoned this place of desolation.

Rumours of the intense fighting spread like wildfire through the trenches, carried by messengers who had seen the devastation first hand; telling silent stories of comrades lost and positions obliterated. It was said that entire sections had been buried alive under the bombardment, swallowed by the very ground they fought to defend. The men of the 9th Battalion, who had already endured days of heavy fire, now braced themselves for the unimaginable. They were about to be thrown back into the inferno.

At 1545 hours on the 4th of May echoes of "Stand to!" reverberated around the companies, the battalion moving off an hour later to Vaulx-Vraucourt from where they departed for Noreuil in order to relieve the 12th Battalion. Due to the massive troop numbers in the town the battalion bivvied at Vaulx, where they and all other units were placed on a high state of readiness. This had been the right decision as at 0630 hours on the 6th, intelligence was received that the German army had broken through; thus the battalion moved forward immediately, making use of the sunken roads on both the northern and southern outskirts of Noreuil. Here they waited until 1600 hours when they were given orders to make a night attack on the Hindenburg Line.

This second Battle of Bullecourt was part of a huge offensive along a sixteen mile front, with the British attacking Bullecourt Village, whilst the 2nd Australian Division was designated the capture of a sector of the Hindenburg Line adjoining the village to the south east. The attack on the 3rd of May, failed, with some key trenches captured and the Canadians on the left and the Aussies on the right the only bodies of troops to hold and remain in the trenches they had captured.

The Australian Division had seized part of the two trenches known as OG1 and 2, after a vicious fight, managing to repel several strong counter attacks. It was now up to the soldiers of the 1st Division. Orders had been issued for the 7th Division to attack the village of Bullecourt, and this was now underway. Simultaneously the 1st Australian Division was to take OGs 1 and 2 up to the outskirts of the village and link up with the British division. After a difficult fight, the 1st and 3rd Battalions, now occupying OG 1 and 2, were exhausted. The 9th Battalion was thus sent forward to relieve the two Aussie battalions in readiness for *their* attack. Zero hour was set for 0400 hours on the 7th, fifteen minutes before the British attack on the village, no doubt distracting the enemy while the British advanced.

At dusk on the 6th the 9th Battalion took over the extreme Australian left flank.

On their way to their positions they encountered unforgettable evidence of the struggle which had ensued over the past few days. The communication trench which led them to the front ran along the foot of a steep road embankment to its right, whilst the actual road was situated on the left of the sap. The sights awaiting them were nothing short of horrifying, the trench having become a graveyard for the fallen, remaining forebodingly silent.

Clancy moved cautiously, holding up his hand to signal a brief halt as he surveyed the trench ahead of them. His usually hardened expression faltered as he looked left and right at the butcher's yard that lay to his front. Not usually being one for taking the Lord's name in vain, the words slipped from his lips as if pulled by some force beyond him.

"Jesus Christ!" he exclaimed as he shakily made the sign of the cross on his chest and mouthed an apology as he glanced to the heavens above.

The sap was a macabre sight; choked with dead bodies...from both sides, the bodies lying thick, tangled, and twisted in unnatural poses, the product of both artillery and bayonet alike; their lifeless limbs draped over each other like broken marionettes, skin waxen and slick with congealed blood. The men who once filled these uniforms were now indistinguishable from the mud itself, their bodies shattered by blasts, missing heads, arms, and legs, their faces contorted into frozen screams of agony. The stench of rot and decay was suffocating, a vile mixture of blood, excrement, and death that clung to everything, seeping into their nostrils and refusing to let go.

In some places, it was evident that the only way to move forward had been to heave the dead out of the trench itself. Corpses had been flung up and over, and now they littered the parapet on all sides, limbs jutting at awkward angles, some impaled on barbed wire. Flies buzzed in clouds over open wounds and the exposed entrails of soldiers, both German and allied alike, intestines spilling from gaping stomachs, glistening with blood that had soaked deep into the earth. Torn off limbs, still in boots or sleeves, lay scattered as if tossed aside by some monstrous hand, whilst chunks of flesh, barely recognisable as human, clung to the walls, smeared in streaks of crimson.

The floor of the trench too was a gruesome mess, a slimy mixture of mud and gore. Pools of blood had mingled with the rain, creating a sickly, sticky mire that sucked at their boots with each step. One body, half buried in the ground, seemed to have dissolved into the mud, its ribcage exposed and hollow, where scavenging rats had already begun their grim feast. In places, the dead were piled three or four deep, creating a grotesque barricade of bloated, decaying flesh, and the colours of their uniforms were now indistinguishable from the brown filth that consumed everything.

As Ponsonby, Archie and Roo approached Clancy to investigate the cause of the hold up, there was no need to ask. The horrific scene before them said it all. There was nothing left to identify these men as individuals; they had been reduced to little more than meat, their humanity stripped away.

"On my God!" Ponsonby said, his eyes instantly welling with tears.

Roo placed his hand on the Captain's shoulder.

"We haven't got time to bury the poor souls," said Roo, "so we'll just have to do our best to step over them".

Ponsonby nodded his agreement and, without a word, because none was required, he waved his Company forward.

Soldiers struggled to hold back their tears as they tried their best to traverse the dead soldiers, but despite their best efforts, physically stepping on the bodies was inevitable. For Corporal Stowe it just added fuel to his fire of hatred for the enemy.

Throughout the endeavour the stretcher bearers from the Australian Army Medical Corps (AAMC) worked studiously on the outer edges of the trench searching for signs of life. All of the time that the battalion was advancing, German shells were raining down on the labyrinth of trenches, skimming across the parapet and banks of earth like stones on a pond, and splashing onto the road. As Roo recovered his stance from such a shell he saw two AAMC parties disappear in the smoke of an explosion; more bodies added to the tally.

By 2230 hours the battalion was settled in to the line, but, despite their terrible march to get there, there was little rest to be had. Whilst the parapet was manned, working parties set out to make dumps of wooden stakes, barbed wire, bombs, and other material near the end of OG1. Telephone lines too were laid to the same point. The battalion was now ready for anything. At 2230 hours the acting CO, Major Neligan, issued final instructions to all Company Commanders, as well as the Officer in Charge of machine guns and mortars.

The hours leading up to the battalion's attack were anything but quiet. Anyone hoping to snatch a few winks that night was out of luck, when at precisely 0200 hours on the 7th of May, the calm was shattered like glass as the Germans launched a ferocious assault on the left flank of OG1, which was held by the 4th Battalion. It was sudden, with explosions and the crack of rifles illuminating the night sky like a thunderstorm. The enemy stormed in, swift and brutal, seizing a short section of the trench with terrifying efficiency. The garrison, under non-stop pressure, had no choice but to withdraw, falling back forty yards under a hail of gunfire and shrapnel.

At 0345 hours the allied artillery added to the night's excitement when it exploded in to life, beginning its pre-attack barrage, which pounded the German positions with a merciless fury. The ground shook violently, tremors running through the men's boots as shells screamed overhead. The haze of smoke hung in the night sky as, at 0358 hours, the first attacking platoon scrambled over the makeshift barrier in OG1 and began its advance along the trench, rushing forward, adrenaline surging, hearts thumping like the artillery still pounding the earth. But the Germans were ready for them. At a distance of seventy yards the platoon ran headfirst into a storm of machine gun and sniper fire, bullets whizzing past like angry hornets. Some of the soldiers were picked off with deadly accuracy, while enemy bombers hurled egg and stick bombs with terrifying precision. The crack and boom of explosives tore through the ground, dirt and debris raining down like hail in a summer storm. As if that weren't enough, to add to the chaos, pineapple bombs lobbed from a Grenatenwerfer, a small trench mortar, landed with deadly thuds, sending shockwaves through the ground and flinging men like ragdolls.

Caught in a murderous crossfire and with no cover to speak of, the platoon was driven back to its start point, under constant fire, their advance crushed in a matter of brutal minutes.

There was no shame, for they had done their best under terrible circumstances and sometimes retreating *was* the better part of valour. As they filed past the next attackers, their mates, there were whispers of "good work boys" as each man received a pat on the back or a hearty handshake.

Now it was the turn of Lieutenant Sargent's platoon, yet, despite being a veteran of the last year of fighting, the young officer still struggled with self doubt. His mind raced as he sought the advice of his SNCOs, Roo and Archie.

"So what do you reckon we should do?" he whispered, his voice betraying his uncertainty.

Roo, sensing his hesitation, spoke with calm authority.

"Listen, Tomo, you're a good leader," he said, locking eyes with the lieutenant, "look down the attack trench. What do you see as the main problem?"

Tomo paused, his gaze scanning the length of the narrow, claustrophobic trench, his heartbeat drumming in his ears; but he focused.

"Well, our immediate problem is the concentration of enemy bombers ahead of us".

"And...?" Roo prodded, his tone that of a patient teacher pushing a student toward the answer.

Tomo's eyes brightened, the flicker of a plan sparking to life.

"So we need to fight fire with fire," replied Tomo, a spark suddenly being igniting in his thoughts, determination replacing doubt, "how many bombs does each man have?"

"Five each. Some a few more," replied Roo.

"Right, we'll leap frog forward, bombing as we go. As each man runs out of bombs the next man will take his place and so on," said Tomo, feeling quite proud of himself.

Roo's mouth curled into a smile as he grasped the officer's shoulder.

"There you go sir, my thoughts exactly".

Feeling a quiet sense of satisfaction, and with a firm nod, Tomo turned and issued orders to the platoon after which they set off down the trench.

Suddenly, the night exploded around them. The earth convulsed under the force of their bombs, flashes of light illuminating the dark trench walls, as dirt and rocks flew through the air. The Aussies were tossing their bombs to the front and sides, with the sharpness of test match cricketers. One after another, they leapfrogged forward, the blasts sending quakes through the narrow trench. As they surged ahead, agonising screams of pain echoed to their front, and the enemy's bombardment faltered. No more bombs came their way. Moving quickly through the trench they came across the Grenatenwerfer, which had been abandoned by its crew.

Their work was not yet complete, but they paused, and Tomo allowed himself a brief moment to breathe.

"This is working a treat eh boys? Not like the bosche to leave behind a trench mortar," said Tomo.

"Don't get too cheery mate, we're out of bombs. I've sent a runner back, so we'll have to hold here for a bit," said Archie.

The platoon's wait seemed like an eternity, but in reality was only a few minutes. The CSM and his ammo party were already poised and ready to move forward when the runner arrived at their location.

"G'day men. I hear you've run out of goodies, so me and me mates have come to replenish you," announced Clancy.

The CSM had brought with him a couple of rifle grenadiers and two gun groups.

"Tomo, what do you reckon to putting the machine guns in some shell holes to the side of this trench to cover your advance?" he asked.

"Sounds like a sensible plan CSM, please arrange that," replied the lieutenant.

"No worries mate...oh...and the OC and the rest of the company will be along soon, so let's get a move on eh?"

Once the gun groups were comfortably settled in they began to send bursts forward at the enemy. This was the signal for the platoon to recommence their bombing run.

Pretty soon the platoon was again halted by a huge salvo of enemy bombs, which rained down like a deadly storm, detonating with deafening booms, throwing some off balance as they stumbled into the trench walls, dirt and jagged shrapnel cascading over them.

"Get down!" Tomo yelled, his voice nearly drowned out by the explosions.

But the troops didn't need to be told as they dived for cover, pressing themselves against the mud soaked walls of the trench, dirt and metal fragments tearing through the air like a swarm of razors.

Archie swore loudly, pulling his helmet tighter as another bomb detonated nearby, sending a shower of earth over his back.

"Bloody hell, *come on*...I've only just got back from the hospital!"

As the platoon weathered the onslaught, Roo crawled up beside Tomo, eyes sharp, face smeared with mud.

"We can't stay pinned down like this mate, they'll tear us to bits!"

The young officer didn't seem fazed at all, and calmly peered over the parapet just long enough to be able to see that enemy machine guns and snipers were occupying shell holes to their front, but he also saw that the Aussie machine gun crews were already on to it and were giving each other mutual support as they advanced in stages towards their German counterparts.

As he ducked back down in to the trench Tomo was very pleased to have such tactically aware troops with him. He wiped the sweat and grime from his brow, and clenched his teeth.

"Don't worry sarge the Lewis Gunners are on to it. Time for us to move forward now don't you reckon?"

As the platoon moved again it was apparent that the enemy was attempting to surround them, but Tomo's quick reactions and assessment of the situation, combined with the arrival of the remainder of the Company, prevented this from occurring.

Again there was a frenzy of bombing between both sides, whilst above ground, machine guns and rifle grenadiers unleashed a deadly volley, firing across the open battlefield. Explosions, bullets, and shrapnel filled the air, the men in the trench staying low as they moved on towards the enemy.

For some the day was about to get interesting as Ten Bob tossed a Mills Bomb forward, resulting in a sight which took the Aussie soldiers by surprise. As his bomb exploded a great flaming spout shot in to the air to a height of about thirty feet, lighting up all around for some distance. It did have its positives in that it illuminated enemy positions for all to see, these being swiftly dealt with whilst the unexpected light display was there to be taken advantage of.

"What the blazes was that?!" exclaimed Roo.

"Blazes? Yeah, very funny mate," replied Clancy.

"Maybe I hit a petrol drum or something," Ten Bob added.

As the men edged their way slowly round the bend in the trench they discovered the body of a German soldier with the remains of something metal strapped to his back. Captain Ponsonby recognised what it was immediately.

"Curses and naughty words!" he exclaimed, "it's one of those flame thrower contraptions".

"Curses and what?" Clancy asked, "and what's a flame thrower?"

Ponsonby leaned in, and quietly and quickly explained to Clancy.

"The Germans call it a Flammenwerfer. It's simple enough. You wear a couple of cylinders on your back. One is filled with gas and the other petrol of sorts. There's a hose with a gun on the end, pull the trigger, a spark ignites the fuel and it shoots liquid fire ahead...voila".

Yet another addition to the arsenal of war, the flame thrower was deadly in close quarter combat, and was especially useful for clearing bunkers or trenches; liquid fire, that sticks and burns wherever it hits, with a range of over one hundred yards.

"It's a nasty piece of kit".

"Crikey! Bullets not good enough now? They're trying to barbecue us," said Clancy.

"Sadly, yes," replied the Captain.

Corporal Stowe thought he had won a raffle when he stumbled upon another undamaged flame thrower in a dugout. After he had tinkered with it for a while, he turned a valve then squeezed the trigger on the nozzle at the end of the hose, causing a stream of sticky liquid to shoot forward.

"Mate you need to light the end," said Roo.

Stowie looked closely at the nozzle.

"How? I can't for the life of me see any form of striker," Stowie replied.

Roo fumbled in his pouch and pulled out a box of matches, which he tossed to Stowie.

"Here...and when you light it, make sure you point that bloody thing *away* from us lot".

Stowie held out his rifle to Clancy.

"Hold on to this for a bit mate will yer?"

"Who am I, your butler?" Clancy joked as he took hold of the weapon.

"Go on mate, give it a blast," Ten Bob called out.

With all eyes on him, Stowie cautiously pointed the nozzle skyward, giving the trigger a soft and gentle squeeze, causing the liquid to trickle out in slow, lazy drops. As he hesitated Clancy, growing impatient, tried to hurry him up.

"Come on mate, the war will be over by the time you've lit it".

"Alright, alright...hold your horses and have some patience," Stowie muttered, striking a match with deliberate care.

As soon as the flame touched the liquid, a tiny flicker ignited, dancing upwards on the end of the nozzle. Stowie nodded his approval.

"Is that it?" said Clancy, "you couldn't light a fag with that!"

Without a word, Stowie firmly squeezed the trigger. A sudden whoosh filled the air as a searing jet of fire leapt forward, crackling and glowing with heat. Stowie's grin widened, a mixture of excitement and anger, as he signalled to the Company to follow him, the nozzle hissing as the flames illuminated his features.

"Come on boys," Stowie laughed, the fire casting an sinister glow over him, "let's give these bastards what for...and for Taff".

There was no time to think or reply as Stowie set off along the trench intending to wreak havoc, suffering and death on any enemy who had the misfortune to get in his way. As he moved, the men of 'B' Company close behind, dirt and rocks were flying from all sides as German bombs and machine guns kicked up the earth with every explosion and burst of fire. For the moment the flames from the flamethrower were limp, dribbling feebly on to the floor of the trench. There was little enemy resistance for some time until Stowie rounded a bend, finding himself firmly in the sights of a German machine gun. There was no time to react as Stowie closed his eyes and gritted his teeth expecting to be torn to pieces...but...nothing...that is except for the cursing of the enemy gun crew who raced to clear an unexpected stoppage.

Stowie and the men close behind could not believe their luck.

"BASTARDS!!" Stowie shouted as he squeezed the trigger with a brutal force, sending a powerful torrent of fuel and flame exploding towards the enemy soldiers; illuminating the trench like a furnace. Sprinting forward, he swept the blazing jet across the machine gun crew, his voice a savage howl that cut through the chaos like a banshee. The unfortunate Germans barely had time to react before they were engulfed, their screams piercing the air as the fire transformed them into human torches, their bodies twisting in frantic, hopeless attempts to escape, as they performed a flaming dance of death, their uniforms and flesh melting from their bodies as they staggered, falling one by one to the ground, silent; their blackened and charred lifeless bodies smouldering like a burnt Sunday roast.

The men behind Corporal Stowe stood frozen, stunned momentarily at the total destruction and sheer devastation left in the wake of this new device. The blackened remains of what had once been men now lay in a twisted heap. Stowie, however, didn't flinch, calmly stepping over the carnage without a second glance, his boots crunching over charred bones and seared flesh, a look of hatred coupled with admiration for the giver of death now strapped to his back. As he turned back to his mates to his rear he simply waved them forward casually as if what had just occurred was an every day event. There was more grisly work yet to be done.

"Come on! TAFF!!" he yelled as he worked his way forward through the trench, calmly firing jets of flame into any dugouts they encountered.

Although a grotesque and ferocious experience for all, the troops kept their composure, surging forward, firing at and bombing all targets of opportunity. Mad as a wasp nest in a paper bag he may have been, Stowie was careful and diligent with his new toy, so much so that when the Company encountered another machine gun nest which was out of range of his flames, the men took over and a fierce bomb fight ensued for about three minutes. As the attackers edged closer, Stowie managed to squirt off some fire in the direction of the machine gun, but the flames fell short, managing to ignite a roll of hessian which then caused a fog like mist in the trench. The machine gun crew foreseeing their own demise, if the mad man with the Flammenwerfer managed to get any closer, took the opportunity to flee using the smoke as a veil. When Stowie and the boys reached the position all they found was a few boxes of ammunition and the lock of the machine gun.

"Good decision boys," Stowie muttered to himself.

Captain Ponsonby was now up on the machine gun position having worked his way through the congested trench.

"Having fun Corporal Stowe?" he enquired.

"Yes sir; I haven't felt this good for a while now," Stowie replied as he spat on the ground.

"Well, in part, thanks to you, we are over four hundred yards forward of our jumping off point, so well done," said Ponsonby.

"Really? Thanks to these men and old Lucifer here," Stowie replied acknowledging his mates with a nod, and gently tapping the flame thrower.

As the enemy fire had died down to nothing, it was time for a quick re-org. Clancy and his ammo party, who had been running up and down the line, ensured that each man was bombed up and replenished with ample rounds. Meanwhile, Captain Ponsonby carried out a quick recce and, through his field glasses, noted that some distance farther along the trench, there was movement. Approximately forty enemy soldiers were withdrawing, their rear being guarded by the machine gun crew and parties of bombers. Some of the enemy had also retreated along two cross trenches leading to OG2.

Ponsonby signalled a temporary halt and organised small posts, with bomb stops, in the cross trenches. The bomb stops, sturdy barriers of sandbags and timber, designed to block the blast and shrapnel from grenades, would prevent the enemy from returning and hurling bombs down the length of the trenches, as well as protect *his* men as they prepared for the next move.

It was still dark and the enemy needed to be seen off. Much to Stowie's disgust "Lucifer" was out of fuel.

"All good things must come to an end I suppose...thanks mate," he said as he kissed the fuel tanks and casually dropped "Lucifer" on the ground.

Clancy eyed "Lucifer".

"Dead is it?" he asked.

"Yeah mate," replied Stowie.

"That's a bit of a shame. It would have been useful right now," said Clancy as he handed Stowie his rifle.

Whilst Captain Ponsonby and the main body strengthened their position, set up Company HQ and ran communications line back to Battalion, Lieutenant Sargent, his platoon and the CSM moved forward to seek out the elusive enemy. Despite the Germans still tossing bombs, the Aussies kept pushing forward. Darkness, however, had not been their friend, as was revealed when dawn's light began to filter through. At around 0515 hours the platoon were moving slowly along the trench lobbing the occasional bomb, and receiving a few in return, when they spied a Gordon Highlander standing boldly on the parapet ahead. The man was Captain Gordon. He was soon joined by another four Scotsmen. Clancy saw the group first and quickly nudged Lieutenant Sargent.

"Hey Tomo...look...a couple of jocks".

The Lieutenant felt a gush of relief as he greeted the Captain with a wave.

"I thought you Australians were known for your cricket," the Scottish Captain noted.

It quickly became apparent that the last bombing exchange had been between the men of the 9th Battalion and the Highlanders. Luckily no harm had been done and the allies quickly saw the irony.

"Well you *jocks* obviously aren't, judging by *your* standard of bowling," replied Clancy.

"Aye...point taken...still no harm done eh laddies?" said Captain Gordon.

The good news was that they had reached their objective and linked up with the 7th Division who had managed to seize part of the village. As for the Germans whom they had been pursuing, they were now trapped between the *equally* terrifying Scots and Aussies, taking refuge in a dugout. Unfortunately for them the Scotsmen were about as unforgiving as Stowie and his new mate "Lucifer", tossing Phosperous Bombs into the dugout, their own version of the flames of hell. None of the enemy escaped the conflagration; the dugout still burning fiercely fourteen hours later.

Whilst 'B' Company had been on the move, 'C' Company in OG2 had advanced at 0400 hours to establish two strong points with two platoons. Once done another two platoons leap frogged them, and captured a further length of trench, setting up two similar strong points. They had met with similar fierce opposition that 'B' Company had endured, but they soon overcame the enemy. The next two platoons then passed by, led by Lieutenant Ramkena and Sergeant Porter, and continued the attack. A Grenatenwerfer positioned at a cross roads two hundred and fifty yards to their front had held them up, delivering heavy fire on the ANZACs, but a Stokes Mortar managed to eliminate the German weapon and 'C' Company carried on forwards, a brave dash along the parapet by a bomb hurling Sergeant Porter contributing to the enemy's flight.

The attack groups successfully pushed forward and established their outposts just short of their objectives at the cross roads; all of this whilst enemy bombing parties bombarded them quite heavily. The Gordon Highlanders had gained a greater part of their line, although they too had not managed to capture their *exact* objective.

The Aussies had got off quite lightly with regard to artillery, however, once they had gained their objectives this suddenly changed when a heavy concentration of shells rained down on both their new and old positions, making it difficult for them to properly organise themselves on their current positions, or to be easily re-supplied.

There was nothing else to do except sit about sheltering as best as they could in their trenches. For the moment it was impossible to have defences laid out on the parapet due to the incoming rounds; but it was extremely unlikely that there would be an enemy counter attack until the barrage subsided or eased a little. Even then it would take mere seconds for the Aussies to man the parapet, and the Germans didn't appear game to risk it at the moment.

As they sheltered, the men kept their heads down as shells fell closer, their explosions sending fountains of dirt and debris into the air, shaking the very ground with the concussion of the blasts, causing the men to flinch instinctively. Some of the soldiers lit cigarettes; others read letters, whilst some, like Roo, got the billy on.

With his usual unexpected magic, Captain Ponsonby, with Tomo in tow, arrived where his Gallipoli mates were huddled.

"Ah...Rueben Taylor," he said as he savoured the aroma of the tea boiling away in the billy can, "I can always rely on you for a lovely cuppa".

Roo glanced up and gave the officer a cheeky smile.

"Yeah, yeah…I should open a trench cafe and start charging," Roo responded.

"That's a top idea dear boy," laughed Ponsonby as he passed Roo his mug.

"We should give it a name," Clancy piped up.

"How about 'Tea Enfield' or 'Dig In Cafe'?" suggested Ten Bob.

"Or the 'Dugout Cafe'," said Tomo, much to the approval of all in earshot.

"I was thinking more on the lines of 'Shithole Cafe' myself," laughed Clancy.

"Charming," added Roo as he thought for a second, "hey…my tea aint *that* bloody bad…is it?"

"No, no, of course not. It's as good as my mother used to make; or better," Ponsonby insisted.

"Ha!" laughed Clancy, "the closest *your* mum ever got to a tea pot was when the maid was pouring her tea *for* her".

Ponsonby grasped his chin with his thumb and forefinger for a moment.

"Yes, you're probably right".

Clancy then suddenly remembered something the Captain had said earlier.

"Hey skip…what was that you said before? Curses and naughty words or something?"

"Oh, that…you know, just trying to keep my language clean…don't want a clip round the ear when I meet Doris".

Archie's ears pricked up suddenly.

"What, you're gonna come and meet mum and dad when all of this is over?"

"Of course," replied Ponsonby, "we're mates, as you say, friends for life".

Archie and Roo smiled at each other then both shook Freddy's hand.

"We'll hold you to that mate," replied Roo.

Clancy cleared his throat very loudly, then flinched as another explosion showered them with dirt.

"Don't forget me, Stowie and Ten Bob".

"And me," said a hopeful Tomo.

"Mum will sure be in her element, afternoon tea on the verandah and all that," replied Archie, as he pondered for a moment, "bloody hell I wish this was all over so we can go home".

Just as Archie finished his sentence another whine of artillery was heard, but this time from their rear. The boys were about to cheer when the friendly rounds slammed into the earth a few yards to their front, showering them with mud.

"You drop short bastards!!" Clancy yelled, to no one in particular, before turning to Ponsonby, "you'd better get on the blower and tell those gunners what lousy shots they are mate".

"Yes, I'll be back in a tick," replied the Captain as he made his way to Company HQ to make his telephone call.

The artillery soon found their range and the boys breathed a collective sigh of relief; not that the Germans had ceased *their* shelling of course. As it was, the trenches in their new position had been badly mauled by the bombing and shelling, some of the walls being almost non-existent.

Stowie kicked at a crumbling section of the trench wall, shaking his head.

"This won't stop a sneeze, let alone a shell".

Clancy inspected a collapsed section and nodded, a satisfied expression on his face.

"We've got the bones of a trench at least so let's patch this up fast eh".

"Too right Clance, there's not much of a barrier if Fritz starts chucking bombs over. I reckon we'll be picking shrapnel out of our teeth," Roo noted.

Mutual support and interlocking fields of fire too were the order of the day with the Aussies and Highlanders agreeing to occupy each others' flanking posts, causing their front lines to overlap and close any gaps to the enemy.

All in all, during the advance, around six hundred and fifty yards of trench had been gained in OG1 and another two hundred and fifty yards in OG2. The Germans, obviously in a bit of hurry to withdraw left a lot of equipment behind, including two hundred and fifty rifles, three mortars, three flame throwers, and a large number of bombs and flares.

"This lot will come in handy at least," Clancy noted, as he surveyed their haul.

"Yes, but at what cost dear chap?" replied Captain Ponsonby.

What cost indeed, with twenty five men dead and one hundred and thirty six wounded.

5

A bloody new chum

Life in the 9th Battalion's part of the line had quietened down for a few hours and the officers and SNCOs had been summoned to Battalion Headquarters for a briefing by the CO. All in all it was hoped that their time here was going to be uneventful...or so they thought, for they had visitors.

The OC, Clancy, Roo, and Archie trudged back to their lines, mud caked on their boots. As they reached the trench, they were met by a snarling British sergeant, from the North Essex Regiment, his voice thick with disdain.

"Ah, the bloody colonials. Now all our hard work in taking this place is gonna go down the pan".

Clancy, not one to take an insult lying down, bristled.

"You wanna watch your mouth, mate, before I fill it with my fist!"

A scuffle almost broke out as Clancy stepped forward, but before it escalated, Captain Ponsonby stepped between the two men.

"You'd better adjust your attitude before you lose those stripes, Sergeant."

Before the sergeant could respond, a scream echoed from no man's land. Archie's head snapped toward the sound.

"Sir, I think there's a wounded man out there. Do you want me and a couple of the lads to go out and take a squiz?"

The sergeant smirked, his expression not lost on Ponsonby.

"What is so funny about wanting to rescue a wounded comrade sergeant?"

"Hah!" laughed the sergeant, "he aint wounded is he?...yet...take a look if you like".

Ponsonby ignored the lack of respect coming from the sergeant.

"Sir, quick. You're not going to believe this," said a shocked Archie as he handed Posonby his binoculars.

The officer scanned the area to his front, his face hardening as he passed the binoculars back to Archie, who then shared them around with his mates.

"Good God," said an angry Ponsonby, as he turned towards the sergeant "what the hell is the meaning of this?"

Archie and the others took turns looking through the binoculars. Their faces mirrored the captain's disbelief. About ten yards from the trench stood a wooden stake, and tied to it, facing the enemy line, was a lone soldier; a British soldier.

"This scum and his mates put him out there just before sunrise," Stowie added.

"He's a bloody conchi aint he," replied the sergeant, a sneer etched across his face.

Clancy clenched his fist, his temper flaring.

"Oy! You bastard, this is *my* officer and you will call him sir!"

Before Clancy could act on his threat, Ponsonby stretched out his right arm to block his path.

"Now, I know what a conchi is but these chaps might not, so do tell sergeant," said Ponsonby.

"A conscientious objector," the sergeant replied smugly, "he refuses to fight. No doubt you blokes have got a few of them yourselves".

That remark caused a few murmurs amongst the Aussie soldiers who were not ones to be called cowards.

"We damn well *have* not!" Ponsonby snapped, "*these* men....*we*.... are *all* volunteers".

"Well more fool you then," the sergeant sneered.

Before he realised it was coming the sergeant found himself flat on his back in the mud, courtesy of Stowie's massive fist. Stowie wanted to save the CSM the embarrassment of a court martial so had stepped in.

"My CSM gave you fair warning you bastard!" growled Stowie as he pointed to the sergeant, whilst tipping a nod and wink to Clancy.

"Right," yelled the sergeant as he staggered to his feet, clutching his jaw, "*you*, laddie, are on a charge. What's your bleedin' name?"

"*You*, sergeant, won't be charging anyone," Ponsonby interrupted coldly, "now get out there and bring that fellow back to the trench...now!"

"No.....sir," said the sergeant defiantly whilst pausing to glare at Clancy and Stowie, "I will not".

The diggers were in disbelief at what they were witnessing. Surely sergeants in the British Army weren't all like this disrespectful man before them? Ponsonby's jaw tightened as he snapped at the sergeant.

"Did you bring an officer with you sergeant?"

The sergeant made no reply.

"He brought a colonel with him sir. He's an even bigger ass than this fella," said Stowie.

"Right. Where is this colonel?" Ponsonby asked.

"In your HQ, probably helping himself to your rum mate," Stowie replied.

Ponsonby was not amused.

"Unbelievable!" he said as he turned to the English sergeant, "Go and fetch your officer NOW!"

Muttering under his breath, the disgruntled sergeant made his way along the trench, his fellow British soldiers shaking their heads in shame and disbelief as he passed them, both NCOs even managing an obscene finger gesture towards him, after he had passed of course.

"I'm sorry about him sir," said one of the English corporals, "he's not much cop as a soldier but got promoted because he has a loud voice and likes to grovel to the colonel".

"Well that doesn't say much about your colonel then, does it mate?" Archie responded.

Ponsonby nodded his appreciation to the corporal.

"Thank you corporal. Tell me what is the situation along the front line in these parts? Do you have agreements with the Germans at all?"

"We try to sir, you know don't shoot unless *we* do, but the colonel and the sergeant think it is alright to play with our lives and insist that we fire a few rounds and lob a few bombs over," said the corporal, "all while they hide in the command post dugout".

Ponsonby raised his gaze skywards and tutted.

"Typical".

Stowie then saved the day, in a manner of speaking.

"Sir?"

"Yes Corporal Stowe, what is it?" replied Ponsonby, feeling a little tense with the whole situation.

"We had a bit of an unofficial truce this morning...you know...for the Germans to collect their dead and wounded. They didn't get them all in though".

"Did you indeed?" Ponsonby replied, a plan beginning to flicker in his head, as he looked towards the German lines, "and who did you deal with over there?"

"A bloke called Werner. He's an officer I think. He seems like a decent fella," Stowie replied.

"Good. That *is* good," said Ponsonby as he looked over to his men, "Archie, has anyone got something white? A handkerchief perhaps?"

"I have sir," announced Roo, "Aunt Doris made it for me and sent it over to Gallipoli the other year".

"Wonderful. Good old Doris eh?" said a smiling Ponsonby, "Roo, now don't damage your hanky, but would you mind tying it to your muzzle for a flag of truce please?"

"Yeah, no worries Freddy, er, sir," replied Roo keenly.

"I don't think Mum would appreciate being called *old* Doris sir," chuckled Archie.

"Oh yes, point taken Archie," replied Ponsonby, feeling a little less tense.

The tension however was about to change as the sergeant and his colonel barged their way along the trench towards Ponsonby and his mates.

"What is the meaning of this Captain?" demanded the colonel, "my sergeant says one of your men struck him".

"That's the man there sir," said the sergeant, pointing at Stowie.

"I was here all the time and didn't see nothin' sir," said the English corporal, as the sergeant, scowled back at him.

"Really Jones? Are you calling Sergeant Anderson here a liar?" asked the colonel, "what about *you* Captain, did *you* witness this assault?"

"No sir, I did not. Perhaps the sergeant had mud in his eyes," replied Ponsonby.

"More like shit," uttered Clancy under his breath.

Ponsonby paused and gave a quick glare to the CSM, then turned to the colonel

"Out of respect for your rank, sir, I am informing you that my men will be fetching in that fellow tied to the stake over yonder".

"You ruddy well will not!" barked the colonel, "he is a damned coward, and if you disobey me I will have you pinched, and court martialled".

Ponsonby could feel his blood boiling as he searched the immediate area of the trench with his eyes, looking towards one of the sleeping dugouts, its door covered with a hessian sack.

"Colonel, I'd like to talk privately with you in that dugout if you please," said Ponsonby.

The colonel smiled defiantly, looking around at the Australian soldiers and their officer with contempt.

"You, young man, and your undisciplined rabble, are not in a position to make demands of me," the colonel replied.

Captain Ponsonby was a likeable and calm fellow, not known for any outbursts of anger, except towards the enemy of course, but today was not a good day. His hand drifted to his revolver, as his anger flared, and before anyone could react, he had it pressed under the colonel's chin, grabbing him by the scruff of the neck, steering him unceremoniously in to the dugout. The men around them, both British and Australian, stood firm as events unfolded, exchanging glances but remaining silent. A code among soldiers... I didn't see it if you didn't.

"Unhand me you buffoon!" cried the colonel.

Once inside the dugout, Ponsonby growled at the colonel.

"You, sir, are supposed to be an officer and a gentleman, someone for these men to look up to and focus their courage on. But I believe *you* to be a shirker and a coward".

"You know nothing of me," responded the colonel, stammering.

"Really?" shouted Ponsonby, "I have heard tales of British regiments who are leaderless because all of *their* officers led from the front and paid the ultimate price, but here you are, not a scratch, and skulking in *my* command post".

The colonel was now feeling uneasy as Ponsonby pushed the muzzle of his revolver deeper in to his neck.

"I...I have just been lucky that's all old man," replied the colonel.

"Lucky?" shouted Ponsonby, "how many times have you climbed over the top, eh? HOW MANY???!!!"

The colonel was now beginning to panic.

"None," he replied, "that is what my officers are for, what?"

Ponsonby could control his rage no longer and back handed the colonel across the face with his free hand, forcing him to fall backwards on to the muddy ground.

"You struck me! That's a shooting offence," announced a somewhat shocked colonel.

"Not in *my* army it isn't, you gutless bastard. Where in Kings Regulations or the Manual of Military Law does it say you can do this sort of thing? Where? How *dare* you stake out a soldier like that. How dare you!" Ponsonby said, pausing for a moment to think, "my name is Ponsonby. Do you recognise it?"

The colonel thought for a moment.

"There was a Ponsonby at Waterloo was there not?"

"Yes, and there is a Ponsonby in the War Office, a General no less, *my* uncle, and he has the ear of the King. I could ruin you with one conversation and you will return home in disgrace. Do you want that?"

The colonel's expression was one of sheer panic. He shook his head vigorously.

"Right. I and my men are going to retrieve that soldier," said Ponsonby, "and when we return I want the official papers signed by you honourably discharging that man from your army, then you and your useless sergeant can return to that rat hole you came from. Do you understand?"

The colonel nodded, terrified, as Ponsonby reached into his desk drawer and flung some paper and a fountain pen at the colonel.

"Here! Now get bloody writing you arse!"

Ponsonby re-holstered his pistol and gestured to the colonel to do his work, then he flung open the hessian door of the dugout and strode out in to the trench.

Archie could see the look of anger and determination on Ponsonby's face.

"Are you right mate?" he asked.

Ponsonby nodded.

"We have some work to do," Ponsonby replied, "Archie can you get a small section of four men together please mate, we're off in to no man's land. Roo, do you have your flag of truce ready?"

Roo looked at the white handkerchief tied to his rifle muzzle.

"Yes mate," he replied.

"Right then, let's get to it. Roo wave your flag over the top of the sandbags, but keep your head down," said Ponsonby as he called out over the gap that was no man's land, "Werner! Werner!"

It took a while for a reply to come back, but come back it did.

"Ja? Was ist das? Er, what do you want?" came a German voice.

"Oh bugger!" said Ponsonby, "my conversational German language skills aren't that good. A truce...er...der waffenstillstand...so we can come fetch that man out there, on the post...der soldat auf dem posten".

He looked back to his friends, who gazed back in awe, and shrugged his shoulders.

"I hope I got that right," he said hopefully.

"Komm bitte hier...freund," a voice called back from the other side.

"It looks like you did," said Stowie, "that is Werner alright".

"Good man," thought Ponsonby.

"Werner! I'm coming over now with four men, please hold your fire. Oh, how do you say this?...wir kommen jetz vorbei, ich habe vier soldaten bei mir, nicht scheezen bitte".

"That all sounds Dutch to me sir but it is doing the trick. Look there's Werner and he's waving you over," announced Stowie.

"Right...Archie, Stowie, Ten Bob and Roo with me. The rest of you hold your fire. Roo, keep that hanky high and dry," said Ponsonby.

As they slowly climbed up the rickety scaling ladders on to the freshly sandbagged parapet, Ponsonby called out to Werner.

"Werner we are coming. Don't shoot......er wir kommen Werner, nicht scheezen".

The five men gingerly made their way across the muddy expanse of ground, gently stepping over the German dead, who lay peacefully in the puddles after a sudden and violent end, moving barbed wire obstacles out of their path as they went. As they walked they watched as a distinguished looking German officer appeared from the opposing trenches. He had his hands raised in the air and was carrying no weapon.

"Alles ist gut," he called out as he and the five Australians cautiously approached the staked out soldier.

As the six men stood before each other, the German held out a hand of friendship.

"Guten morgen. Ich heiße Hauptmann Werner Plath. Wie gehts?" said Werner.

"Good morning Captain. Sprichst du Englisch. I'm sorry but my German is very limited," replied Ponsonby.

Werner smiled.

"You have been doing well my friend," he replied.

"Thank you. I'm sorry, my manners escape me. I am Captain Ponsonby and these four fellows are my friends," said Ponsonby.

The German officer, a stocky, serious looking fellow, clicked his heels as he exchanged formal nods and a few words with the Australians.

"These Britishers think my army is a firing squad. All along the front line they do this, but we refuse to do their work for them," said Werner, "I am happy that you have come for him. Had he been left we would have fed him at night, but it is not safe".

"Well, thank you all the same," said a grateful Ponsonby.

"And *we* were told that *you* blokes were baby killers mate," said Archie, looking back to the battalion trench, "but really it's those English bastards over there".

"Nein, nicht baby killers. Like you we are just fighting for our country and our kommerades," replied Werner.

"You're a good bloke Werner," said Archie as he offered his hand in friendship.

"Danke," replied Werner, accepting Archie's outstretched hand, "we have heard that you Australians are fearless animals in battle".

"Animals?!" exclaimed Stowie with a cheeky smile, "that's not very friendly, mind you I've seen bigger brawls in the pub back home at closing time than here".

"Ich verstehe nicht," replied a confused Werner, not understanding the larrikin humour.

"Don't mind him Werner he's only joking with you....er....scherzen," explained Ponsonby.

"Oh yes, ha, ha, I understand now," replied Werner, hesitantly, "so, where are you going to? Will you be stationed here now?"

As Stowie opened his mouth, Ponsonby skilfully and quickly jumped in.

"Now, Captain; that would be telling wouldn't it, and we don't want your side plastering us with artillery rounds now do we?" said Ponsonby.

Werner smiled innocently and shrugged his shoulders like a naughty child who had just been caught out by the Teacher. Ponsonby turned to his men.

"Right chaps let's cut this fellow down and take him back to the trench".

Once the boys and the British soldier were safely back in their trench, there was a noticeable tension in the air. Archie crouched beside the man, giving him a once over and offering him water.

The soldier was of medium build, standing around five foot ten, but it was his face that drew the eye. Although he was only in his mid twenties, his hair was prematurely grey, framing features that might have once been lively. His face, worn from both the war and a tough upbringing, still carried a hint of mischief - a friendly, cheeky expression that seemed out of place given his ordeal. His blue eyes, though dimmed by exhaustion, retained a welcoming warmth, betraying the kind of man who might have shared a laugh in better times.

His uniform, the same pattern as that worn by the AN-ZACs, was quite ragged, torn in places and missing any markings, strands of cotton betraying where they had been ripped off. From the threads in the centre of his forearm it was obvious that badges of rank had once sat there. On his collar was a single brass collar title, the one on the other side missing. As Archie inspected it he saw a prancing horse with the word "Kings" inscribed on a scroll at the bottom.

"What's your regiment mate?"

The soldier gulped down the water and, still catching his breath, finally spoke.

"I'm from the Liverpool Pals Battalion, part of the King's Liverpool Regiment," he said, his thick scouse accent barely understandable, "I enlisted with me mates."

Archie raised an eyebrow.

"Pals Battalion? So you volunteered, like us?"

The soldier nodded, but before he could answer, Archie pressed further, searching for answers.

"Then why are you refusing to fight?"

The soldier looked taken aback, his eyes widening.

"Is that what those twats told you?" he asked, almost incredulous.

"Yeah, mate, they said you're a conchi," replied Clancy.

The man's face became stern, and he straightened his back as if summoning the strength to tell his story.

"I'm no bloody conchie. Me and me mates were at the Somme last year. We're soldiers".

"Yeah mate, we were there too," said Clancy.

Archie's expression softened a bit, but his curiosity remained.

"So what's the story then?"

The soldier's voice grew grimmer as he explained.

"A couple of weeks ago we were in the attack at Arras. At first, things were going good, but the artillery barrage didn't take out the barbed wire like it was supposed to, and bloody hell did we pay for it. We lost over seven hundred blokes just from our battalion. But the officers, they kept sending us forward...murdering bastards!"

The Aussies exchanged uneasy glances. Archie could already feel where the story was heading, but he stayed silent, letting the man continue.

"Us NCOs asked the officers, no, pleaded with them, to hold off on another wave until we could clear the wire properly with the big guns, but these toff's wouldn't have it. They had us arrested instead. Couldn't sully the name of the regiment see by taking advice from *our* sort. So they shipped some of us down here, to this mess, where they figured these buggers wouldn't care and would do this to us".

The man's voice was steady but filled with bitterness, as though he was long past anger and now left with a kind of tired resignation.

"An unofficial execution..." Ponsonby muttered from the side, his eyes narrowing in disgust.

The soldier nodded, confirming Ponsonby's grim realisation.

Clancy let out a low whistle.

"Some of our blokes had a similar problem at the Nek," he said quietly, his voice weighed down by memory, "but they just went over the top...straight into hell; but they did eventually see sense...you know...and stopped the attack".

The trench fell into silence for a moment, each man reflecting on the insanity of war and the cost of following orders that made no sense, the quiet finally being broken by the voice of the English colonel.

"Here is this man's discharge, Captain," the colonel said, his tone thick with condescension as he offered Ponsonby an envelope. He tilted his chin slightly, his eyes narrowing with the kind of surprise one reserves for something beneath them. "And we'll say no more about it, what?"

Ponsonby snatched the envelope from the colonel's hand with an air of impatience, barely hiding his disdain, and read the letter, giving a cursory glance at the rescued soldier's sleeve.

"Yes. This will do nicely," he said, his voice edged with sarcasm as he cast a disdainful stare at the colonel and his entourage, "*you* may go".

The colonel, visibly affronted, straightened his posture, clearly unused to such dismissive treatment, his eyes flashing with indignation, and without a word, he turned on his heel, and went on his way, his small band following in his wake.

Ponsonby held the discharge letter in one hand, as he read the document again before extending it to the soldier.

"Here are your discharge papers...sergeant," Ponsonby said, his tone flat, "you're free to go".

Philip Bartholomew - or Pip, as his mates had called him - didn't move to take the letter immediately. His grey hair, an uncommon sight for a man of his age, seemed to tell more of his story than words could. His face, worn from a hard life, spoke of years in the Brownlow Hill Workhouse, growing up as a foundling, an orphan; a man with no family and no place to go.

"Go home to your family," Ponsonby added, with a slight hesitation as he searched for a glimmer of relief in the soldier's eyes.

Pip's lips twitched, not into a smile, but something more solemn. His blue eyes, once perhaps full of hope, held only a tired emptiness now. He spoke softly, almost to himself.

"I have no one. I'm an orphan. The army was the only family I've ever had. I joined up with all of me mates from the Work House...and they're all dead".

Roo knelt beside Pip.

"I'm Roo, what's your name mate?"

Pip had never seen a person of colour before, let alone one wearing sergeant's stripes, and stared at Roo marvelling at his facial features and almost desiring to reach out to touch his skin just to see if it felt the same as his.

"Sorry sarge, I've never seen a black man before...sorry again...er my name is Philip Bartholomew," Pip replied, his hand offered to Roo, "very pleased to meet you, all of you; and thank you".

Roo laughed.

"Don't worry about it...neither had I until I looked in the mirror".

"Philip Bartholomew...that's a bit of a mouth full," said Clancy.

Pip nodded and explained how he had been left on the steps of a convent twenty four years ago on the 1st of May, the feast day of Saint Philip, one of Jesus's disciples, so the nuns had named him after the saint.

"What about Bartholomew?" Archie enquired.

"Another saint and disciple," Pip replied, "but me mates call me Pip for short or Sergeant Bart...well Mister Bart now I suppose".

Captain Ponsonby thought for a moment.

"Pip...just like in 'Great Expectations'...by Dickens?"

His words fell on deaf ears.

"Sorry Freddy, if it's a book we don't have much time for that sort of stuff on the station," replied Archie.

"Well, perhaps you should make some time. It doesn't hurt to be well read you know," said Ponsonby.

"Er...I know the book sir," Pip replied, "it was in the orphanage library. Quite a long read, and it has an Australian connection".

"That it has," said Ponsonby as he pondered for a moment, "how do you fancy an Australian connection?"

Pip was confused.

"Sir?"

"Join us and come back to Australia after the war," replied the Captain.

"Can I *do* that?" asked a surprised Pip.

"Well, I don't know for sure, but I'll certainly find out," Ponsonby replied, a new sense of vigour in his demeanour, "you'd have to be a Private soldier though".

Pip nodded, a smile appearing on his worn face.

"But where would I live? Australia's miles away".

"Can you ride a horse?" asked Archie.

"No," replied Pip.

"Well...neither had I...until I could," said Archie, "don't worry we'll teach you".

"Looks like Doris and Ray have gained another waif and stray," Ponsonby noted.

Roo glanced at Clancy, who gave a nod.

"A bloody new chum. You'll figure it out. We all did".

Pip stared at the discharge papers in his hand, as if they meant something far greater now. Not freedom, but a new beginning. A fresh start. Perhaps even a family. The weight of his past wasn't gone, but the burden lightened just a bit.

Ponsonby watched the exchange in silence, then nodded, allowing the soldiers to offer Pip something he had never been given: a choice, a future beyond the trenches.

6

Born out of the ashes of destruction

The weather had remained reasonably fine during the fighting but now it was bucketing down with rain, turning the trenches in to a muddy quagmire again; much to the delight of the men...or perhaps not. The men were managing to keep more or less dry and had been able to scrounge some wet weather gear for Pip, as well as a rifle and bayonet.

As Archie looked up at the grey clouds and felt the rain soaking his skin, he suddenly thought of home.

"Bugger me...and I haven't even seen any black Cockatoos".

"Black what?" asked Pip feeling confused, "is this an Australian thing I need to know about like?"

"Yes mate, one of many," replied Stowie, "you'll get used to it. I sure did".

"So what does it mean?"

"Well, back home if you see a black Cockatoo, which is a bloody big parrot by the way, then you know it is going to rain," Archie explained.

"Yeah...*and* it does; fair dinkum Pip," added Roo.

Pip was becoming more confused by the minute.

"Fair dinkum? Yous fellas speak a different language".

"They...er we do," replied Stowie, "but it just means that a person is telling the truth, or that they are not joking about it".

As they spoke the OC and CSM returned from an orders group with the Commanding Officer. Roo looked over to the two men and smiled.

"We're just teaching Pip here a few Aussie words".

"Yeah mate, we'll make an Aussie out of you...just like old Freddy here," laughed Archie.

"Hey...less of the *old*, dear boy," replied the Captain, "any way I have some news. Pack up your kit and prepare to move out of the line in the early hours".

The men breathed a sigh of relief and at 0230 hours the next morning the 9th Battalion departed from the line, having been relieved by the 5th Battalion. Returning to Noreuil where they had started a few days earlier, the battalion settled into the sunken roads. The rain, however, was still not their friend and continued to pour down; their new position offering no protection from the deluge whatsoever.

"Hey Pip. I bet this is a home from home for you eh?" asked Roo.

"What do you mean?" replied Pip.

"I hear its always raining in England," said Roo.

"Not all the time but it does rain a lot".

"Back home you'll find a big change then because it is hot and sunny most of the time, but come January you get a year's worth of rain in one day," said Roo.

Pip looked surprised.

"Yeah mate, dad sometimes jokes that we should build an Ark," laughed Archie.

The rain was playing havoc with their surroundings as everything gradually turned in to mud. Their stay was set to be an unpleasant one until yet another unexpected move on the 9th of May sent the battalion on a three and a half hour march to Bapaume.

"Blimey, with all this marching I'm sure I'm about six inches shorter," Roo noted.

Archie laughed.

"Ha, at this rate the only thing left of us will be our heads".

Despite the constant sounds of war in the distance, once at Baupame the men managed to sleep all day. Pip was kitted out with his Australian uniform and equipment, soldier for the use of, whilst everyone was treated to a bath and a change of underwear. For most, the emersion of their filthy bodies into the bath water sent the water a murky greeny brown colour. Clancy of course was on form as ever.

"Hey fellas, if you think the water is a funny colour, you should see me undies".

As he picked up his newly issued slouch hat, Pip hesitated for a moment, turning it in his hands. It felt strange, foreign, yet somehow fitting. The Rising Sun badge, gleaming proudly on the turned up brim, caught his attention. He'd seen it before, of course, and laughed at the men's jokes about it being an emblem from a jam jar, but now it was his to wear. He traced the outline of the sun's rays with a roughened finger, feeling the weight of what it meant. His eyes dropped to his collar where the same badge sat, small but unmistakable.

After all those years in the British Army, with its stiff uniforms and rigid rules, this felt different, making him feel like part of something freer, something new. He adjusted the hat to sit at a slight angle, like the Aussies did, even though the fit still felt unfamiliar. The brass 'Australia' shoulder titles caught the light as he smoothed down his tunic, and he ran his thumb over the word. 'Australia'. It still felt odd, like he wasn't quite meant to wear it. Raised in a Liverpool workhouse, Pip had never imagined himself in *any* army, let alone this one, but the Aussies had taken him in, and, here he was, wearing the uniform and symbols of a nation he wasn't born into but had chosen to fight alongside. He was finally home.

At Baupame the 1st Division was now Corps Reserve and during this stay fatigue duties were fewer, thus the men, for once, managed an *actual* rest. Including Pip, as of the 11th of May, the Battalion strength was forty one officers and eight hundred other ranks.

The 9th remained at Baupame for two weeks managing to squeeze in the odd sports day, plus a visit by General Birdwood. The Gallipoli veterans were particularly pleased to see him.

By the 23rd of May the battalion had moved on to Ribemont, the whole brigade being billeted in the village. The troops were relieved as many thought that the longer they remained at Baupame the more likely it was that they'd be in the front line again. To the men the sight of green fields and villages was preferable to the sounds of battle that they had marched away from.

A highlight of their stay was pay day, music to the ears of the men who had not had much in the line of luxuries for some time. The Australian troops were the highest paid of the British Empire troops and were known by their counterparts as "six bob a day tourists". A Private soldier was paid six shillings a day, compared to the miserly one shilling and one penny a day of a British soldier of the same rank. Even a British infantry sergeant received a mere two shillings and six pence per day. When an Australian soldier was paid, one shilling of their daily pay was held over as "deferred" pay, to be paid out at the end of their service, a great savings plan. The men could also choose how much was allocated to Australia and their family, and how much they received on the Front.

Pip stood in the ranks patiently as each man waited to be called forward. He glanced around at the familiar, now slightly more relaxed faces of his fellow soldiers, the only sound being the clink of coins and the steady murmur of soldiers as they eagerly counted their money. The barn they were using as a makeshift pay office smelled faintly of hay, a small comfort compared to the muddy trenches they had come from. Billeted in this quiet French village, the troops took what small luxuries they could get, even if it was just the feel of dry ground underfoot.

Pip's thoughts wandered to the whispers he'd heard about the Australians being called "six bob a day tourists". The name had made him laugh the first time he'd heard it, but now, standing in line for his first payday, he was curious to see what the fuss was all about.

Finally, it was his turn.

"Private Bartholomew!"

"Sir!"

Bringing himself smartly to attention he marched up to the desk where the Pay Officer sat, the Pay Sergeant beside him. He halted, as only a British soldier could, stamping his right foot in next to his left, and saluted the officer, who barely looked up as he gestured to the four bank notes in front of him.

"Count it," he instructed.

As he stared at the small pile of notes he quickly searched the desk for the stack of coins he was used to receiving, then picked up the bank notes and started counting, his eyes widening as he reached the total.

"Four pounds?" he muttered under his breath, disbelief creeping into his voice.

He blinked, counted again, running the notes through his fingers. There it was; four pounds, just as shocking the second time. He'd been a sergeant in the British Army and had never seen this much pay in a month, let alone sixteen days. This felt like robbery, but of the good kind.

The Pay Sergeant, noticing his hesitation, smirked.

"Well? Do you want the money or not?"

Pip nodded his head quickly.

"Yes, sir!" he blurted, quickly stuffing the four one pound notes into his pocket before they could realise their mistake.

"Sign here," said the sergeant.

Pip dutifully signed then saluted again.

"Pay correct, sir!"

The Pay Officer gave a satisfied nod, and Pip turned and marched away, his mind still spinning from the shock. Four pounds. For sixteen days. It was hard to believe.

He found Archie, Roo, and Clancy leaning against a stone wall nearby, all of them grinning as they watched him approach.

"Well, how did you find your first pay day?" Archie teased, raising an eyebrow.

Pip shook his head, barely able to keep the sceptical expression off his face.

"Four pounds," he muttered, "it used to take over a month as a sergeant to earn that much!"

"Yeah, it's not bad, is it? Six bob a day for marching around France. Could be worse," said Roo.

Archie looked at his wounded leg and then elbowed Roo in the side.

"Just marching?!"

Pip rubbed the back of his neck, still staring at the notes in his hand.

"No rank, no responsibility, *and* I'm getting paid three times as much; I'm dead chuffed".

Clancy grasped his shoulder.

"Well, mate, welcome to the AIF. As long as you don't let the pay go to your head, you'll do just fine".

Pip pocketed the money, finally managing a smile.

"I think I'm going to like it here with you fellas," said Pip, a curious realisation springing into his thoughts as he eyed his mates' rank insignias, "hey...if this is what a private gets how much do *you* lot get paid?"

Clancy, grinning, put a finger to the side of his nose.

"Wouldn't *you* like to know, mate?"

The men chuckled to themselves for they might have been fighting the same war as everyone else, but it seemed the Australians were doing it their own way - and getting paid handsomely for it.

On the 18th of May, during an 'A' Squadron patrol near Sausage Ridge, almost on the Turkish line, heavy fire had broken out and Corporal Langridge was killed. Despite a valiant attempt by Corporal Geddes to retrieve his body, he was driven back by an enemy barrage and had to withdraw, minus Corporal Langridge.

Four days later, on the 22nd of May, the 2nd Light Horse, accompanied by the New Zealand Mounted Rifles, embarked on a critical mission. Tasked with acting as a screening force, they moved into position between Beersheba and the line stretching from Hadaj to Wadi Inkharuba. Their objective was clear – provide comprehensive protection for the engineers working to demolish the old Turkish railway, which snaked its way from Beersheba towards Auja near Magdhaba. It was a dangerous operation, and one that required constant vigilance, as the enemy could strike at any moment; but the troops knew what was at stake.

The existence of this railway posed a significant threat to the EEF's right flank, enabling potential enemy movements and supply lines. To eliminate this danger, the engineers worked swiftly and meticulously, their every move shielded by the ever watchful mounted troops.

The screening patrols established a defensive perimeter, their positions strategically dispersed to guard against any possible enemy incursions. The forward patrols kept a sharp eye on the horizon, scanning for any signs of Turkish forces, whilst flanking patrols moved along the sides, ensuring no surprise attacks from the wings, while patrols to the rear monitored any threats from behind, securing the engineers', and their own path of withdrawal.

As the sun climbed higher, its blistering heat bearing down mercilessly on the soldiers and their mounts, their mission proceeded with staunch precision, with the engineers, under this protective umbrella, methodically planting explosive charges along the railway.

By midday, the final charges were set, and with a series of thunderous explosions, the railway was rendered inoperable. As the dust settled and the twisted remnants of the railway lay shattered, a cheer erupted from the lighthorsemen, pleased with a job well done. The engineers, their task complete, signalled to the mounted troops, and in an ordered and well practised manoeuvre, the 2nd Light Horse and the New Zealand Mounted Rifles began their withdrawal, ensuring the engineers were safely on their way before falling back themselves.

Their journey to the bivouac area was an arduous and taxing one, spanning sixty four miles across uneven, hostile and unforgiving terrain, but despite the fatigue setting in from both the mission and the terrible heat, they pressed on filled with a mixture of exhaustion, pride, and unspoken mateship.

The rhythmic sound of hooves pounding the rough ground was the only constant in the dark, broken by the occasional muttered curse or groan as the men shifted in their saddles, trying to find some relief from the mounting discomfort. Every muscle ached, and the heat of the day had only been replaced by the biting chill of the desert night. Although fatigued, there was no room for complacency, for, with threat of ambush ever present, keeping their senses on high alert despite their bodies begging for rest was a must.

Each man battled his own private war against sleep. Eyelids drooped, only to snap open again at the slightest sound, while minds wandered back to thoughts of home or the familiar faces of fallen mates. They relied heavily on one another, not just physically but mentally, their shared hardship knitting them closer together with every passing mile.

Some found comfort in the stars above, tracing constellations that felt oddly out of place in this foreign land. Others stared ahead into the blackness, their focus narrowed to the horse in front of them, the only guide in the disorientating void of the desert night. They rode in silence mostly, the occasional low murmur of encouragement passing between them, as officers and NCOs rode up and down the column, exchanging witty remarks which helped keep the men's spirits up.

For thirty one hours, they rode through the night and into the next day, the sun's scorching heat bearing down on them again, yet, despite their weariness aching bones and dry throats, they maintained their vigilance and discipline until they finally reached the safety of their encampment. Beyond exhaustion they may have been, but there was a quiet satisfaction in their eyes, for they had done what was asked of them and more. The railway was destroyed, and they had brought themselves and their engineers back in one piece.

The demolition of the railway had not only disrupted the enemy's logistical capabilities but also solidified the EEF's strategic position. The efforts of the mounted troops had once again proven invaluable in the long march towards victory.

On the 25th of May, despite the arrival of Lieutenant Brett and thirty recruits, the regiment's strength was very weak. But nothing could be done unless more men volunteered back home.

Life for soldiers in the Middle Eastern deserts was an ongoing battle against the elements, disease, and monotony, with each day bringing new challenges and hardships.

There was *some* good news however, when the regiment moved to Kazar at the end of the month for a musketry course; the good news being the relatively short distance from the beach. Swimming parades were very popular and far outweighed the weapons course, which was really for the benefit of the new comers.

Camping in the open during the scorching summer months, soldiers from both sides faced almost unbearable conditions. Food shortages plagued the camps, and the prevalence of debilitating sand fly fever further weakened the troops.

Rations for the EEF too were notoriously lacking in variety and quality. While in camp, soldiers could access rice, peas, dates, porridge, jam, bread, meat, and bread pudding, whilst army canteens offered sardines, pears, chocolate, sausages, milk, coffee, cocoa, and biscuits for purchase. However, during operations, the troops relied on "iron rations" of Bully beef and army biscuits, occasionally making a stew from tinned pressed beef and onions. Tea was a constant companion, consumed at every opportunity.

The only respite for the troops came during rest periods on the Mediterranean coast at places like Kazar.

In contrast, morale among the Ottoman forces on the Palestine front was problematic, particularly among Arab units, who were vulnerable to enemy propaganda. Logistical difficulties led to shortages of food and water during the hot summer of 1917, and the lack of postal, recreational, and health services, coupled with high desertion rates, further depressed morale.

Not surprisingly, dust was a constant adversary for both sides. The regular onslaught of the khamsin - the hot desert winds sweeping in from the Negev Desert - carried billowing clouds of pulverised road dust, enveloping everything in its path. The winds, capable of raging for days, tore down tents and marquees, leaving drifts of sand and fine dust around Gaza, which felt like red hot needles during sandstorms, infiltrating every aspect of life, from food and drink to sleep; clinging to perspiring skin, unlike the more manageable sand.

The area behind the front lines was always a hive of activity. Traffic broke up road surfaces, creating deep layers of fine dust that lifted with the slightest breeze, cloaking everything in a white cloud. To manage this, traffic was restricted to main roads, which were swept clean and marked with wire netting and boards to guide troops.

Septic sores became a significant issue during the summer, particularly in the ANZAC Mounted Division. A poor diet lacking in variety and vegetables, along with fly and mosquito bites, contributed to the prevalence of these painful, hard to treat sores. Flies were everywhere, infesting food, drinks, and tents, making minor cuts and scratches easily infected. These sores, typically treated with antiseptics, required frequent bandage changes, which quickly became filthy due to the dust. The troops were in dire need of the vitamin C from fresh oranges, but as yet these were not available.

As at Gallipoli, delousing and washing were daily routines, but only when there was water available. Soldiers hunted for lice whenever they had spare moments, burning the minute offenders with candle flames and matches. Water was a precious resource, with deep wadis and wells providing necessary supplies. Extensive efforts were made to drill for water and establish pumping stations and pipelines to ensure a steady flow to various locations, but, despite these efforts, water quality varied, with some sources causing stomach troubles among the troops.

Medical support was essential in these harsh conditions. The daily Sick Parade allowed soldiers to receive immediate treatment for minor ailments, while more serious cases were referred to field hospitals.

Yet another coastal holiday beckoned on the 19th of June when the entire brigade moved to Marakeb, on the beach, near Khan Yunis. Despite the many inspections and other military necessaries and distractions, their ten days in situ was a welcome rest for the weary ANZACs. Various forms of entertainment, including a boxing tournament assisted in livening up the men's evenings and distracting them temporarily from the thoughts of war.

On one of the evenings, in the midst of the makeshift camp, a vibrant Pierrot troupe had set up their temporary stage. This travelling concert party, known for their lively variety shows, had drawn a curious crowd of ANZAC soldiers eager for a diversion.

The Pierrots were dressed in traditional costumes and were a sight to behold - each performer wearing loose fitting, brightly coloured garments adorned with large pom poms and pointed hats. The show began with a classic Pierrot song, "Au Clair de la Lune", a familiar tune from the men's school days, setting the tone for the evening through a wide ranging mix of songs, dances, and comedic skits. Their leader, a hook nosed man with a talent for banjo playing, led the ensemble with a spirited and contagious energy. His white face paint, marked by exaggerated eyes and lips, highlighted his expressive gestures and exaggerated expressions.

As the concert unfolded, the audience of ANZAC soldiers, including Percy, Chugger, Davo, and Boggy, watched with mesmerised attention. For many of these men, hailing from remote country towns and outback farms and cattle stations, this was their first experience of such a performance. The Pierrots sang melodious tunes, their voices harmonising beautifully under the evening sky, whilst interspersed between the songs were comedic routines filled with slapstick humour and clever pantomime, drawing hearty laughter from the war weary men.

Jugglers too tossed colourful balls and rings into the air with impeccable skill, whilst dancers moved gracefully across the small stage.

Percy nudged Chugger, a grin spreading across his face as the antics of the Pierrot clowns brought a rare moment of laughter.

"Now I know what those shows were that Mum and Dad said they saw back in the old country" he said, his eyes twinkling.

"Well, we never had anything like this in the bush," Chugger replied, chuckling, "to be honest, I didn't even know what a parrot troupe was until today".

"It's Pierrot, mate," Percy corrected Chugger with a laugh. "not parrot...Pierrot".

Chugger shrugged, still smiling.

"Whatever it is, they're bloody funny".

Davo, usually the most quiet and reserved of the group, couldn't suppress a laugh as one of the Pierrots exaggeratedly tripped over his own oversized shoes, much to the delight of Boggy, who clapped enthusiastically.

"Look at that, Davo's actually smiling," Boggy teased, giving him a friendly nudge.

"Bloody hell Davo, you wanna watch that smile doesn't crack your face mate," added Chugger.

"I reckon its wind," said Boggy.

"Yeah, well, don't get used to it," Davo retorted with a smirk, but his eyes betrayed his amusement, "these fellas *are* good, though. It really takes your mind off things".

"Cheers to these Parrots," Chugger said, raising an imaginary glass, "for giving us a night to remember".

"Cheers!" the others echoed, their spirits lifted, if only for a moment.

As well as travelling concert parties there were also sports meets which kept the troops, and the bookies, interested.

Percy was mates with one of the athletes, Private Scouller, and was aware of his athletic prowess and accomplishments.

"There's some money to be had here boys," announced Percy.

"Really? What do you know?" asked Boggy.

Percy said nothing but simply touched the side of his nose with his right forefinger.

"Fellas, I'm a bit short, but can you all afford to club together for a bet on Scouller?" asked Percy.

"Is it a sure thing?" asked Davo, "I never was good at betting and I'm trying to save for my own place once this is all over".

"I reckon it is mate. Just a couple of pennies should do the trick I reckon," replied Percy as his three mates reached into their pockets.

The boys managed to scrape together two shillings, not a great sum, but all that they were willing to risk, and approached a "bookie" from the New Zealand Mounted Rifles.

"We wanna put a bet on Private Scouller," said Chugger, quite gruffly.

The Kiwi soldier eyed the boys up and down.

"Yeah mate, which event?" the Kiwi asked.

Percy rubbed his chin.

"What's he in?" he asked.

The Kiwi bookie thought he was on to a good thing with these seemingly naive Aussies and reeled out a list of events that Scouller was competing in.

"Oh mate...the one hundred, two twenty, four forty and eight hundred and eighty yard runs, and the high jump, long jump and hurdles," replied the Kiwi, "he must be a fit bugger eh?"

"Can we bet on everything he's in to win?" asked Percy.

"Everything? Really?" said the Kiwi, feeling stunned, but sensing an easy profit, "how about I give you five to one odds on each event, and your winnings from one rolls over to the next and becomes the stake?"

Percy pondered whilst his mates looked apprehensive.

"Yeah, righto...you're on," announced Percy as he offered his hand to the Kiwi and handed over the two shillings.

"There goes our money boys," whispered Boggy.

"See you later for our winnings," said Percy.

"Yeah right," the Kiwi soldier thought to himself.

As the four men made their way to the makeshift sports field Chugger, Davo and Boggy were not confident at all in the bet which Percy had just placed on their behalf.

"Who is that Greek bloke...you know the one who rode the flying horse?" asked Chugger.

"Hercules?" asked Davo.

"Yeah, that's the one," replied Chugger, "well I hope that Scouller is as strong and fit as Hercules today or we are buggered".

Remarkably Private Scouller was, and won all of his events. The boys were stunned. Boggy was trying hard to quickly tally up their winnings.

"That can't be right!" he exclaimed.

"What can't be?" asked Percy.

"Well, two shillings at five to one on all those races works out to almost eight thousand quid!" replied Boggy.

"You're joking mate!" said a stunned Davo, "that's nearly two thousand pounds each. That's my home sorted, and more".

"Yeah, well I reckon that bloody bookie won't have that much money on him. Let's go and find him and see," remarked Chugger.

After a long search through the bustling crowds of soldiers, the boys finally found the bookie skulking near the YMCA canteen tent.

The Kiwi soldier immediately recognised the four Aussies and seemed a little worried.

"Fellas...come to collect your winnings have you?"

"Yeah. Got our eight thousand quid have you?" replied Chugger, impatiently holding out his open hand.

The New Zealander looked left and right for a possible escape route, but there was none.

"Er...no. Sorry boys but I didn't count on you winning eh?" he said.

"I bet you bloody didn't," growled Chugger, "well, you should have done your sums before you took our bet mate!"

Boggy too was annoyed and began slowly punching his right fist into his left hand.

"Come on...how much have you got?"

The soldier stepped back, reached in to his tunic and produced a thick wad of bank notes.

"Just this..."

Chugger snatched the pile and quickly counted it.

"A thousand pounds!?" snapped Chugger.

"Take it boys and we'll call it square," announced the bookie.

Percy wasn't convinced.

"Mate, you took bets from a whole brigade. You'll have more than this. Empty your pockets; boots off!"

The Kiwi soldier obeyed, and the boys discovered another five thousand pounds.

"That's the lot boys...honest...take it *please*," said the Kiwi.

Percy noticed that the soldier had kept his lemon squeezer hat firmly on his head throughout his ordeal.

"The sun in your eyes is it mate?" Percy asked, frowning, as he snatched the Kiwi soldier's hat from his head.

"Well, well, stone the crows...look at this!" exclaimed Percy as he examined the inside of the hat, "there must be fifteen thousand pounds here!"

Chugger grabbed the fifteen thousand and added it to their six thousand pounds haul.

"Twenty one thousand pounds...not bad for a two shilling stake eh. What do you reckon?" Chugger said, winking at his mates.

"Come on fellas that's all I've got!" said the bookie.

"Tough bloody luck!" shouted Chugger.

Percy had a sudden twinge of guilt and beckoned for Chugger to hand over the money.

"I'm no thief...unlike you," said Percy as he glared at the bookie, "so here's our winnings, plus a thousand each for our trouble *and* our initial stake".

The Kiwi was nonplussed.

"So you're leaving me with just nine thousand?"

"Take it or leave it you bastard!" growled Percy as he tossed the remaining bank notes at the Kiwi, who quickly scuttled to pick them up before they were caught by the breeze and lost forever.

"Here, have a drink on us," said Chugger as he flicked a six pence at the soldier.

As the four mates turned and began their journey back to their lines they couldn't believe their luck.

"Twenty one thousand pounds he had! There must have been some big bets today," said Davo.

"That's twelve thousand pounds for us though for a stake of two shillings," said Boggy in disbelief.

"Not a bad return eh?" said Percy, nodding.

The next day the boys reported to the unit pay office to arrange to send their money home. A few eyebrows were raised, but nothing was said.

The four mates were set for life. All they had to do now was to keep those lives safe, which in a war was no easy feat.

As the mates wandered back to their bivvie area, their rifles slung over their shoulders Percy admired the town of Marakeb, which was only a short walk away.

"Anyone fancy a stroll in to town?" he asked.

"Oh mate, I don't know. I get sick of the bloody Gyppos try-ing to sell you stuff," replied Chugger, still mulling it around in his head.

"And trying to steal your wallet..." added Boggy.

"You bunch of bloody miseries. Are you coming or not?" asked Percy.

"Oh bugger it. There's nothing else to do anyway," replied Chugger.

So the five mates headed in to the village, which was much the same as any other that they had visited. As they walked, the distant hills surrounding the town appeared dry and rugged, dotted with olive groves and ancient terraces, reminders of the land's deep agricultural roots. Above them, the sky was a bril-liant, cloudless blue, the mid morning sun casting long shad-ows across the stone buildings, which radiated the day's heat. The buildings, made of sun bleached stone, rose with weathered grace, their thick walls etched with centuries of wear. Narrow, winding alleyways snaked between the structures, some just wide enough for two men to walk side by side. The doorways were arched, many of them framed by intricate stonework, while ironwork balconies jutted out from the upper levels, draped in washing drying in the sun, or decorated with vibrant potted plants. Some houses were capped with domes or flat roofs, where locals would sit and chat, escaping the heat of the day.

Marakeb felt timeless, a place where the past and present uneasily coexisted. As the mates passed through, they saw local men huddled together under the shade of olive trees, smoking strange pipes and discussing matters in low, melodic voices. The women, who were dressed in traditional robes, their faces hidden, hurried along, balancing clay pots on their heads or carried baskets filled with bread from the communal oven. Stray cats darted between their feet, seeking food or shelter in the nooks and crannies of the town's labyrinth of streets.

Percy was in his element and marvelled at the streets, a patchwork of cobblestones, uneven and worn smooth by the feet of countless generations. In the distance, the haunting call to prayer echoed from the minaret of the town's mosque, a tall, slender tower standing in contrast to the low, sprawling buildings, whilst the voices of children laughing and playing in the alleys filtered through the ancient town, and the occasional bray of a donkey or the clatter of a cart rattling over the cobbles added to the pleasant and peaceful sounds of civilisation.

As the men walked, the sound of sandals scuffing the stones mixed with the distant echo of merchants calling out in Arabic, led them to the bustling marketplace. Even Chugger, who despised these places, was impressed with the colourful stalls which lined the central square, each overflowing with baskets of spices, fresh produce, and handmade goods. The mouth watering scent of cumin, cinnamon, and roasted coffee beans was wafting through the air, blending with the sharper smells of tanned leather and charcoal from nearby cooking fires.

Boggy inhaled the cooking smells with vigour, savouring each odour, whilst imagining the local delights that awaited them.

"I could eat a camel boys," said Boggy, turning suddenly upon hearing footsteps running up behind them. It was young Alfie.

"Wait for me Aussie cobbers," he called out.

"Bloody hell Alfie, don't sneak up on blokes like that...not around here anyways," said Percy.

Chugger coughed and glared at Percy following his lapse in language, then nodded his head towards the boy.

Percy held out his open hands as if to indicate that it was too late now.

"Sorry Mister Percy, it would have been a bastard if you had shot me eh?" replied Alfie, whose head recoiled as Chugger landed a smack on the back of his head.

"Alfie! What have we said about your bloody language...oh bugger!" said Chugger as he realised what he had just said.

Boggy quickly lifted Alfie up and nodded to him, as Alfie, not wanting to miss an opportunity, slapped Chugger in return, much to the delight of all present.

"There...what is good for the goose is good for the...er...what is it you say?" asked Alfie.

"Gander mate, its gander," replied Percy.

"Oh yes. I remember now," said Alfie with a wink, "bad Chugger!"

Chugger gave the boy a scornful glare, and then smiled.

"I bet you're hungry mate," he asked.

Alfie used to visit the men at meal times in the hopes of a few morsels. Bully beef was the usual fayre, but he also sampled horse and donkey meat, which he enjoyed.

As the boys continued down the narrow, dusty street, a sudden commotion erupted, a mixture of frantic shouting and the unmistakable sound of a woman's terrified scream. Instinctively, the five soldiers unshouldered their rifles and fixed bayonets, the metallic click slicing through the noise. Chugger grabbed Alfie by the arm and pulled him behind the group.

"If anything happens to us run like the blazes back to camp... don't stop, don't look back...do you hear?"

Chugger's voice was firm, no trace of humour or his usual cheeky grin.

Alfie nodded, the fear in his eyes betraying his age. The soldiers advanced slowly forward along the narrow street, the tension increasing with every step. The screaming and shouting grew louder, the wails of the woman now sharp and desperate. Then, without warning, a young Arab woman darted out from an alley, running swiftly into Chugger's arms; trembling like a leaf.

Chugger, caught off guard, managed a crooked smile.

"Ease up girlie, what's the rush?"

The woman, her veil slipping from her face, was barely twenty. Her eyes were grey and her face was beautiful, sculpted and flawless like the Roman statues they had seen in Alexandria.

"Ease up, what's the rush?" he asked again, his voice softer now, trying to calm her.

Although she couldn't understand his words, the sheer panic in her eyes spoke volumes as she clung to Chugger like a limpet, her eyes darting left and right, as the noise from down the narrow street became louder and closer. Then, in a terrified burst, she cried out, "Musaeidat eayilati sawf yaqtuluni!"

Alfie understood and stepped forward, his eyes wide, gesturing for the woman to stay behind them.

Percy turned to the young boy.

"What did she say mate?"

"She say her family is going to kill her," replied Alfie.

Percy's eyes widened in shock.

"Get away mate, that can't be right," he replied, then as if on cue, a mob of townspeople appeared, armed with knives and clubs.

At their head was a grim man wielding a massive, curved scimitar sword. The five lighthorsemen instinctively formed an extended line across the narrow street and charged their bayonets in the direction of the mob, steel flashing under the midday sun. The crowd paused, hesitating for the first time, sizing up the khaki clad foreigners with rifles levelled at them. Silence fell as the man with the scimitar stepped forward, his voice dripping with venom.

"Give us the woman!" he demanded.

"Why?!" Percy snapped back, his stance unyielding.

"She has dishonoured her family and must die," the man answered, his eyes straying to the sword in his hand.

Chugger stepped forward a pace waving his bayonet at the man.

"Says who?"

"Allah, peace be upon him, and the Prophet Mohammed," replied the man, his gaze shifting skyward, his voice carrying the weight of centuries of tradition.

"Bugger off!" said Chugger, "what has she done?"

The man looked left and right, unease in his eyes, darting between the mob and the soldiers.

"She is my daughter and refuses to marry this man...Nasir," he replied, pointing to a fat, toothless Arab who looked like he was on his last legs.

Percy acknowledged Nasir with a slight bow and smiled, letting out a low whistle.

"She refuses to marry *him*? I *am* surprised," he retorted sarcastically, "and you want to kill her for it?"

"Yes. I want her head," the man growled, pointing at his sword.

As he listened to the exchange Chugger's blood was boiling and he could contain himself no longer.

"*You* are her *father* and she is a defenceless woman, you gutless pack of mongrels," Chugger shouted as he struck the girl's father between the legs with the butt of his rifle, causing him to crumple in agony as his sabre clattered to the ground.

Seeing her chance, the girl burst out from behind her protective khaki wall of Aussies and picked up the sword, raising it to finish off her father, her eyes burning with years of pent up rage. The mob gasped, horror stricken by the sight of a woman defying a man.

"No!" shouted Chugger, as he grabbed her sword arm before she managed to swing the mighty weapon at her grimacing father.

"Alfie, tell her to get back," said Percy.

"Eud alan!" said the boy; and the woman obeyed, stepping back behind the soldiers, sword still in hand, her knuckles white.

The mob suddenly bristled with new anger, their murmurings vociferous and threatening, until Percy shouted for the boys to take aim; then they went quiet.

"Amazing what a loaded rifle can do eh boys?" laughed Boggy.

The girl's father, still clutching his groin, spat through clenched teeth.

"Give me the woman!" he man demanded.

"Or what?" demanded Percy.

The man was silent for a moment.

"Five pounds and she is yours," he announced, hand outstretched.

Percy's eyes narrowed, disgust curling his lips.

"A fiver?! You wanted her dead a minute ago...now bugger off...the lot of you...imshee!!" Percy shouted as he waved his rifle at the crowd.

"'Iidha ra'aytuk maratan 'ukhraa, fa'ant mayit jmyean," the girl's father muttered as he and the mob turned and walked away.

Alfie quickly translated the comment for his friends.

"He says if he sees you or the woman again, you are all dead".

"Is that right?" said Percy, "well he'd better bring a few more *men* with him, because there were none *there*!"

Chugger was livid and called out to the retreating mob.

"I haven't seen any of *you* blokes on the battlefield! Gutless bastards...only good when you're ganging up on one girl!!!"

As the mob retreated into the shadows, their angry murmurs fading with the dusk, the boys felt a sense of relief. Bayonets were still fixed, rifles gripped tightly, but the danger was past...for now. Percy wiped the sweat from his brow, looking around at the others.

"Well, that was a bit close for comfort," he muttered, shaking his head, "let's head back to camp, eh?"

The others nodded, their hearts pumping fast, adrenaline still coursing through their veins. They unclipped and sheathed their bayonets, and slung their rifles back over their shoulders as they began to walk away from the narrow street, their boots crunching on the dusty cobbles.

But Chugger didn't move, standing there, rooted to the spot, his gaze locked on the girl who had collapsed onto her knees in the dirt. She was trembling, her eyes fixed on the ground where the mob had stood moments before. Alone now, utterly abandoned, she looked like a lost bird, fragile and terrified, the weight of her fate hanging heavy in the air.

"Chugger?" Percy called over his shoulder, "are you coming mate?"

But Chugger remained silent. He couldn't bring himself to leave her there, standing all alone. His mates had already taken a few steps forward, but he remained by her side, his expression betraying his worry for the girl.

"She's got no one," he muttered under his breath, glancing from the girl to his mates. "They're gonna come back for her, you know...and when they do...she's dead".

Percy paused, turning back to face him. The others did the same, exchanging uneasy glances.

"Yeah, but what can *we* do?" Percy asked, a hint of frustration in his voice, "it sounds harsh, but she's not really our problem Chugger. We did what we could".

"She's got nowhere to go, Percy," Chugger replied, a steely edge creeping into his tone, "look at her. If we leave her here, she's as good as dead".

The girl's eyes flicked toward Chugger, her gaze full of fear and uncertainty. She didn't speak their language, but she didn't need to - her situation was written all over her face.

Boggy stepped forward, scratching the back of his head.

"Yeah, but what are we supposed to do with her, mate? We can't just drag her back to camp like a stray dog".

Chugger clenched his jaw, glancing down at the girl again. Her veil hung loosely, half off her face, but she didn't seem to care anymore. She looked broken, like she'd lost everything, her life hanging by a thread. Her eyes met his, pleading silently.

"We *can't* leave her, and *I'm* not going to!" he repeated firmly, his voice low but sure.

Percy sighed, rubbing his temples.

"So what, we just bring her back with us? What if they don't let her stay? She's not a soldier. I don't want to leave her either mate, but...bugger it...I don't know."

"We've got a bloody camp full of soldiers. Someone's gotta know what to do," Chugger argued, "if we leave her here, they'll kill her...and I'm not letting that happen, and I know you blokes don't want that either".

There was a pause as the group stood in the fading light, the weight of the decision playing on their thoughts. Alfie looked from the girl to Chugger and then back to Percy.

"The people here are not good...very superstitious...she is safer with us than out here," Alfie said quietly.

Boggy sighed, shifting his weight.

"Oh, bugger it. Fine...let's take her back. The worst thing that can happen is the higher ups will send her off somewhere safe".

Percy gave a reluctant nod.

"Alright. But this is on you, Chugger. She's your responsibility".

Chugger smiled then knelt down next to the girl, his hand extended toward her. She hesitated for a moment, then slowly reached out, taking his hand. He helped her to her feet, his grip steady and reassuring.

"Come on, miss. You're with us now," he said softly, though he knew she didn't understand the words. She didn't need to - his tone said it all.

As the tension seemed to ease, the girl suddenly grabbed Chugger's hand, her grip firm and urgent. Before anyone could react, she started pulling him down a narrow alleyway, her pace quick and determined.

"Oy! Where's she taking you?" Percy called out.

Chugger glanced over his shoulder.

"No idea, but I reckon I'd better go with her".

The others hurried to catch up, Alfie running alongside them. The girl led them through the maze of dusty streets, her veil fluttering loosely as she ran. They weaved past crumbling stone walls and open market stalls, the scent of spice and sweat hanging in the air. Every so often, she would glance behind her, eyes wide with fear as the clatter of hurried footsteps echoed behind them.

"She's leading us somewhere," Percy muttered, "but where?"

Before anyone could answer, Alfie turned, his face paling.

"It's them...look...they're following us!"

Chugger cursed under his breath as they reached a small, flat roofed stone house tucked at the edge of the street. The girl stopped abruptly and pointed to the doorway. Through Alfie, she spoke hurriedly, gesturing for the boys to stand guard.

"She says to wait here while she gets her things," Alfie translated.

Boggy scoffed, unshouldering his rifle and clipping on his bayonet.

"This lot again? Just full of hot air. Look at them, gutless wonders...they won't do anything".

The sound of angry murmurs grew louder as the mob, led by the girl's father, closed in. Most were still armed with knives and clubs, while the father clenched his fists, his eyes burning with rage.

"Bayonets up, lads," Percy ordered.

The soldiers snapped to attention, rifles at the ready, their bayonets glinting in the sunlight as they formed a protective barrier around the narrow entrance to the house, the steel tips of their weapons gleaming like the fangs of some cornered animal.

The girl's father stepped forward, yelling in Arabic, his voice commanding the crowd as he pointed toward the house. The mob took a step closer, encouraged by his words.

Boggy let out a low laugh.

"See? Gutless wonders, the lot of 'em. They won't do a thing".

His eyes flicked to Chugger.

"But I reckon they'll keep trying if we don't scare 'em off for good".

Percy's eyes narrowed as the mob inched closer.

"Maybe it's time we show them we mean business?"

Without hesitation, Percy fired a shot into the air. The sharp crack echoed down the alley, reverberating off the stone walls. The mob flinched, a ripple of fear passing through them.

The girl's father yelled something again, but his voice wavered this time. There was hesitation in the mob now, their steps faltering as they glanced between the soldiers and their leader.

"Hold the line," Percy growled, "no one's getting through".

Minutes later, the girl re-emerged from the house, her expression happy yet defiant. Clutched in her arms was a woven blanket, her few belongings neatly tied up with a thin cord. She looked at Chugger and the boys, then back to the mob. In her hand, gleaming under the sun light, was the scimitar.

Chugger raised an eyebrow.

"Alfie, ask her if that is all she's got".

The girl nodded. The blanket contained nothing more than her essentials, but the scimitar was the most precious. Her father's protests grew louder as he pointed furiously at the sword, but she held it firmly, refusing to let go.

"It's a family heirloom," Alfie translated, as the father spat more curses their way.

Percy gave a grim nod.

"Then she keeps it. Let's move."

They fired a few more shots into the air, the deafening cracks sending the mob scattering like rats. The girl's father remained, obstinate, but even *he* took a step back as the soldiers surrounded her, bayonets outward like a shield of sharpened steel.

As the mob melted away into the darkness, Percy signalled that they should move, and, together, they began the trek back to camp. The five soldiers, and Alfie, surrounded the girl, keeping their eyes on the streets and alleys ahead, wary of any more threats lurking in the dark. Chugger stayed close by her side, his presence a silent promise of safety.

When they arrived at camp, there were a few raised eyebrows as the group marched in with the girl in tow, her curious eyes taking in the sea of khaki uniforms and rows of horses and canvas tents. But no one said a word. Chugger's determined expression and the girl's obvious distress were enough to keep any questions at bay, at least for now.

Inside one of the tents, they sat her down, offering her water and food, which she accepted with shaking hands, still wary, though the tension in her shoulders had eased slightly now that she was away from immediate danger. Her presence among the men was unexpected, but the men accepted it with curious amusement. The atmosphere was more relaxed, but the events of the day lingered in the air.

"So? What now?" Percy asked, breaking the silence, "we can't just keep her here forever, she needs somewhere safe, but...she can't stay with the regiment".

Chugger crossed his arms, looking down at the girl.

"She can stay with us for now. We'll think of something".

Alfie had been translating on and off throughout the events, though the girl, through her eyes and gestures, was communicating more than words could ever say.

"What's your name, miss?" Chugger asked, leaning towards her, careful but intrigued.

Alfie translated.

"Ma asmak?"

The girl hesitated, her eyes darting toward the ground. Finally, she responded in a soft voice.

"Rachel".

"She says her name is Rachel," Alfie relayed, his own eyebrows lifting in surprise.

Chugger laughed.

"Yeah I think I got that bit mate".

"Rachel? That's an Aussie name if I ever I heard one," said Johnno.

The men exchanged puzzled glances.

"You big dill Johnno...it's a Biblical name," Boggy muttered, scratching his head, "if I remember correctly she was the wife of Jacob".

Percy grinned.

"Well, look at that, an Arab girl with a name straight out of Sunday school".

Chugger smiled and looked at the girl.

"Rachel...it's a beautiful name," he said, the words coming slow and careful, as if testing how they sounded on his tongue.

He saw her smile, as she met his gaze, her expression softening for the first time since they'd found her; and that was enough. There was something unspoken between them, something Chugger couldn't quite put into words, but it was there - a quiet connection, fragile yet unmistakable.

"She can stay with me," Chugger finally said, his tone leaving no room for argument, "she's not safe anywhere else".

"Oh yeah?" asked Percy, with a cheeky smile, "the last time I looked we all shared a tent".

Chugger thought for a moment.

"Well I'll have to try and scrounge *her* a tent from the QMs then".

The others nodded, some still unsure but unwilling to challenge him. Rachel had found her place, at least for now, within the strange fold of soldiers who had become her unlikely protectors. And Chugger, standing by her side, knew in his gut that this was only the beginning.

Over the next few days, Rachel became a constant presence, following Chugger everywhere. His mates teased him almost non-stop, with Percy winking and saying, "Looks like you've found yourself a shadow mate". Chugger would brush it off with a smirk, but inside, he couldn't help but feel protective of her.

Rachel still wore her veil, tightly wrapped, her face half hidden behind the cloth. It was a part of her, as much as the scimitar she carried with pride, the very sword she'd been prepared to use to defend herself. Chugger found himself staring, sometimes wondering what lay behind the fabric, the mystery of her beauty only making him more drawn to her.

Whilst sitting by the fire one evening, Chugger nudged Alfie.

"Ask her why she keeps the veil on, mate. She's beautiful. She doesn't need it".

Alfie translated, his young voice careful not to offend, though his own curiosity matched Chugger's. Rachel listened, her eyes thoughtful, before responding quietly.

"She says she wears it because her god, her dignity, and her father demand it," Alfie said.

Chugger nodded, understanding in a way he hadn't expected. There were rules he didn't understand, faith and tradition that were foreign to him. Still, he reached out, gently brushing his fingers over the veil.

"Tell her she doesn't need to hide. Not with us. Not with me".

There was a long pause. Then, slowly, Rachel reached up and pulled the veil back, revealing her face fully for the first time. Her dark brown hair tumbled free as she shook her head, cascading over her shoulders, her skin smooth and radiant under the flickering firelight. She looked at Chugger, meeting his smiling gaze directly, and for a moment, everything else disappeared.

Boggy gulped.

"Blimey...she's a bit of all right eh?"

Chugger didn't say a word, but the smile on his face spoke volumes. From that moment on, Rachel moved with a new found confidence, though her loyalty to her faith was still strong. She was never far from Chugger's side, the scimitar always slung across her back like a warrior queen.

The men took to her quickly, not just because she could ride a horse as well as any of them, but because of the fierce pride she carried, a pride that matched their own. When it became clear she had nowhere to go and would always be in danger, the boys scrounged up what they could - a slouch hat, boots, a tunic far too big for her, and a pair of trousers that had to be pulled in tightly with a belt.

Rachel beamed when she saw the uniform pieces, slipping them on with a strange mix of pride and amusement. The slouch hat sat crooked on her head, her dark hair spilling out from underneath, but she wore it as if it had been made for her.

"She looks better in that get up than half you lot," Percy joked, earning a round of laughter from the men.

Rachel's new life among the soldiers began to take shape. Chugger and Percy had found her a place in the field kitchen, working alongside the cooks. The work kept her close to the regiment, and no one questioned her presence, and she now had something that as an Arab woman she could have only dreamed of...a wage; her own money. As far as the boys were concerned, she was one of them now, and at night, when the fires dimmed and the desert cooled, she would sleep next to Chugger, in the tent he had scrounged, wrapped in her own sense of safety for the first time in her life. He never spoke of it, but Chugger was always the last to close his eyes, his hand resting protectively on the scimitar that now lay beside her.

As the weeks passed, Rachel's integration into the camp became smoother. Though the language barrier still stood between her and the soldiers, Alfie took it upon himself to teach her English. They often sat together during quiet moments, Alfie pointing at objects and pronouncing their names while

Rachel listened attentively, her brow furrowed in concentration.

One afternoon, as the sun dipped low over the camp, Alfie grinned mischievously and leaned in closer to Rachel, speaking in a lowered voice.

"Right, now try this one...," he said, whispering in her ear, the cheeky twinkle in his eye unmistakable.

Rachel's face lit up with excitement, eager to try out the new phrase. She glanced at Chugger, who was busy cleaning his rifle, and in a clear voice, she called out, "G'day, you old bastard!"

All in earshot fell silent for a moment as the soldiers exchanged shocked glances. Chugger spun around, his eyes betraying his surprise and shock. Alfie was barely containing his laughter, but the look on Rachel's face, innocent and proud of her newly learned words, made it all the more hilarious.

Chugger marched over, his face a mix of amusement and exasperation, and gave Alfie a swift clip round the ear.

"You cheeky little bugger," he muttered, shaking his head.

Rachel, confused at first, quickly realised something was off when she saw the smirks on the other soldiers' faces. Her eyes narrowed as she looked at Alfie, who was still grinning like a schoolboy caught pulling a prank. With a playful huff, she swatted him on the shoulder, muttering something in Arabic that probably wasn't too polite.

"Ladies don't swear..." said Chugger as he glared at Alfie before leaning down to Rachel, smiling softly as he explained. "Maybe don't say that one again, alright?"

Her cheeks flushed with embarrassment, and she nodded. But despite the moment, communication was getting easier by the day. Slowly but surely, Rachel picked up more words and phrases, and though she still struggled with the language, all who came to know her felt a little more connected to her.

Even Chugger was constantly surprised with the speed of her learning, especially one evening when she approached him, her voice soft as she uttered "Wilbert…"

Chugger looked up, a little surprised to hear his first name, one he hadn't been called in years. The way she said it, with a touch of shyness, caught him off guard. A warm smile spread across his face.

"You got it right, Rachel," he said, tipping his slouch hat at her, "not bad at all".

She smiled back, sitting beside him. The two of them exchanged jokes and laughter, often stumbling through the language, but always finding a way to understand each other. They teased and laughed like schoolchildren, tossing words back and forth, their bond growing deeper with every passing day.

Percy watched them from afar, a faint smile tugging at the corners of his mouth. The playful banter, the shared looks, and the laughter; it all took him back to his own youth. He could almost hear the giggles of him and Lil, his childhood sweetheart, and now his wife, running across the paddocks with Archie and Roo, chasing after one another without a care in the world.

Percy looked over to Davo and Boggy.

"Reminds me of the old days, that does," Percy muttered, a touch of homesickness creeping into his voice as he looked at the pair. There was something about young love, about the unspoken bond that grew stronger with every word, every look. It was a feeling he knew all too well.

On the Western Front, the 1st, 2nd and 5th Divisions finally found themselves with their longest stretch of rest from the fighting since disembarking from Australia. Stationed now in the old Somme battlefield and the areas surrounding Amiens and Hazebrouck, the landscape had a different air to it - quieter, almost deceptively calm.

Pip surveyed the countryside, markedly more peaceful than the last time he was here.

"This is quieter than when I was here last".

Roo, standing beside him, nodded.

"Yeah, us too. Feels strange, doesn't it?"

Despite the lull, the army kept them busy. Throughout June, they were slipped into a 'best trained battalion' competition under the guise of routine training exercises. Naturally, the 9th Battalion were the victors, rising to the challenge, eager to demonstrate their prowess and solidify their reputation as some of the finest soldiers on the front.

On the 23rd of June decorations were presented to soldiers of the 9th Battalion, with 'B' Company receiving their fair share. Captain Ponsonby was awarded the Military Cross for his stoic and fearless leadership over their time in France and Belgium, whilst Roo and Archie were each awarded the Distinguished Conduct Medal, their valour under fire earning them respect from every man in the ranks. The prize that everyone expected, the Victoria Cross, was not awarded however, but Stowie *did* receive the Military Medal for leading the attack with his captured flame thrower, which pleased him either way.

Two days later, the men had a reunion of sorts with an old friend in one Lieutenant Colonel Butler, their former Medical Officer, and Kilcoy GP, who now commanded the 3rd Field Ambulance. Butler had come to lecture them on the importance of physical fitness - an ironic topic, given how much marching they'd been doing of late.

By the end of June, the Battalion had swelled back to full strength with thirty four officers and nine hundred sixty four other ranks. The rest continued, though it felt like a moving feast, with the Battalion constantly relocating - first to Ribemont, then Bronfay Farm, near Frau, and Camp 165 just down the road.

"I reckon all this marching is Doc Butler's idea...to keep us fit," Clancy noted, earning a few weary chuckles from the men around him.

No one was complaining, though. After all they'd been through, a bit of marching was a small price to pay for a few moments of peace.

As for the Lighthorsemen, the 29th of June saw the brigade move out to Gamli and Ghabi. From here, four days later, they were to become the covering force for a recce by General Chetwode, of part of the Turkish line at Irgeig.

Leaving their bivouac at 0100 hours, they moved to Wadi Hanafish on the 4th providing a protective screen to all sides of the main party, keeping an eye out for enemy patrols. They came into contact with the enemy at Hill 550 just before dawn, and again at Wadi Sufi at 0700 hours. From this point they were subjected to ineffective shell fire throughout the day, but pushed on, some of the men managing a two fingered salute and other obscene gestures towards the distant enemy.

The exploding artillery shells were an unwelcome addition to the day, with five men being wounded. Random explosions of sand and rubble here and there were an unnerving experience for both men and horses, with some struggling to keep their spooked mounts calm. Percy rode up and down the line offering words of encouragement to the troops; words which were gratefully received. Riding past Boggy, Percy noticed that his mate looked uncomfortable, fidgeting and moving uneasily in his saddle, so slowed his horse and trotted alongside.

"What's up mate?" he asked.

"I've got a sore backside mate with all this riding for hours on end," replied Boggy.

"Yeah, I know what you mean," replied Percy, "I ride a lot on the station at home, but this is more like being on a long cattle drive eh?"

"It is mate. I reckon by the time this is over my arse cheeks will just be a pad of hard skin, you know like you get on the soles of your feet," said Boggy.

"Perish the thought mate," replied Percy as he spurred his horse in to a canter and continued up the line, trying to rid his thoughts of that unfortunate picture.

The regiment finally arrived at the sector, which encompassed Hill 730 to 770, in the late afternoon and, once the recce was completed, they withdrew at 1800 hours, still under artillery fire.

Percy shook his head as he observed the many falls of high explosive shells bursting uselessly on the hard terrain, and thought to himself that had the Turks used shrapnel rounds instead, the story for the regiment might have been different.

On the 8th of July a memorial at Pozieres was unveiled. The 9th Battalion, along with other units, sent a detachment to represent them. Major Neligan was promoted to Lieutenant Colonel and was appointed as the Commanding Officer of the 10th Battalion. A great sense of loss was felt by all with his departure. A former member of the Royal Horse Artillery before moving to Australia, he joined the 9th Battalion as a Private. At Gallipoli, when a Sergeant, he acted as Adjutant, later being commissioned. He was a brave and gallant soldier who was highly respected by all.

On the 24th of July the battalion marched to Albert and entrained to Steenbecque in the north, marching on to Staple, near Hazebrouck, a town with vital rail links. Three days later they were bussed to Lumbres, twenty five miles east of Boulogne. The local landscape of the area was marred by vast quarries, but the town, known for its industrial heritage was built on former marshes at the crossroads of the valleys of the rivers Aa and Bléquin, another key area for the allied armies. Throughout the week, the reason for the previous sodden nature of the area became apparent as while they were there it rained constantly and they returned to Staple having accomplished none of their planned training.

A further five weeks was spent at Vieux-Berquin, a Flemish rural village in the district of Dunkirk. It was here that four months of training came to an end, not only learning new doctrine and methods of attack and defence, but bringing the new men up to scratch. Various inspections and tests were now carried out to confirm the effectiveness of the training. They even managed to squeeze in a brigade sports day on the 22nd of August, as well as a march past General Birdwood.

For the 2nd Light Horse Regiment July was taken up with patrols in various parts of no man's land around the town of Gamli. The brigade now considered themselves the owners of no man's land, and had what they termed as grazing rights. Turkish trespassers only ventured out occasionally, under the cover of darkness but, nonetheless, the Light Horse's time was taken up with Jacko patrol drives.

"This is just like driving cattle," remarked Johnno.

"The good old Queensland Drover eh?" added Chugger, as he broke into song, "pass the billy round boys, don't let the pint pot stand there, for tonight we drink the health, of every overlander".

The Regiment moved out to Goz Lakhleilat, four miles south of the Karm road, which was frequently used by the enemy. Working alongside the 3rd Light Horse, who were in position further south, the regiment formed an extended line approximately three miles long, north east to south east to commence droving of the Turks. As the sun rose on the new day the regiment, as yet unseen by the enemy, discovered two regiments of Turkish cavalry and a battery of artillery at Karm. The order to concentrate the regiment was immediately passed left and right along the line. Turkish flanking patrols were about and soon the Light Horse were forced to reveal themselves.

The sun now blazed high in the cloudless sky, casting long shadows over the arid expanse of the Palestinian desert, the air shimmering with intense heat, making the horizon waver like a mirage. Dust kicked up by cantering hooves formed a billowing trail behind 'C' Squadron of the 2nd Light Horse Regiment. Their mounts, a mix of wiry Walers, surged forward with powerful strides, their riders urging them on with determined shouts.

Leading the squadron, Major Stodart squinted through the haze, eyes fixed on the faint silhouettes of a patrol of Turkish lancers.

"There they are, boys!" he called out, his voice steady despite the pounding of his heart, "Sergeant Taylor!"

"Sir?" replied Percy.

"Take your boys and invite those blokes to join us will you?" said the Major.

Percy gave a thumbs up sign to the officer then turned to his Troop.

"Come on boys let's get at 'em!" he called out as he spurred his horse into action.

The lancers, eleven in total, on sight of the advancing Australians, promptly turned their horses and began to race towards a distant rise, hoping to lose their pursuers in the rugged terrain. Their dark uniforms and fluttering pennants stood out starkly against the pale sand, marking them as Ottoman soldiers. The gap between the two groups was closing rapidly, the lighthorsemen gaining ground with every passing moment.

Chugger, riding at Percy's side, leaned forward, urging his horse to greater speed.

"We're almost on them, Perce!" he shouted, his words only just heard over the thunder of hooves.

"Don't forget...we want them alive mate, so go easy," Percy called out to Chugger.

With a swift hand signal, Percy directed his men to fan out, creating a wide arc to encircle the lancers. The manoeuvre was executed with precision, the lighthorsemen forming a tightening noose around their quarry. As the distance shrank to mere yards, Percy raised his rifle, the glint of gun metal catching the sunlight.

"Hold your fire!" he ordered. "We want them alive!"

The surrounded Turkish lancers, realising their predicament, reined in their horses, bringing them to a skidding halt. They glanced around wildly, eyes darting between the encroaching Australians and the empty desert stretching out all around them. The inevitability of capture settled over them like a heavy shroud.

One of the lancers, a young officer with a fierce, defiant expression, raised his lance in a futile gesture of resistance. But before he could issue a command, the muzzle of Percy's rifle was pointed squarely at his chest.

"Drop it," Percy growled, his tone tolerating no argument, "drop your lances!"

The officer hesitated for a moment, then signalled his men to comply. One by one, the lances clattered to the ground.

"Imshee!" shouted one of the lighthorsemen, using the Arabic word for "move" to command the lancers. The Turkish soldiers, understanding the order, reluctantly began to move as directed, some glaring at the Aussie soldiers, others, their heads bowed in defeat and relief that *their* war was finally over.

The tension in the air began to melt away as the immediate threat faded. Percy surveyed his men, their faces flushed with the exertion and excitement of the chase.

"Good work, lads," he said, a cheeky smile breaking through his stern demeanour, "let's get them back to the rear".

As the Troop regrouped and began the trek back, the prisoners rode silently among their captors, the sun continuing to beat down without mercy.

The enemy was now warned of the 2nd's presence, but as the regiment was still forming they had the appearance of a larger force than they actually were. The Turks fearing an attack from this far greater force immediately withdrew. Heliograph messages having been sent, prompted reinforcements from the whole of the ANZAC and Australian Divisions, who arrived after the Turkish withdrawal.

Watching the huge numbers of Aussies arriving, albeit too late, Boggy waved and sarcastically commented, "thanks for coming boys".

The area of no man's land formed a triangle, with Gaza being the apex and Beersheba and Gamli being the two other corners. In order to keep the enemy out of the triangle, yet more night patrols were carried out.

On the 2nd of August the regiment laid an underground telephone cable as far as Karm, which would assist greatly with communications with the rear echelon and rear guard units and reinforcement units. They also carried out several long patrols and recces south of Beersheba, one of which included the new Commander in Chief, General Sir Edmund Allenby, and two of the Corps Commanders, Sir Harry Chauvel and Sir Phillip Chetwode. To all it appeared that the long awaited third battle of Gaza would soon be upon them.

7

Mud and sand

Following detailed inspections by the Brigadier and staff, the brigade marched passed the General Officer Commanding (GOC), 2nd Army, General Plumer. The General had been posted to France in February of 1915 and given command of 5 Corps which he led at the Second Battle of Ypres in April 1915. Upon assuming command of the Second Army in May, he was promoted to full general on the 11th of June 1915, and during that month his command was the overwhelming victor over the German Army at the Battle of Messines. The battle had opened with the simultaneous explosion of a series of mines, placed by the Royal Engineers' tunnelling companies beneath the German lines, which created nineteen huge craters. It was the loudest and largest explosion ever known, and allowed Plumer's men to leave their trenches and advance three thousand yards.

The 9th Battalion was well over strength now, numbering fifty three officers and twelve hundred and four other ranks. It was by far the strongest battalion in the brigade.

"With these numbers I reckon we will be back in the line soon," said Clancy.

Clancy's prediction was unfortunately accurate as intelligence officers had been carrying out recces on the front line over the past few days, a sure sign of a return to the battle grounds.

In the mean time many underlying tests were being carried out to confirm the mens' readiness and fitness, such as a battalion route march of fifteen miles, plus a drill competition to test their re-actions on receipt of verbal orders, their memories and overall team work.

All officers were shipped off to Devonshire Lines, near Busseboom, in the support area behind the Western Front and Ypres, lying between Poperinge and Ouderdom, in north west Belgium. They had been sent here to view, of all things, a large scale model of their next target. The model had been expertly constructed, on the open ground, showing all of the physical and topographical features of the area.

It appeared that nothing was being left to chance, with the CO briefing each individual company on the details of the forthcoming attack. He was even equipped with a very large and detailed map. The men were indeed impressed with these new methods and organisation, and felt that finally they were well prepared and informed of what lay ahead, with many walking round the diorama, which would later become known as a mud map, with their notebooks and making detailed sketches.

On the 13th of September the 1st Division began to move back to the front line. On the first night the 9th bivvied at the village of Thieushouk, moving on the next day to the Belgian frontier village of Abeele, where they spent the next two days. Abeele, with a population of just a few hundred was unusual for the fact that it straddled the border of France and Belgium, its main street being the border between the two countries, so that houses located on different sides of the street were located in a different country.

As part of the planning and easing in stage, both officers and NCOs inspected the front line and the scale model of this particular battlefield. Clancy and Ponsonby were impressed.

"I reckon each NCO should draw a plan from this for the briefing to the platoons and sections," said Clancy.

The suggestion however, was not required as each man was already doing just that.

Ponsonby smiled.

"You know CSM, for once I feel really good about this".

Clancy nodded.

"Me too mate".

Ottawa Camp, situated just north of Ouderdom, became the battalion's next destination on the 16th of September. Here even more visits were made to the front line and all equipment was thoroughly inspected to ensure that it was all in good working order, and supply.

Two days later the men were on the move again, this time to Chateau Segard Camp, one and a half miles south of Ypres.

Here they began to make preparations for their latest operation at a place known as Menin Road, taking its name from the route that linked the towns of Ypres and Menin.

"WIPERS! I hate this bloody place," said Stowie.

"Yeah, a bit close to the Somme and Pozieres for my liking," Roo agreed.

"What I don't understand is why they don't attack in the summer when the ground is firm. Surely this will all be mud soon now the autumn is setting in," said Archie.

"And it was all going so well," laughed Clancy.

"Chin up chaps, the weather is splendid at the moment and, hopefully, it will remain just so," said the ever positive Captain Ponsonby.

The battalion's latest battle was to be part of the second stage of the 3rd Battle of Ypres; another great offensive designed in order to gain control of the area around Zonnebeke, east southeast of Ypres. It would mark the first major Australian involvement in a series of British "bite and hold" attacks, a tactical approach devised by General Plumer.

The fifteen mile front had opened up on the last day of July, in the middle of summer. Although a number of attacks had been carried out, in light of the unusually wet weather it appeared that Haig was allaying Archie's fears , deciding to allow the ground to dry out before re-commencing the offensive; so right now they were at a standstill.

At this time the British line was located on Westhoek Ridge, three and a half miles east of Ypres. The final objective was AN-ZAC Ridge, approximately a mile further on.

"ANZAC Ridge? That has to be a good omen," said Archie.

The two intermediate objectives were known as the Red and Blue Lines, whilst the Green Line was the final objective; the prize.

Eleven Imperial Divisions, plus the 1st and 2nd Australian Divisions, were to make the assault. The men were very pleased as the two Australian Divisions were to attack side by side, the first time that this had been done.

New tactics were also to be employed, in this case the leap frog method, which basically meant that when the Red Line had been taken, the attackers would hold the captured ground whilst the next unit leap frogged past them to take the Blue Line. Once the Blue Line was taken a third attack wave would take the final objective, the Green Line.

For the seven days leading up to the attack over three thousand and ninety one artillery pieces bombarded the enemy positions, twice the amount of artillery support than that was used on the Somme, with one gun placed on every five yards of the front line. All was planned meticulously. It was a mammoth task to utilise road corridors to bring forward the immense numbers of troops, but this was solved by borrowing roads from other formations occupying sectors not involved in the attack.

As well as the bombardment, the artillery, under the unsuspecting noses of the enemy, practised the creeping barrage, which was to be employed to shield the attackers, and to destroy enemy positions to their immediate front as they pressed forward.

On the 19th General Plumer passed down a decree that all troops were to be given as much rest as possible. The 9th Battalion were still located at Chateau Segard Camp so enjoyed a rare lull with the front line far enough away that the men could sit and take a breath. The mood was quieter, more thoughtful. Around the camp, soldiers were hunched over scraps of paper, pencils scratching out letters to distant homes and loved ones, trying to bridge the miles with words that could never fully describe the horrors they'd faced. But it wasn't the mud and death they wrote about - it was the familiar comforts of home, small reassurances sent across the seas.

Archie and Roo sat side by side, using crates as desks. Their letters were nearly done, both writing to Archie's parents, Doris and Ray, back in Australia. The air smelled faintly of wood smoke, and though the clouds hung low, the day felt peaceful - almost like home.

Roo finished a line and looked up.

"Do you think we tell them the same stuff as each other?" he asked, half amused.

Archie chuckled.

"Probably. I reckon Mum will be saying to Dad that we might as well write one letter and both sign it".

"I don't think they mind," Roo replied, glancing at Archie with a wry grin, "at least they know we're both still in one piece".

Archie nodded, tapping the end of his pencil on the paper. As his eyes drifted for a moment, they settled on Pip who was sitting off to the side on an overturned crate, his gaze wandering between the other men as they scrawled their letters.

Archie nudged Roo, nodding toward Pip.

"Look at Pip. He looks a little lost".

Roo followed Archie's gaze.

"I don't reckon he's got anyone to write to".

Archie pondered that for a moment, then called out to Pip, raising his voice just enough for him to hear.

"Hey Pip, are you not writing to anyone?"

Pip looked up, his eyes meeting Archie's for a second before glancing at Roo, then shifting awkwardly on his crate, a smile appearing on his face.

"Nah mate, no one, not a sausage," he muttered, shaking his head slightly, "and besides who wants to write to this old scouse scally?"

"No one at all?" Roo asked, his voice gentle.

"Nah mate. If I went home the only bods that would be waiting me is the bailiffs".

Archie felt a pang of sympathy.

"Well, that's no good," he said, softening his tone, "I'll tell you what, Pip, we're writing to our parents, so if you want to drop them a few words we'll stick it in the envelope with ours...what do you reckon?"

Roo grinned.

"Yeah, mate, they'd love to hear from you. Aunty Dot will probably send you something as well, she's like that, just ask Clancy over there".

On hearing his name Clancy joined in.

"Oh mate...fruit cake, gloves, hats, all sorts. She is a wonderful woman".

Pip looked between them, a flicker of confusion crossing his face. It was clear that being included like this was unfamiliar to him. He gave a small, uncertain nod, managing a faint smile.

"Thanks lads," he said, his voice low but grateful.

Archie grinned, returning to his letter, whilst Roo laughed.

"I reckon she'll be knitting you a scarf before you know it".

Archie scribbled a quick note about Pip in his letter, whilst Roo leaned over, checking Archie's writing, nodding in agreement.

"We'll make sure they know all about you mate," Archie said as he folded his letter, "you're part of the family now".

Clancy paused for a moment thinking about his letter but also about their new chum.

"Hey mate, to be honest we don't know much about you. What's your story?"

Pip wasn't one to talk much about his past, not because he didn't want to, but because he didn't think that anyone cared to hear about it. But the eyes of his new mates were now upon him, expectant but kind.

"I dunno," Pip muttered, rubbing the back of his neck, "not much to tell, really".

"Come off it, mate," said Clancy, "everyone's got a story; even me".

Pip hesitated, glancing down at his feet. The silence stretched a little longer before he spoke.

"Well, as you know I was left on the steps of an orphanage," he began slowly, "and I grew up there until I was too old and then they sent me to the work house".

The boys exchanged a few glances but said nothing, letting Pip continue.

"It wasn't a place anyone would choose to live," Pip said, his voice steady, "the work was hard like, but the food was worse. You weren't treated like a person, more like...like an animal they had to keep alive just enough to get the work done and fulfil their Christian duty".

He paused, his eyes distant, as if seeing those harsh days again.

"We started early in the morning. Dirty jobs, long hours. You got a bed, but not much else. No family to care about you. No future; just more work".

Roo whistled softly under his breath.

"Bloody hell, Pip I wish we hadn't asked now...sorry mate".

Pip shrugged.

"Nah...that's alright lar...you got used to it. Didn't know any different really, but when the war came, I thought...well, maybe this was my chance to get out of it, see something else. Maybe even make something of myself, which I did, me being a sergeant like".

He gave a bitter smile.

"I *do* love the army, but it turns out, it's just a different kind of hard life...except that no one shoots at you in the slums eh?"

Archie scratched his chin, feeling the weight of Pip's story settle on him.

"Sorry mate. I didn't realise. You've really been through the wringer".

Pip gave a small nod but didn't seem eager for sympathy.

"Its fate I suppose, and besides a lot of blokes have had it worse. I got through it, and now here I am".

Roo passed Pip his notepad and pencil, tapping the paper.

"Well, why don't you write some of that down? The oldies would love to know the man that we are fighting alongside. Tell them everything. I reckon they'd be glad to hear it".

Pip stared at the page for a moment, the idea of writing to someone who cared, even if it was Archie and Roo's parents, seemed strange. But after a beat, he picked up his pen, fingers tightening around it.

"What do I say?" Pip asked, glancing between Archie and Roo.

"Just tell them what you told us," Archie said, smiling.

"Yeah," Roo added with a grin, "you can tell them the truth about me too, mate, you know, that I'm the real brains behind this whole company".

Archie rolled his eyes and gave Roo a playful shove, but Pip couldn't help the small smile that crossed his lips. He hesitated a moment longer, then finally began to write.

He wasn't sure what to say, or how much to share, but as the words started flowing, something eased in his chest. For the first time in a long while, someone cared to listen to his story, and he was grateful for it.

On the 20th of September, after pushing through Ypres, the 1st Australian Division, along with the 2nd Division, relieved the British troops and positioned themselves on the front line at Westhoek Ridge, facing Glencorse Wood. In the lower areas, the ground was like a swamp, bogged down by water, but elsewhere it was holding firm. The Australians were to hold there until the time fixed for the attack, so spent the next few days improving their trenches and overhead cover.

As part of the 3rd Brigade, the 9th Battalion, along with the 10th, 11th and 12th, had departed Chateau Segard at 2345 hours on the 19th and moved to the jumping off tapes which had been laid in no man's land just forward of the front line. Being the Red Line attackers the 11th Battalion were placed closest to the enemy, followed in order by the 12th, 9th and 10th respectively.

Up until this moment the weather had remained fine and the battlefield was dry, but, by mid evening a fine drizzle had set in, turning into steady rain by 2300 hours. Corps and Army Headquarters had been considering whether or not to call off the attack, but General Plumer gave the order to go ahead when the rain suddenly stopped at midnight.

"Thank God for that," said Clancy on hearing the news.

As the 9th formed up Pip felt like there was a ton of bricks on his shoulders. After all, he *had* been accused of cowardice. Grasping hold of Archie and Roo he whispered to them.

"I won't let you down fellas...honest".

Archie smiled.

"None of us doubt that mate. Just do what you have to and we'll see you at the end".

The 9th experienced a delay on the way forward as the 28th Battalion had wandered onto the wrong track, causing a thirty minute delay for the 12th Battalion and all those following it, but they were soon approaching their forming up positions. Opposite they faced elements of the Bavarian Ersatz Division and the bulk of the 121st Division.

At 0420 hours an enemy flare was launched, bursting over Glencorse Wood, casting a ghostly light over the landscape. It was the signal for a twenty minute barrage which fell on the incoming soldiers. The 9th Battalion at this moment, was passing through Chateau Wood when the enemy artillery opened up with a thunderous roar. In the darkness the men had kept tightly together so as not to lose touch, but in an instant, chaos erupted as the men sheltered as best they could, scrambling for cover, behind shattered trees and other vegetation, while others instinctively threw themselves to the ground as the first explosions tore into their ranks. The blasts sent jagged shrapnel flying, striking men where they stood. A soldier to Pip's left cried out, clutching his arm as blood seeped through his sleeve, while another collapsed nearby, motionless. Others, in the confusion, huddled together against the onslaught, their eyes wide with fear as explosions ripped through the wood, turning trees into splinters and the air thick with dirt and smoke. The barrage seemed to last for an eternity and when it finally petered out the men, grateful for its end, stumbled to their feet and, although dazed, reformed ready for the off. Some were wounded, staggering with cuts and burns, while others lay still, their lives ended in the flash of a shell. As the stretcher bearers dealt with the many casualties the battalions continued on, only to be hit by a second volley ten minutes later. This time, it was even fiercer. The ground erupted once more, sending men sprawling. One man was thrown back by the force of an explosion, his helmet clattering to the ground, while another fell silently, hit by a piece of flying metal. Each man gritted their teeth and held their breath, bracing for the worst, as the storm of artillery fire pounded the earth around them again.

The two bombardments took out all Company Commanders, with Captain Ponsonby being left unconscious after being knocked for six by the exploding concussion of an incoming round.

The stretcher bearers did their best in evacuating the wounded, whilst Lieutenant Meyers took charge and led 'A', 'C' and 'D' Companies to the assembly point at Jabber Trench.

'B' Company who were carrying ammunition and supplies had to scramble around in the darkness to find their loads which they had tossed aside during the shelling. Lieutenant Thomas Sargent was the only company officer left standing and, although he knew in his mind what he needed to do, he felt panicked, clutching his head as he looked left and right. Fumbling in his breast pocket he pulled out his compass, which was secured round his neck by a lanyard, and, straining to see the luminous numbers in the dark he began to orientate it, watching as the dial turned with every movement.

"East north east," he whispered to himself, "there you go…"

To his rear there was a clicking sound as Archie, Roo and Clancy tried to attract his attention.

"G'day Tomo, are you alright? You're *it* by the looks of things. Good to go?" Clancy whispered reassuringly.

Tomo was relieved at the sound of a friendly voice and gave a thumbs up sign to the three men.

"Clance, we need to get the men and ammo up to Jabber Trench," Tomo whispered, pointing into the darkness, "according to my compass bearing it is that way, but what do we do then.....?"

"Good mate. As for Jabber, just calm yourself and think about that one as we walk. You're doing good," replied Clancy as he squeezed the officer's shoulder.

"Well, I know we need to take the Green Line just to the front of Polygon Wood," Tomo whispered confidently.

"There you go," replied Clancy, "you're the skipper now. The boys will follow you".

Tomo smiled and paused.

"I think the sergeants need to take charge of the platoons".

"Already on it mate," replied Clancy, "righto let's go eh?"

The enemy shelling had caused the various companies and battalions to become intermingled, but there was no time to re-organise, so on arrival at the tape all of the troops kept absolutely silent until the allied bombardment commenced at 0540 hours on the 20th of September. As soon as the three thousand plus guns unleashed their crashing barrage, the line immediately moved forward. Each man knew where he had to be, so all mix ups would be undone in the leap frog stage.

The first rays of sunlight were slowly bursting forward over the horizon. As the men rose to their feet nearly every one of them lit a cigarette; and why not? The Germans *knew* they were coming but were currently sheltering from the allied barrage which was now creeping slowly towards them. What a sight it must have been though as hundreds of red fireflies eerily danced in dawn haze. In their path was the wooded swamp of Nonne Bosschen, where two German divisions had been halted by the British three years earlier. As they trudged through the sucking mud and soaking vegetation they were shrouded by the dawn mist which hovered like a host of butterflies over the woods, blending in with the smoke from the creeping barrage, which was moving forward at a speed of one hundred yards in six minutes. This was the rate that the men needed to travel in order to keep pace, yet despite the quagmire in which they found themselves, they managed to move like a knife through butter.

"Bloody hell, this is harder than I thought," said Tomo.

"Yeah mate, but look around you, the blokes are keeping pace with you *and* the barrage," replied Clancy.

The Lieutenant's face showed that he was proud of himself, and, although a veteran of many battles before this, he finally had the confidence to call himself a leader; helped and encouraged by a few mates of course.

The leading battalion, the 11th, captured the first objective with surprising ease, at just after 0600 hours, unleashing grenades and phosphorous bombs with devastating precision, forcing many enemy troops to surrender. The Germans were occupying concrete strong points, which became known as pill boxes because of their resemblance to a box which held pills; unsurprisingly. This was the first time that the Aussies had seen such a structure, but pretty soon they were making prisoners of their contents, the Germans, who surrendered nine times out of ten, as soon as they were reached. At this point in the advance the occasional scrap broke out when a pill box refused to surrender.

"Are these the same Huns we were fighting a few months ago?" asked a surprised Tomo.

"Yeah, it is a bit weird. But don't count your chickens mate," replied Clancy, as a lone enemy machine gun was heard rat tat tatting down the line somewhere.

Clancy scoffed and raised an eyebrow.

"See what I mean?"

The expertise of the gunners' new methods and interoperability with the infantry, meant, for many, that today's barrage was the best that the men had witnessed so far, with the infantry comfortably walking behind it to their objectives.

Once the Red Line had been taken it was a time for all battalions to re-organise, re-supply and find each other. As this was going on, the shelling of the enemy continued, ready for the next stage in an hour.

Roo even had time to make a quick brew.

"Bloody hell Roo, I reckon you should definitely open that cafe or milk bar when we get home," Clancy joked as he held out his mug in anticipation.

"Why's that then?" asked Roo.

"Well, you're the fastest tea maker I've ever known," replied Clancy.

Roo pondered.

"Freddy is usually here on the scrounge for a cuppa. I hope he's alright".

"Yeah, me too...eye, eye, here comes the stand in skipper," replied Clancy, "where's your cup mate?"

Lieutenant Sargent glanced at Roo and passed him his tin cup.

"Gosh Roo, I don't know how you do it...all hail the Dugout Cafe eh?" said Tomo.

"Hey...I like *that* name...good on yer sir," replied Roo, smiling.

The lieutenant explained to the NCOs that the next creeping barrage would begin at 0708 hours, so all the men needed to be re-plenished and ready to go by 0700 hours.

"Right mate I'll get on to it," replied the CSM as he began passing the message down the line and confirming that the men had a full supply of ammo and bombs.

At 0708 hours on the dot, the 12th Battalion departed the Red Line, followed by the 9th and 10th Battalions. The 11th were now holding the newly captured Red Line.

The shelling reverted back to a creeping barrage, the three battalions following it steadily. Not a shot was fired and the three battle groups reached the Blue Line at 0740 hours.

On arrival there were no enemy soldiers in situ, most likely because the ground was undigable due to the abundance of tree stumps and roots, which made digging an impossible task. The 9th and 10th Battalions remained on the line, lying prone, whilst the 12th moved one hundred yards to the rear and quickly began to dig in. It was a good position with commanding views and good fields of fire. The 9th and 10th, whilst awaiting their advance, decided that as there was a lack of enemy fire, it was a good time for a spot of breakfast, although most of the boys *had* been munching broken biccies and other goodies in their grab bags as they walked. The wait stretched to two hours, which was a good thing for re-organising again. The 9th also ensured that it was in contact with the units on its flanks, the 10th Battalion on the right and the 28th, part of the 2nd Division, on their left.

At one minute to ten the advance re-commenced with some of the 9th so eager to reach the objective that they carried on marching forward before the creeping barrage had *itself* moved on, becoming casualties themselves.

"Stop! Stand still!" Clancy shouted, frantically waving his hand to slow the men down, "follow it...don't run into it!"

But a few didn't hear, still pushing ahead. The ground shuddered with each explosion, and suddenly, the concussive force of a nearby blast pushed through the air, knocking men off their feet as if an invisible hand had swept them away. The shockwaves slammed into their chests, sending them sprawling into the mud. Shouts and curses followed, soldiers clutching their rifles as they scrambled to stand, shaken but still alive.

Roo ran up, grabbing a stumbling private by the shoulder.

"Pull back, you dag or you'll end up flat on your face again if you don't wait for the barrage to move!"

More shouts echoed down the line as NCOs tried to regain order.

"HALT! Don't move until the barrage moves on!"

Clancy ran alongside the men, still waving his arm to hold them in place.

"Stand bloody still, Fritz will still be there when you get there, there's no rush!"

The concussive blasts continued ahead, close enough to the troops to feel them in their bones, but far enough that no one was seriously injured. A few men staggered, like drunkards, dazed, wiping the mud from their faces.

"Hold steady! Don't move until I bloody say so!" Clancy shouted along the line.

The men, bruised but not broken, fell back into line, their eyes fixed on the distant explosions. They had learned their lesson, keeping pace now, as they moved forward again.

It took ten minutes to occupy the Green Line, even though enemy resistance was now stronger, bullets cracking and thumping to the front and sides whilst artillery rounds whined overhead.

One pill box in particular was causing havoc, its machine gun raking across the field, holding the advance at bay It had to be dealt with - and quickly. The boys had never attacked a fixed position like this before, but Tomo was on to it; surprised by his own decisiveness. Assessing the situation, the lieutenant quickly gathered up a small section of men, issued a snap briefing, then set off. With the rest of the company laying down covering fire, the enemy gun was kept busy, its crew unaware of what was about to unfold. Splitting into two groups the section dashed towards the pill box, running forward on either side of the structure, the pounding of their boots drowned by the gunfire as they pressed on, closing in from behind. They reached the rear of the structure, unseen and unheard. The German machine gun crew, completely unprepared for an assault from behind, were caught off guard. The sight of Tomo's men emerging from the smoke, rifles and bayonets pointing directly at them, left them no choice—they surrendered on the spot, hands raised in a mix of shock and defeat.

This lesson in new tactics had been watched closely by all in sight of it, and very quickly the six pill boxes in the battalion area were captured or destroyed.

Whilst all of this was occurring, the 28th overran the Green Line and communications were lost with them for a short while. They were located on the edge of Polygon Wood, and it was here that the advancing battalions dug in, in full view of the enemy, placing Lewis Gunners in shell holes fifty yards to their front.

The barrage had now ceased and the battalions settled into their new positions, feeling well, and confident. Communication lines were laid back to Battalion and Brigade Headquarters and the men were prepared for anything that could be thrown at them. This came in handy when, during the afternoon, the enemy made a few attempts to overrun the Aussies, but each time carefully planned artillery barrages saw them off, along with rifles with some guts behind them. The Aussies were fully replenished and even found a dump containing German barbed wire, which they utilised and used in their defences. But all was not quiet as the battalion was suddenly hit by a furious artillery bombardment by the enemy, a respite coming at 2300 hours when they were relieved by the 2nd Battalion.

In this action the battalion had lost thirty five dead, one hundred and forty nine wounded and fifty six missing. The total allied casualties during the battle of Menin Road Ridge, or the Battle of Polygon Wood as the men of the 9th preferred to call it, were between twenty and twenty five thousand, five thousand of those being from the two Australian divisions.

Despite the high number of casualties, it had been a stroke of luck, combined with bad intelligence, that the Germans had been caught napping. Making too many assumptions they were completely surprised by the offensive, believing that the Ypres offensive was about to resume, and that the 1st Australian Division had been transferred to Egypt.

8

The blackest day

After a week of training and re-organising at Dickebusch and Steenvorde, the battalion was again on the line at ANZAC Ridge. The latest attack by the four ANZAC Divisions fighting side by side, was to be on Broodseinde Ridge.

On the 1st of October on ANZAC Ridge, the 9th's positions were shelled heavily, but the casualties were relatively low. 'A' and 'C' Companies, acting as a cable laying party came under a particularly heavy bombardment. Captain Knightley, an original battalion member, was assisting in the rescue of the wounded from the mud when a 5.9 inch shell catapulted him into the air. Unfortunately his leg was badly broken in three places and had to be amputated; thus ending his active service career.

Following the successful laying of the cables the entire battalion moved to a huge, deep dugout known as "Halfway House". Here they sheltered for a few days, from the rain, and death.

At 2000 hours on the 3rd of October the battalion moved forward to its reserve positions, two companies on Westhoek Ridge and two on ANZAC Ridge.

The Battle of Broodseinde took place the next day, part of the broader struggle for Passchendaele. Following the successful advances at Menin Road and Polygon Wood the previous month, the objective was to seize Broodseinde Ridge, which the Germans had held since 1915. All four ANZAC divisions - the 1st, 2nd, 3rd Australian, and the New Zealand Division - were set to fight together for the only time during the war.

Thousands of ANZAC soldiers had marched through Ypres along the Menin Road, passing the infamous Hellfire Corner, preparing for the battle to come. The whole road was a terrible and macabre sight, bordered by dead mules and mud spattered horses, smashed wagons and limbers, and freshly killed men tossed off the track to leave it open for the never ending stream of traffic.

At 0600 hours the battle commenced, and within roughly three hours, a substantial part of Broodseinde Ridge had been secured, with all attacking brigades capturing their objectives. On either side of the ANZAC forces, British infantry also took their objectives, with tanks exploiting the unusually dry conditions to support the assault. Very soon prisoners poured in over the Battalion's positions, many of the unwounded Germans being used as stretcher bearers.

The German military would later record the 4th of October as the "blackest day" of the war, whilst for the Allies, the victory at Broodseinde Ridge was seen as a breakthrough, raising hopes that German control in the Ypres Salient might finally collapse.

However, these hopes soon faded as German reinforcements flooded the second line between Broodseinde and Passchendaele, and by noon, the weather turned against them, with torrential rain beginning to fall. The downpour would continue for days, and during the tough month that followed, only five days passed without rain - an ominous sign for the Allies' advance toward Passchendaele.

On the 5th, in the drizzling rain, the battalion relieved the 8th in the support trenches. The surrounding countryside was now becoming extremely boggy.

Clancy wiped a hand across his brow, flicking away the water.

"Looks like we timed that one just right eh?" Clancy noted, glancing at the sky.

"Bloody rain!" replied Stowie, shaking the mud from his boots.

On the morning of the 6th, the battalion huddled in the muddy support trenches, the drizzle now a steady downpour. The rain soaked earth clung to boots, pulling them deeper into the bog. The German artillery which had remained relatively quiet and sporadic for about twenty four hours suddenly recommenced, turning its attention to the support lines.

Suddenly, the earth shook violently. A deafening crack split the air as the German artillery woke with a thunderous roar, shells screaming overhead, exploding with blinding flashes along the ridgeline. Dirt, debris, and the occasional mangled tree stump shot into the sky, raining down over the men.

"Take cover!" came the shouted order, though it was barely heard over the explosions, and those who *did* hear it laughed to themselves at such an obvious instruction.

"Christ, they're onto us now!" Clancy shouted, glancing toward Roo and Ten Bob who were crouched nearby.

Stowie spat some mud out of his mouth.

"Bloody hell, it ain't the rain we gotta worry about no more".

The ground beneath them heaved like a living beast, every blast closer than the last. Men tightly hugged the sides of the trench, hands gripping their helmets as the shells pounded ceaselessly, their hearts racing, feeling each explosion vibrating through their bodies.

Through the smoke and rain, the Germans were pouring their wrath into the support lines. They'd been waiting, and now, they were striking hard. The trenches, already soggy and crumbling, were beginning to collapse under the weight of the bombardment.

A few yards to the rear, a shell landed, its detonation throwing a cascade of mud over the men. Stowie cursed, wiping his eyes, but no one had time to joke. The bombardment raged on, each shell tightening its grip on their nerves.

Pip, crouched down and, covered in mud, grinned at the soldiers around him.

"I don't think these Geermans like us very much," he said, in his thick scouse accent, "I thought we'd at least get a cup of tea or something".

Clancy shot him a look, barely suppressing a laugh at his pronunciation of "Germans".

"Keep your head down, mate, or you'll get more than tea!"

Another shell slammed into the ground nearby, shaking the trench. This time, a section of the wall collapsed inward, burying a few of their mates, including Roo and Ten Bob, up to their necks, under a heavy mass of mud and debris.

Shouts of "Stretcher Bearer!" cut through the chaos, but the barrage gave no quarter.

"Over here! Quick, help dig 'em out!" Clancy shouted.

But no order was needed as, without hesitation, the men sprang into action, scrambling toward the collapse. Pip, seeing the situation, tore off his helmet and started using it like a shovel, scooping up the heavy mud in frantic swipes.

"Come on, you lot!" he shouted, slinging mud aside with his helmet, whilst managing a cheeky wink, "this'll be the fastest you'll ever see *me* dig, so make the most of it".

Clancy and Stowie clawed at the mud with their bare hands, while Pip tossed his helmet full of dirt over his shoulder, making quite a dent in the mud pile. His grinning face was streaked with mud, but he didn't stop.

"Hold on, lads, we'll have you out in a mo!" Pip called, pulling away debris.

The rain made everything slimy and hard to manage, but they kept going, determined. As Pip scooped another helmet full of sludge he grinned at Roo and Ten Bob as they struggled in the mud trying to free themselves from within.

"Come on, you lazy pair, wakey, wakey. Stop your nappin', it's *your* turn to make a brew".

The men worked fast, ignoring the shells pounding around them. Stowie and Clancy yanked free one of the trapped soldiers, his face caked in mud, but alive.

"There you go, mates," Pip said with a wink, tossing his helmet aside as they hauled Roo and Ten Bob out, "I don't know...I leave you alone for five minutes, and you go and get yourselves buried...and I won't mention the state of your uniforms".

"You silly bugger," Roo laughed as he wiped mud from his hands and face and brushed himself off.

Despite the mayhem, a few of the men couldn't help but laugh, Pip's antics, a breath of fresh air, cutting through the tension like a warm breeze. His helmet now dented, he shook the mud from it and jammed it back on his head.

Another shell hit closer, shaking the ground under their feet, but by then, they'd freed their mates.

Roo slapped Pip on the back and shook his hand.

"Thanks mate. Do you reckon we'll live through this, Pip?"

Pip adjusted his muddy helmet with a grin, as the dirty liquid dripped down his face.

"If we do, mate, first round of tea's on you. And get me a new bloody helmet while you're at it!"

The 7th of October was equally appalling with heavy squalling rain pelting down on the weary soldiers. Despite this the 9th were gradually working their way up to the front line, relieving the 11th Battalion in the left sector. Arriving in the dark they were greeted by boggy ground, which made it difficult to move around or, indeed, sleep. Here they remained for three days being drenched by torrential rain on the afternoon of the first day.

"Well this is a bloody good start! I swear this rain's trying to drown us before the bloody Germans get a chance!" Clancy growled.

"I reckon we'll be swimming outta here if this keeps up," said Pip, "anyone fancy a dip in the Somme?"

Roo laughed.

"With all this rain, I reckon we were better off staying buried. Warmer down there, eh?"

The next day began with an unusual break in the weather. The clouds parted, letting a pale sun spill over the battlefield. The men, relieved for once, took the opportunity to dry out their rain gear with wet weather capes and trench coats spread out along the parapets, flapping in the light breeze as they caught whatever warmth the sun offered. Pip referred to his cape as a poncho, but no matter the name it was a versatile piece of kit, doubling as a ground sheet or overhead shelter.

Stowie, eyeing his own soaked cape, stretched it over the top of the trench wall with a grunt.

"Hope this sun lasts long enough to dry these bloody things out".

"Fat chance," Clancy muttered as he draped his kit over a sandbag.

Pip leaned against the parapet, watching the men fuss over their waterproof capes, and began to sing.

"The maid was in the garden hanging out the clothes...and down came a blackbird and pecked off her nose".

Clancy laughed.

"I don't know about nursery rhymes, I'd settle for some bloody dry boots, mate".

Roo paused for a moment and thought of his childhood days.

"I remember Aunty Doris singing that to me when I was about three," he said, "my mum and dad were still alive then".

Pip's ears pricked up, sensing something in common with Roo.

"So you're an orphan too?"

"In a manner of speaking. My mum and dad are dead, but I have Aunty Doris and Uncle Ray...and Archie and Percy of course," Roo replied.

For the better part of the morning, the troops occupied themselves with small tasks, keeping an eye on their drying uniforms and equipment, hopeful that the fine weather might hold. For a moment, spirits lifted, and the usual chatter of the trenches returned.

But by mid afternoon, the peace was shattered. They had been lulled into a false sense of security when a strong gale suddenly blew up in the afternoon, out of nowhere, sweeping across the landscape, whipping through the trenches like a furious beast. Capes and trench coats, carefully laid out to dry, were snatched by the wind and sent flying.

"Oy! My bloody cape!" Clancy shouted, chasing after it as the wind tore it from the parapet.

Pip stood up, holding his own rain gear in place with one hand, laughing.

"No rest for the wicked eh?"

The wind howled through the trench, tugging at everything in its path. Men scrambled to gather their drying clothes before they were lost to no man's land, Stowie managing to grab his cape just in time, folding it over his arm.

And then, as if on cue, the sky darkened, and heavy rain began to fall once more, within moments, turning the trenches into muddy rivers.

"Bloody typical!" Clancy shouted over the downpour, pulling his, once again, wet cape back on.

Pip, grinning through the rain, slapped on his soaking helmet.

"And it's not even bath night!"

Clancy, now drenched again, shook his head.

"At this rate, Pip, we'll all be floating down the trenches before the day's done".

The rain poured non-stop, soaking everything and everyone. Not even their capes could keep them dry. They were drenched, their uniforms heavy and cold against their skin.

Pip laughed.

"Well, lads, it could be worse..." as he was suddenly hit by mud bombs hastily thrown by his mates.

Then, in the evening...more heavy rain.

The battalion was finally relieved on the 10th of October.

The previous day the first attempt had been made on Passchendaele, known officially as the Battle of Poelcapelle, when the French 1st Army and the British 2nd and 5th Armies launched an attack over a thirteen thousand five hundred yard front, stretching from just south of Broodseinde to St Jansbeek. The aim was to advance halfway from Broodseinde Ridge to Passchendaele, but the assault came at a heavy cost, with many casualties on both sides. While the British and French troops managed to hold their gains in the northern part of the front, most of the ground captured near Passchendaele and on the Becelaere and Gheluvelt spurs was soon lost to fierce German counter attacks; the return of heavy rain and the thick, clinging mud being the primary reasons they couldn't hold onto the captured positions. For the Germans too the fighting had pushed their forces to the limit, managing to prevent a break-through - though replacing their own mounting losses was becoming ever more difficult.

Following their relief the 9th Battalion moved out to Dominion Camp where they spent two weeks. Here they received two batches of reinforcements and a visit from General Birdwood, not to mention the return of a certain Captain Ponsonby, who was quite apologetic.

"Sorry to be away. I tried to get back but those nurses were holding me prisoner I'm afraid".

"Lucky you," said Archie.

Clancy gave the captain a cursory glance and scoffed.

"Huh! I thought you were stuck on the dunny or something. Besides, we've elected a *new* skipper".

"Elected?" replied Ponsonby.

"Yeah, Tomo here has proven himself to be a good bloke...and he's an Aussie...so off you trot," said Clancy, waving Ponsonby away.

All became silent. Ponsonby was lost for words...until the whole group burst into laughter. Clancy held out his hand.

"Welcome back you old bastard," Clancy announced as Lieutenant Sargent whispered in the captain's ear.

"We missed you".

"You've missed me...really?" asked a surprised Ponsonby.

"Yeah, but some practise on the ranges would sort that," joked Clancy.

Ponsonby smiled, trying to hold back the tears..

"Thank you Tommy, and I've missed you all too".

"So how are you skip?" asked Roo.

"Oh, you know, so, so," replied Ponsonby, "but what a day to return".

"What do you mean?" asked Roo.

"It's my birthday today," replied the captain.

"Many happy returns mate," said Clancy, "so, how old are you then?"

"Thirty seven".

"You *old* bastard! I thought you were younger than that," replied the CSM.

Roo glanced at Clancy, grinning.

"We don't *all* look as worn out as you mate".

"And there I was thinking I was a handsome rooster...you know...in a rugged sort of way," Clancy replied.

"Next time we get some leave we'll have to test you on the local ladies CSM," added Pip.

Clancy shrugged his shoulders.

"Anyone got any grog to toast the captain's big day?"

With the help of Alfie and the boys, Rachel's command of the English language had improved greatly over the last few months, although with the fact that her father spoke some English, the boys suspected that she had had some exposure to it at home. Needless to say communication was much easier, and she always had Alfie at her side to assist her if she needed it.

In the early weeks after Rachel had joined the regiment she was slowly discovering many customs which were foreign to her, especially when it came to food.

Bacon was something she had heard of, but had never seen, or tasted. In her religion Pigs were unclean animals and thus their meat was considered to be unhealthy, and therefore not eaten. She had also been taught that it was a sin to consume such meat; unless of course you were starving and this was the only food available.

On occasion bacon was available from the field kitchen and the men would lap it up, the smell of sizzling bacon in pans filling the air and bringing, to many, thoughts and reminders of home. Rachel would often watch with curiosity as Chugger and his mates gathered around the campfire, her nose wrinkling with surprise as she inhaled the aroma of the cooking smells.

On one of these mornings Alfie was nearby sorting wood for the fire.

"What is that?" she asked, her brow furrowing, "Alfie, what are they cooking?"

Alfie looked up.

"It's bacon, Rachel...pig meat".

Chugger, overhearing the exchange, stepped closer with a grin, aware of the significance that bacon possibly played in Rachel's beliefs.

"Smells good eh? Do you want to try some?"

Rachel, tempted but unsure, shook her head and crossed her arms.

"'Iinah najs," she replied.

Alfie, seeing her distress, translated for her.

"She says it is unclean".

Chugger scratched his head, half understanding and half not.

"Unclean? Well, what sort of meat *does* she eat?" he asked.

Alfie spoke to Rachel then turned to Chugger with her response.

"Mainly goat and sheep".

Percy joined in the conversation.

"Have you not seen the dags on the arse end of a sheep mate? I wouldn't call *that* clean...and besides the meat is skinned, washed and cooked before we eat it, so no worries".

Rachel seemed to accept the explanation but was still hesitant.

Chugger held out a piece of bacon on his fork, his eyes dancing with anticipation.

"Just one bite. You'll never know unless you try".

With a hesitant sigh, Rachel reached for the piece of meat, her fingers trembling slightly. As she took a bite, she braced herself for disappointment. But to her surprise, the salty, smoky flavour flooded her senses. It was unlike anything she had ever tasted.

She chewed slowly, grappling with her conflicting emotions.

"It...it is good," she admitted, her voice a mix of disbelief and reluctant acceptance.

Chugger laughed gently and nodded.

"See? You're getting the hang of it. You're a true blue Aussie now!"

Rachel met his gaze, the warmth of the fire contrasting with the uncertainty in her heart.

"Aussie...yes...very good," she said as she took another bite, a flicker of a smile breaking through, "perhaps I *can* eat bacon...yes?"

Chugger smiled and gently caressed her arm.

"Good on yer Rach".

Having her own income too was a blessing to her and the little that she spent was never on herself, but was used to buy food from local markets whenever the regiment was located near a town. In her mind Chugger and his mates could not exist on bully beef and hard biscuits alone and she often appeared, carrying a pot of aromatic, bubbling liquid, which without a word, she would set down in front of the men, the rich scent of spiced stew wafting through the air.

Eyebrows would be raised, but Rachel would say nothing. Her expression was clear enough to all. She wasn't taking no for an answer, as she ladled out a portion for each man, making sure Chugger's bowl was piled high. The men were impressed and grateful, for the food was better than anything they had tasted since the war began.

Percy took note of Chugger's bowl which was often overflowing.

"Looks like someone's got a soft spot for you, mate".

Chugger felt a strange warmth in his chest, though he grunted.

"She's just sick of watching us eat like animals mate, that's all".

Rachel caught his eye, and for a moment, a cheeky, yet shy smile appeared on her face.

"Where's all this come from anyway Rachel?" Chugger asked.

Rachel understood exactly what he had said but in reply she innocently pointed to herself, then mimed handing coins to an invisible merchant, a proud smile tugging at her lips.

"You bought it? With your pay?" Chugger asked, stunned.

Rachel nodded, watching carefully to see if he was pleased.

Chugger shook his head, eyes softening.

"You don't have to do that for me...for us".

Rachel's expression turned serious, and she touched her hand to her heart, then pointed to Chugger and all present, then quickly turned to Alfie and whispered, hoping for a suitable explanation in English. Glancing towards the sky she briefly practised the sentence in her head before saying it out loud.

"For you...because you matter to me".

Chugger felt a wave of warmth rush through him and looked around, making sure the boys weren't watching too closely to see his blushes, as he blew a quick kiss in Rachel's direction.

Rachel's face lit up at this universal sign of love, and she smiled broadly, feeling more at peace than she had ever felt.

But looking after one another worked both ways, for Chugger was always watching Rachel from a distance whenever he could, the familiar sight of her moving around camp a strange comfort. Her scimitar was, as usual, tied loosely around her waist, the blade awkwardly bouncing with her every step. He'd noticed how cumbersome it looked, especially for someone who moved with such quiet grace. It was time for Chugger to do something about it, something kind for Rachel.

He had been planning his special surprise for a while now, ever since speaking to one of the regiment's saddlers. For just a few shillings the leatherworker had crafted something special; a sturdy, handmade scabbard with a strap to sling over the shoulder, allowing Rachel to carry the scimitar on her back. The handle would rest within easy reach, ready for her to draw it in an instant, should she ever need to.

Chugger cleared his throat as he approached, the brand new leather scabbard held carefully in his hands. Rachel looked up, her dark eyes meeting his, and offered a small, questioning smile.

"I've, uh, got something for you," he said, his voice unusually hesitant.

He was good at making people laugh, but this felt different - more serious, more personal.

Rachel's eyes flicked to the scabbard in his hands, her brows raised in confusion.

"For...me?"

"Yeah," Chugger said, rubbing the back of his neck, suddenly unsure, "I noticed you've been carrying that sword tied around your waist, and well, I thought it could be easier for you with this. It's a proper scabbard, see? You can wear it on your back, and keep your sword handle within reach. Thought it might be more practical".

Rachel's gaze shifted to the leather scabbard, and she reached out, hesitating, as if unsure whether she was allowed to accept such a gift. Her fingers brushed over the smooth leather, the craftsmanship undeniable. She looked up at Chugger, eyes wide with surprise.

"No one has ever..." Rachel began softly, her voice faltering. She swallowed, searching for the words. "No one has...er...how you say...er...ever done something like this...for me. Not even my family".

Chugger shuffled his feet, feeling a bit awkward under her intense gaze.

"Well, it's nothing fancy...just thought you could use it, you know?"

To Rachel this was more than just a practical gift. It was thoughtful, considerate. It was someone seeing her- really seeing her - and caring enough to help in a way that no one ever had before. Her family had always treated her like a servant, with no thoughts or opinions of her own; to endure. But here was Chugger, showing her kindness she had never known.

She inserted the scimitar into the scabbard then slipped it over her shoulder, adjusting the strap. It fit perfectly, the sword handle resting just where she could reach it in a single motion. She drew the sword once, testing the ease of the draw, and smiled - a genuine, warm smile that she hadn't shown in a long time.

"Shukran jazilan...thank you very much," she said, her voice quiet but full of meaning. She stepped closer, her hand resting on his arm.

"Wilbert...thank you".

Chugger grinned, feeling his cheeks warm slightly at the use of his real name.

"No worries...glad you like it".

For a moment, they stood there, the war forgotten as Rachel looked at him, her gratitude evident not just in her words but in her eyes. But what to do? Both wanted to throw open their arms and hug each other but were uncertain as to whether it was the proper thing to do, so for now unspoken words and looks were the acceptable way to go. In the end, it was a small gesture in the grand scheme of things, but to Rachel, it meant the world, and to Chugger, seeing her smile like that made everything worthwhile.

9

The last charge

Revolution in Russia had caused the collapse of the Russian armed forces and thus any further assistance on *any* front. The result was the freeing up of Turkish troops to bolster the Gaza line quite considerably.

The plan was for the 20th Corps to attack Beersheba from the south and the west, and the enemy line as far north as Irgeig, whilst the Desert Mounted Corps attacked from the east and north east. Once Beersheba had fallen, the 20th Corps was to roll up the line from the south whilst the 21st Corps attacked Gaza, and the Desert Mounted Corps simultaneously swept up in the rear of the enemy, cutting off communications, supplies and reinforcements. Allenby was an inspiring leader and there was a cheery confidence in the troops. He knew how to use the mounted troops and for the first time they were to be doing what they had been trained to do. Logistics too had been meticulously planned and organised.

On the 24th of October each unit began to move out in stages to their positions of assembly. A squadron of the 3rd Light Horse Regiment was despatched to Hill 840, six miles west of Beersheba, with orders to dig in and hold it at all costs. The reason; to deny observation to the Turks.

The 2nd Light Horse Regiment reached Asluj five days later, but despite the magnificent logistical operation there was still not enough water to amply supply an entire mounted corps. Yet again they had to make do and ration what they had. The regiment moved out again on the night of the 30th, with rumours of an impending attack on Beersheba in order to capture its garrison and seize its vital wells, which had provided water to the local inhabitants for thousands of years.

The horses were tethered in lines and the sentries had been set. It was to be cold rations tonight as no fires were allowed due to them potentially giving the regiment's positions away. Young Alfie still rode his donkey at the rear of the column but did not enjoy the shelter of the regiment that Rachel did. He was consequently low on both food and water, but not low on friends.

As he wandered around the camp seeking out Percy and the boys, he was relieved when he finally found them, as were the soldiers on seeing him.

"Alfie mate, where have you been, I've been worried about you?" said Percy as he fumbled with his tin of bully beef, finally managing to prise open the lid.

Alfie smiled and sat down amongst his friends.

"I have been looking for you Mister Percy, but in your uniforms you all look the same".

"Except Rachel of course," added Chugger.

Alfie turned his gaze to Rachel who was sat next to Chugger.

"Oh yes... as-salamu alaikum," he said, offering a small bow of his head.

Rachel returned Alfie's bow and smiled at the young boy.

"Wa-Alaikum-Salaam".

"You look knackered mate...have some water," said Boggy as he tossed his canteen to Alfie who caught it and immediately began to drink.

"Thank you...very thirsty," replied a grateful Alfie.

Percy ruffled the boy's hair.

"I bet you are Alf. Got any grub?"

Alfie shook his head, an almost hopeful look on his face, betraying his hunger.

Percy rummaged in his pack and produced a tin.

"Here you go mate, have some bully".

Alfie's eyes widened as he nodded his thanks and tucked in to the beef.

"You don't be shy in future mate. If you're hungry or thirsty just let us know. We'll see yer right," said Percy.

The evening before a battle was always filled with tension, and this night was no different. After dinner Chugger sat in front of his tent sharpening his bayonet, his jaw clenched, the weight of the impending battle heavy on his thoughts.

Rachel, noticing his quiet demeanour, approached him cautiously. She knelt beside him, touching his arm. When he looked up, she could see the worry in his eyes, something he rarely let show.

"Safe," she said softly, pointing to him, then to her heart, "you...be safe".

Chugger swallowed hard, forcing a smile.

"I can't promise that, love. But I'll do my best".

Rachel shook her head firmly, repeating, "Safe." She then placed her hand gently over his, her grey eyes full of quiet strength.

For a moment, Chugger just stared at her, feeling the worry ease just a little. He wasn't used to people looking after him, but Rachel seemed to make it her mission.

"I'll be right," he said quietly, gripping her hand.

Rachel nodded, a silent understanding passing between them.

Alfie had gulped down his food and water and settled down for the night, having erected his small tent next to the one occupied by Percy and the boys. Percy and Davo were still awake, enjoying the cool desert breeze that swept through the camp, a welcome relief after the day's heat.

"Do you reckon Alfie will be alright when this blasted war is over?" Percy asked, his voice low as he gazed at the stars, distant and cold, "I worry about that little bloke. He's only eight, for pity's sake, no family, and God knows what'll happen to him once *we* pack our bags".

Davo lay back on his elbows, shaking his head.

"I doubt it, mate. He'll probably end up on the streets of Cairo again... poor bugger," he replied, his tone as heavy as the silence that followed.

Percy fell quiet, his thoughts drifting to the boy sleeping just yards away. He'd seen how Alfie had adjusted to his rough life of following the regiment, working hard for every penny whilst learning quickly from the men, almost like a sponge soaking up every word. But in the end, Alfie was still just a boy, a few years older than his own son - his whole life ahead of him, and that life filled Percy with concern.

War had a way of twisting people, and Percy feared what might become of the lad if they left him behind, alone in a land that was essentially foreign to him.

His thoughts wandered home to Lil and their young son, Frank, and he imagined the two boys playing together, laughter ringing through the yard. He wondered what Lil would think if he brought Alfie back to Australia with him. A brother for Frank, maybe...It would be a lot to ask of her, but if anyone had a heart big enough to welcome the boy, it was Lil.

Percy stared out into the desert, the outline of the tents barely visible in the moonlight. Tomorrow's battle was on his mind, but so was Alfie's future. He was just a lost boy, one who needed a proper family, a place to belong. Percy felt a knot tighten in his chest as he thought of Alfie being left behind, lost in a world that had already taken so much from him.

He made up his mind.

"Tomorrow, I reckon I'll write to Lil," Percy said softly, more to himself than to Davo, "see what she thinks about me bringing Alfie home. He could have a chance with us, maybe be a brother to Frank".

Davo glanced at him, surprised, but said nothing for a moment. Then he gave a nod.

"That'd be good, Perce. The lad deserves a go at something better than this bloody life".

Percy didn't respond, his gaze still fixed on the horizon. Tomorrow, the battle would come. But tonight, he allowed himself a flicker of hope. Maybe, just maybe, Alfie's future didn't have to be as sorry as the war torn world they were living in now.

He'd write to Lil after the battle. He had to.

The third battle of Gaza commenced at daylight on the 31st of October...All Hallows Day. The enemy forces held Tel-el-Saba, one of the many hills of around one thousand feet in elevation, and only three miles east of Beersheba.

As the section surveyed the area they were hopeful that the 2nd would be selected to attack the prize...Beersheba.

The obvious course of action for this moment in time was to surround the hill and cut its occupants off; but not today. Instead, the 3rd Light Horse Regiment and a regiment from the New Zealand Mounted Rifle Brigade were ordered to go straight at it in a frontal attack. Major Markwell was placed in temporary command of the 2nd Light Horse Regiment whilst the CO was detached to command Brigade Advanced Headquarters.

The 1st and 2nd Light Horse Regiments were ordered to support the 3rd if required and to secure their left flank, which was at risk. Tel-el-Saba was pounded by allied artillery, but no impression could be made. It was expertly defended by machine guns which prevented the frontal attack from making any headway.

At 1400 hours the 2nd came in to action on the left of the 3rd Light Horse and galloped towards Tel-el-Saba, reaching some mud huts approximately eight hundred yards from the town. Here the regiment dismounted and the horses were led to the rear. Unfortunately the regiment could not advance any further as their arrival had caused the enemy to move towards them in force. This manoeuvre had been a serious error on the Turkish part as it had left their right flank exposed. The New Zealand Mounted Rifle Brigade were quick to exploit this and pushed upwards. The Turkish position, now surrounded, quickly fell to the ANZACs, but not before Major Markwell had been killed by a low bursting shrapnel round.

"BASTARDS!" shouted Chugger, "we need to finish these Abduls".

Percy had been observing to the east of Beersheba where the 4th Brigade was assembling.

"Looks like something's going on over there boys," he announced.

The section members each glanced over to the direction in which Percy was pointing and could see that behind the distant ridgeline there were light dust clouds, indicating possible troop movement.

"Hopefully its more ANZACs coming to finish the fight," said Davo.

"I bloody well hope so boys," Chugger added, as he noticed Lieutenant Weller trotting towards them.

"Sergeant Taylor, I need your section to escort some of these field ambulance carts over to the 4th Brigade. They are located behind that ridge over there," he said.

"But sir, if we go over there we might miss the final push here," said Johnno.

The mates all shook their heads in a combination of disbelief and disappointment.

"Come on fellas just treat it as a quick Sunday ride. You'll be back in no time," said the Lieutenant reassuringly.

"Righto sir, no worries," replied Percy.

"And Sergeant..."said the officer.

"Sir?" replied Percy.

"If you can't make it back for our advance on Beersheba, just mind you stay out of trouble and don't get mixed up in any other fights," said the lieutenant with a wink.

It was almost dusk as Percy and his party approached the 4th Brigade positions. The ancient city of Beersheba was still there for the picking and the Turks knew it, and were preparing to fly the coup. The majority of their artillery pieces had departed and the south and western outer edges of the town had fallen to the 20th Corps.

It was now up to the Light Horse.

As the mates trotted up to the 4th Brigade position much seemed to be happening and a feeling of both excitement and foreboding seemed to fill the air.

That afternoon, General Allenby had sent a telegram to Chauvel, instructing him to capture Beersheba "before nightfall." However, Chauvel had already planned this very move after aerial reconnaissance had confirmed that it *was* possible, as the trenches in the immediate path of the charge were not fortified with barbed wire or horse pits. The eight hundred men of the 4th and 12th Light Horse Regiments were now preparing for their mounted assault.

"Ah, the 2nd Regiment. What are you blokes doing here?" asked a young lieutenant.

"Oh, just escorting some field ambulance personnel. What's going on with you fellas sir?" Percy replied.

"Well, it's no secret now, but we're going to charge Beersheba," replied the officer.

A feeling of excitement and pride came over the five soldiers as they glanced at and nodded their approval to each other.

"Charge? You mean like cavalry?" asked Boggy.

"That's right corporal," replied the lieutenant.

Percy thought to himself, then winked at his mates.

"Got room for five more sir? We've got nothing else to do this arvo," Percy enquired.

"Fill your boots boys, but don't get knocked. I don't want to be explaining to your CO," the officer replied.

Such an event was unprecedented; a mounted charge spanning over two miles of open terrain against entrenched infantry, bolstered by artillery and machine guns. However, with the sun nearing the horizon and many of the horses having been deprived of water for nearly forty eight hours, Chauvel had given his consent.

The 4th and 12th Light Horse Regiments formed up behind a low ridge, their silhouettes distinct against the fading light, the lighthorsemen sitting atop their huge Waler horses, a blend of several breeds, including the Clydesdale, a resilient horse with exceptional endurance, even under extreme stress from food and water shortages. Troopers tightened the chinstraps on their slouch hats that were topped proudly with their full and flowing emu plumes, whilst passing the time with the usual gallows humour of men about to go in to battle. Anticipation was in the air, *and* the smell of horse dung, each soldier acutely aware of the momentous charge ahead. The horses, too, seemed to sense the tension, and pawed at the ground and snorted softly. The men exchanged glances, a mixture of eagerness and apprehension etched on their faces.

The five mates couldn't contain their smiles as they rode along the ranks of the 4th Brigade, finding themselves a gap to slot in to, their mounts falling into line with practised ease. The group caught the attention of a Sergeant Major, who trotted up to greet them.

"Welcome the 2nd, come to join in have we?" he asked.

Percy felt uneasy, aware that he and his mates could easily be sent away and back to their own units.

"Yes sir," he replied, "if you are fine with it of course?"

"Well, the more the merrier sergeant. Sling your rifles over your shoulders and prepare to draw your bayonets when the order comes...I hope they are sharp," said the Sergeant Major as he pointed at the town to their front, "our objective is Beersheba about two miles or so just beyond that line of trenches there. Be aware boys, we aint stopping for buggery. No dismounting and going in on foot, we're riding in all the way. Watch out for hand signals, and give 'em what for".

As the Sergeant Major trotted away Chugger noticed their own regiment in the distance preparing to advance.

"Riding in all the way? Well I'll be buggered," announced Boggy.

"Looks like we have a race on our hands too boys!" Chugger remarked.

Percy thought for a moment.

"Once we reach Beersheba we'll head off to the 2nd and join up with them," he said.

His four mates nodded in agreement, not wanting to let their own unit down.

As the lines of light horsemen waited, Percy adjusted his grip on the reins, his heart pounding in his chest, whilst Chugger couldn't resist a whispered quip to ease the tension; earning a few muted chuckles from those around him. Davo checked his rifle one last time, slung it over his shoulder then checked his bayonet; his eyes scanning the horizon where Beersheba lay shrouded in the distance.

Boggy felt a shiver of adrenaline course through him, the weight of what lay ahead pressing down on his shoulders. He took a deep breath, steeling himself for what was to come, whilst Johnno, beside him, tightened his grip on the handle of his bayonet, ready to draw it when the order came, his jaw set in determination. All was quiet now as each man whispered a silent prayer and a promise to watch each other's backs in the chaos of the charge.

The officers and NCOs moved along the lines, offering last minute words of encouragement, their voices steady and purposeful. General Grant, the Brigade Commander, spoke as he rode up and down the ranks of the 12th Light Horse Regiment, just like Kings of bygone days.

"Men, you're fighting for water. There's no water between this side of Beersheba and Esani. Use your bayonets as swords. I wish you the best of luck".

Rachel's heart thudded in her chest, a knot of dread twisting tighter with every moment. She had always worried for Chugger and the boys, and today was no different. As the regiment made ready for the assault, she felt an overpowering pull; she had to find him, to see him before he rode off. But when she mounted her horse and rode towards the lines of lighthorsemen, it was too late. They had already left on their escort.

As she galloped among the ranks of soldiers, her panic rose with every empty face she passed. The troopers, now used to seeing her in her light horse uniform, with the giant scimitar slung over her back, barely glanced at her today. They had their own individual worries, their thoughts consumed with the battle to come. Even the usual light hearted banter with Alfie was missing, for he too was nowhere to be seen, left behind for safety with the QM staff, and she was alone in her frantic search.

Spotting one of the Troop Commanders, Rachel trotted up, her voice trembling with urgency.

"Where is Wilbert...please?"

The officer, distracted by the preparations, didn't recognise the name at first.

"Wilbert?"

"Yes, please...Wilbert...er...er...Chugger," she stammered, the anxiety obvious in her voice.

Realisation flickered in the officer's eyes.

"Ohhhh...Chugger... he's off over that way with Sergeant Taylor," he replied, pointing towards the ridge which, for the moment, shielded the 4th Brigade, "I wouldn't be surprised if he didn't end up in a battle there either".

Rachel's eyes widened as the thought of not seeing Chugger again entered her thoughts.

"Battle?"

The officer nodded.

"Yes...Beersheba".

Rachel's stomach lurched. Battle. The word echoed in her mind, her worst fears coming to life.

"Thank you...er...mate...very much," said Rachel as she turned her horse sharply and kicked it into a gallop, riding towards the 4th Brigade, armed with her huge and terrifying sword.

Dirt flew beneath her horse's hooves as she sped toward the ridge, the weight of her scimitar slapping against her spine, a cold reminder of the danger Chugger was riding into. Her thoughts were beginning to spiral as she raced forward. What if she never saw him again? What if this battle took him, like so many others had taken their friends? She gripped the reins tighter, her knuckles white as she pushed her horse harder.

Behind the distant ridge the low murmur of preparations gradually fell into a hushed silence as the men focused their minds on the task at hand. The sky above was beginning to darken, and although it was still daylight, the first stars began to twinkle faintly, as if in silent witness to the impending assault.

In those final moments, the world seemed to hold its breath. The excitement and anticipation built to a fever pitch, the collective energy of the regiments poised like a coiled spring. The signal to charge could come at any moment, and when it did, they would surge forward as one in a thundering wave from hell.

Percy glanced at his friends, seeing his own determination mirrored in their eyes. Whatever lay ahead, they would face it together, bound by the bond of mateship forged over three years in the fires of war. As the order finally came, they leaned forward in their saddles, ready to unleash the full fury of the Light Horse upon Beersheba.

As each man, their breath misting in the cooling air, gently squeezed their horse's sides with their heels, the lines of light horse set off in a traditional three line charge formation, slowly moving forward as one, at the trot, for about a quarter of a mile up a slight rise. On the brow of the hill the regiments paused for a moment, almost defiantly revealing themselves to the Turkish infantry and artillery who awaited them at the edge of the town. But the Turks, recognising the distant soldiers as Australian Light Horse expected a mounted advance, followed by a dismounted attack, and thus adjusted the sights on their rifles accordingly and readied their artillery pieces.

After the brief pause the two regiments calmly walked their horses forward, and then broke into a trot, which finally sped up to a canter, the sound of steel on steel echoing across the open landscape as hundreds of ANZACs drew their bayonets from their scabbards.

As the charge signal came, one of the officers let out a yell, which spurred the men on. The ground was rough, causing the line to twist, but the lighthorsemen remained calm and steady as they spread out slightly in order to avoid mass casualties from both artillery and small arms fire.

Percy kicked his horse into a gallop across the vast, dusty desert, adrenaline surging through his veins. The pounding of hooves echoed across the open plain, mixing with the roar of hundreds of horses charging alongside. He looked left and right for his four mates, ensuring they all kept close as they raced toward Beersheba. The sun glinted off his blade, as he waved his bayonet above his head, letting out a blood curdling yell which mingled with the hundreds of shouts of vengeance echoing from the stampeding ANZACs. As they galloped, the wind rushed past, carrying the heat of the desert and sounds of distant gunfire.

The smell of sweat, dirt, fear, excitement and determination filled the air as the Lighthorsemen spurred their mounts on toward Beersheba, causing the ground to shake beneath them as their horses thundered forward, the pounding hooves echoing through their bodies. The horses, with wide eyes and flaring nostrils, galloped at full speed, their mouths frothing from the effort. The ANZACs could taste the sweat on their faces, mixed with the gritty dust kicked up by the horses, the dust hanging in the air like a thick cloud, stinging their eyes and filling their lungs, sticking to their uniforms and skin, grinding between their teeth.

The noise was overwhelming. Men shouted, but the wind carried their words away. They were fixated on the enemy positions to their front. The only sound they could hear was the thunder of hooves, the clinking of their equipment, and the rattling of weapons. The horses were fearless and kept pushing forward, their sides covered in white foam, whilst dirt and small rocks, thrown up by the charge, stung the men's skin and bounced off their hats.

As they got closer to Beersheba, time seemed to slow down. The charge was both thrilling and terrifying, the landscape a blur. The men knew this was a critical moment. Everything depended on their speed and bravery. Yet, despite the chaos, a strange calm took over as they focused on the task ahead, urging their horses on with hearts pounding in time with the charge.

In the Turkish trenches, which mainly faced south, with a few shallow ones facing east, the defenders saw the lighthorsemen charging, and their artillery immediately opened fire with shrapnel. As the advance turned into a gallop, the 12th Light Horse Regiment came under fire from the trenches on the high point of Ras Ghannam. The Nottingham Battery responded, targeting the machine gunners in those trenches, and after a second shot, the Turkish soldiers were seen running for their lives.

Percy breathed a sigh of relief as he observed the explosions ahead.

"Go the gunners!" he shouted, his voice unheard in the thunder of battle that engulfed them.

As Rachel galloped, her horse's hooves pounded the ground, churning up earth in a wild spray. Ahead, the Turkish guns roared to life, belching fire and smoke towards the mass of Australian Light Horse charging full tilt toward Beersheba, their bayonets waving about their heads, flashing like silver teeth in the sun.

"Alqarf!" she screamed, the word tearing from her throat in her native tongue, then, without slowing, she ripped her scimitar from its scabbard, the enormous blade glinting wickedly, as she yanked her horse to an abrupt stop, breathing hard, eyes darting between the galloping Aussie horsemen and the entrenched Turkish positions on the forward edge of Beersheba. Her mind raced, calculating the distance, timing the charge.

There was no time to waste.

With a fierce kick, she was off again, veering sharply to the right, her heart pounding with adrenaline. She angled her horse toward the flank of Beersheba, determined to reach the town at the same moment as the Australians thundered in. Dust clouded around her as she rode hard, her sword gleaming in her hand like a beacon.

Dressed in a rag tag collection of Australian army uniform, Rachel cut an imposing figure, her massive blade raised, ready to strike. But the Turkish defenders barely noticed her, paying no attention to this solitary figure galloping towards them on their flank, when hundreds of Light Horsemen were barrelling toward their front like men possessed, bayonets raised high, riding as if hell itself was at their heels.

Rachel leaned low into her horse's mane, her heart hammering in her chest, every second bringing her closer to the madness ahead.

Beersheba was looming closer as the Turkish artillery continued to roar in to life; shrapnel bursting above the horsemen, whilst high explosive shells whistled and whined as they soared over head, detonating harmlessly behind the charging lines. They were now apparently under the guns and out of reach of the death giving missiles, but above them two German bi-planes swooped menacingly like a pair of mating magpies guarding their nest, strafing and bombing, yet their explosives landed ineffectively between the widely spaced formations. Saint Barbara, the patron saint of armourers and artillerymen, was *not* on the side of the Turks that day.

As the leading squadrons, led by scouts seventy to eighty yards ahead, came within range of Turkish riflemen defending their position, several horses were struck by sustained rapid small arms and artillery fire. This fire came from an effective range that could have been devastating, but the vigilant officers of the Essex Battery quickly acquired the position of the enemy guns and silenced them with their first few shells of battery fire. The charging regiments faced more fire about a mile east of Beersheba, where the Nottingham Battery neutralised and drove out a garrison in a redoubt at Point 980, which was flanking the charge.

Although it was broad daylight the galloping lighthorsemen were lit a bright amber colour by the blazing light of the sun slowly setting in the west, and the flash of the shrapnel as it exploded high above them. It was as if fire was erupting from the horses' nostrils and from the shimmering blades of their bayonets as they waved them menacingly at the distant Turks.

As the lighthorsemen closed to within about a mile of Beersheba, the crackling of rifle fire and the rat tat tat of machine guns cut through the air. The bullets thickened, and three or four horses went down. Men ran for cover behind dead horses, whilst riderless horses continued on in a ghostlike charge, their saddles splashed with blood. The enemy trenches were about one hundred and fifty yards to Percy's right, but some of the Turks, unnerved by the sheer audacity of the charge, had forgotten to re-adjust their sights, and their bullets cracked and thumped harmlessly overhead.

Percy and his mates were each screaming like excited children. Never in their lives had they known such elation, albeit deadly. The ground seemed to tremble at the pounding of hundreds of hooves, whilst all around him a torrent of khaki clad horsemen and their mounts raced forward at full killing speed. The horses, their teeth bared like demonic creatures, seemed to soar across the open expanse. Sand and stones kicked up by the hooves ahead peppered and stung Percy's face. A wild symphony filled the air, the pounding hoof beats, the shrill cries, the rasping sounds of horses' lungs, the fading screams and shouts behind, and the louder, urgent warnings ahead.

With a final surge, the horses hit, leaping over the sandbagged front line trenches of the enemy. Some troopers dismounted, engaging in brutal hand to hand combat with the Turkish defenders, whilst others galloped on, plunging into the heart of Beersheba as explosions began to rock the town.

As Percy reached the Turkish defences he swung his bayonet at the first man he encountered. The Turk was standing in the trench as Percy's horse flew over the top like Pegasus. The enemy soldier clutched his rifle, bayonet fixed, and tried to level it at Percy's horse, but in that split second Percy's bayonet lunged downwards and caught him on the side of the head, and as his horse landed on the ground to the rear of the trench he lifted his bayonet and swung it at another man without bothering to see what damage he had done, then just spurred on in an attempt to provoke more fear amongst the enemy. The ANZACs had surprised the Turks with their charge, for they had expected the Australians to dismount and attack on foot, and for a brief glimpse of time they were the kings of the killing as they reached the enemy lines and leapt from their horses cutting down the defenders in all directions. Percy, still aboard Sandy, named after Sandy Creek where his family's cattle station was located, watched as Chugger hammered a man's head with the flat of his bayonet blade, knocking him momentarily to the ground. The Turk yelled in both pain and anger, blood pouring down his face, as he staggered to his feet, only to be overridden by a rush of lighthorsemen, their horses' hooves throwing up a stream of sparks and Turkish blood.

Chugger, Davo, Boggy, Johnno and Percy were all together now as they rode amongst the chaos. Percy was shouting all manner of obscenities as he charged into the mass of Turks who were attempting to flee the carnage, his bayonet swinging as a bearded Turk deflected the blow with his raised rifle before being impaled by the bayonet of a dismounted Aussie soldier; the blade tearing through the wool of his tunic and into his belly. Percy heard a thud as something struck the rear of his saddle, but had no time to look because a Turk with rotten teeth was trying to stab his bayonet through his horse's neck. Percy stretched forward and knocked the Turk's blade away with his bayonet, then began slashing violently at the soldier's arm. The ANZACs were mixed in with the enemy now, unable to manoeuvre their horses any further due to the risk of trampling their dismounted mates. But more Aussies had reached their objective and were eagerly entering the fray. Percy was still engaged in an awkward fight with the bad toothed Turk, frantically lunging at the unexpectedly agile man who was quick on his feet, managing to intercept every swing of Percy's blade with the stock of his rifle. But then he stumbled and Boggy was on to him, stabbing and slashing until blood gushed from a gaping head wound and the Turk crumpled to the ground, dead.

Percy and the boys were desperately trying to keep their horses moving, for there were dismounted Aussies and Turkish infantry amongst the riders now and a slash across a horse's legs could bring a man crashing down to the ground, where a dazed man would be easy prey to a stabbing bayonet.

A bayonet tip appeared from Percy's left, skimming across his belly, but causing no damage, whilst Percy instinctively back swung his blade into a moustachioed face, shattering teeth and sending brain fragments in all directions. Men and horses screamed. All of the lighthorsemen were deep in the fight now, their charge having confused and split the Turks. Mayhem and confusion reigned. Whilst some of the enemy were running for their lives, others were now reforming and began to come at the Aussies from three directions, bellowing their cries of "Allah! Allah!" as they attacked. But, despite this, the Aussies still held the advantage and were now fighting like rabid animals. The Turkish line was a confusion of trampling horses, shouting soldiers and the sound of gunshots and steel on steel as bayonets clashed.

Daylight was slowly slipping away, and the sun on the horizon was both glaring and blinding. Many of those still mounted, including the 2nd Light Horse boys, were now making their way towards Beersheba to drive the Turks out of the town and to capture the vital wells. But the Turks it seemed were having none of it and were intent on slaughtering the invaders. The Turkish infantrymen had now been joined by a handful of cavalrymen who appeared determined to make a name for themselves. Chugger managed to parry a blow from a Turkish sword with a grunt, the blade scraping off his bayonet in a jarring clash, its owner gritting his teeth as he apparently tried to remove Chugger's head from his shoulders.

"YOU BASTARD!" shouted Chugger as the clash of sword and bayonet caused a vibration which rippled up his arm, as he leant forward and punched the Turk square in the face with his free hand.

The Turk wobbled in his saddle, almost losing his balance, but recovering quickly he swung his sword wildly again, managing to hit Chugger's head with the hilt, causing bells to ring in his skull as he swung at and punched the Turk a second time.

"YARRACK!" exclaimed the Turk as he landed a blow to Chugger's right arm with the flat of his sword blade, causing blood to seep through his sleeve.

There was anger in the Turk's eyes. He wanted Chugger's death so badly but did not bank on the skill of the Aussie lighthorseman. Chugger watched as the cavalryman clenched his teeth again. The death blow seemed imminent as he tried to slice his sword at Chugger's face, but then his expression changed as a look of shock and horror filled his face, his eyes widening and his mouth gaping open in a gurgling gasp as blood spewed from his mouth. Rachel had appeared from nowhere and, without a word, she had plunged her scimitar into the Turk's spine, the massive blade slicing clean through and emerging from his chest. She sat there, powerful and silent, her breath heavy, as the Turk shuddered in front of her.

Chugger blinked, his mind racing to catch up as the Turk's sword slipped from his fingers, clattering to the ground. The Turk then whimpered and let out one last dying gurgle as he toppled from his saddle.

Rachel didn't move, her scimitar still dripping with blood as her eyes met Chugger's.

For a long moment, the battlefield seemed to fade away. Chugger, still breathing hard, stared at her, his eyes full of gratitude and something deeper. She had saved his life, and the look in her eyes showed she knew it. Rachel gazed at him, a loving, protective look in her grey eyes. The blood on her sword told one story, but the tenderness on her face told another.

Chugger, battered, bruised, and surprised at Rachel's arrival, gave her a weary smile, his eyes softening.

"I owe you one..." he muttered, his voice rough but full of affection.

Rachel didn't say a word, but the warmth in her gaze spoke volumes as she reached out, briefly placing her hand on Chugger's arm, before turning to face the battlefield once more, her scimitar ready for whatever came next.

But for that moment, the connection between them was undeniable - Rachel, the fierce protector, and Chugger, grateful and alive because of her.

As the noise of battle raged around them Rachel nodded and turned her horse, urging it deeper into the heart of the Turkish soldiers. Her fight had only just begun as she waved the long, curved blade of her scimitar in the air frantically slashing at Turkish cavalrymen and infantry alike. As she rode, her slouch hat was caught in the wind and blew from her head, the chin strap snapping tight under her chin. The hat now flapped wildly behind her, but she paid it no mind. Her face was flushed from the heat of battle, and her long, dark hair spilled free, whipping in the breeze as she galloped amongst the enemy soldiers.

"'Ana áleanukum jamiean!" Rachel shouted, informing the Turks that she cursed them all, her voice sharp and commanding as she swung her blade, cutting down at the enemy with deadly precision.

Turkish heads turned as she rode through their ranks. At first, they were confused by the sight of this lone rider slicing a path between them. But when they saw her face, when they realised she was a woman, their expressions changed from confusion to sheer terror.

Rachel knew why. Some Muslim men believe that if they are killed by a woman, they will never reach paradise. Of course this is a myth, but superstition and mob mentality is enough to make something so, and now she could use it to her advantage.

As she swung her sword she shouted at the Turks to fight her, but instead they stepped back, scrambling to get out of her path. She pressed on, cutting downwards again, but no one dared face her. The Turks, who had been so determined a moment ago, were falling back, fear of a myth overtaking their will to fight.

From nearby, Chugger and Davo watched in total surprise as Rachel rode through the Turkish lines.

"What the bloody hell?" Chugger muttered, shoving his bayonet into an enemy soldier, "they're running from her!"

Davo was equally baffled, landing a blow of his own before glancing over.

"Why won't they fight her? They don't care about us, but they won't touch her?"

Chugger shook his head, panting as he fought off another attacker.

"No idea, mate. It's a first for me".

Rachel, meanwhile, rode with grit and determination, striking hard at the soldiers who scrambled away from her. She could feel their fear and used it to push forward, her scimitar a blur as she continued hacking. The Turks were retreating from her reach now, some abandoning their weapons, too terrified to face the consequences of her blade.

Chugger turned to Davo, his voice edged with awe.

"They're scared of her. Look at 'em!"

Davo grunted, shaking his head.

"Whatever it is, they don't want anything to do with her that's for sure".

Rachel swung her sword at another soldier, but again, he backed away, eyes bulging with terror as he fled. The battle continued to rage, but wherever Rachel rode, the enemy fell apart.

They would rather flee than risk the fate they believed awaited them at the hands of a woman.

The lighthorsemen couldn't understand why, but it didn't matter. Rachel had become a terrifying figure that the Turks refused to confront. She had become something from their nightmares, and she knew it.

Most of the lighthorsemen were now on foot where they could tackle the Turkish soldiers on a level playing field.

Still in his saddle Percy glanced around the battleground.

"This is no good," Percy called to his mates, "time to dismount I think".

At the very moment that Percy spoke there was a loud bang as a grenade exploded nearby, causing Percy's spooked horse to rear up and help Percy on his way to the ground with a thud, momentarily stunning him. As his four mates dismounted they slapped their horse's behinds causing them to gallop away, with the intention of rounding them up later. The battle was still chaotic as a horse stepped within inches of Percy's face, but Percy managed to roll to the side desperately fumbling for his rifle and bayonet which had fallen to the ground with him. A horse stepped on his bayonet and Percy cringed at the sight, praying that the blade was still in one piece. It was, and he quickly snatched it up and clipped it on to his rifle, whilst scrambling to his feet. His current reality was confusion, a drumming of hooves and the echoes of screams all around.

"Are you right mate?" asked a concerned Davo.

Percy rubbed his head.

"Yeah mate...LOOK OUT!" Percy shouted suddenly as a Turk appeared behind Davo, who instinctively threw himself on to the dusty earth, leaving Percy to duel with the enemy soldier.

There was no time to aim as Percy pointed his rifle, from the hip, at the Turk and pulled the trigger.

CLICK!

There was nothing. Had Percy cocked his rifle or did he have a stoppage? As the Turk inched closer Percy fumbled with the bolt, pulling it back, ejecting a jammed round, and forcing it forwards again, inserting a fresh round in to the chamber.

BANG!

This time it worked as the enemy soldier spat blood and fell forward on to the ground.

The fighting seemed to be dying down as Percy removed his slouch hat and used it to wipe the sweat from his brow.

"Thanks mate. I owe you one," said a grateful Davo as he clambered to his feet and looked briefly at the dead Turk.

"I think you owe him ten mate, but who's counting eh?" laughed Chugger.

The 1st and 2nd Light Horse Regiments had almost dead heated with the 4th Brigade's arrival at the edge of town, and were now engaged in a savage struggle of their own.

"Do you hear that?" asked Percy, "I think our mates need us on the other side of town".

Chugger was nonplussed.

"Mate, I don't know how you can distinguish *any* sounds with this racket, but I'm with yer," he replied, pointing at their horses standing nonchalantly in a group by a crumbling stone wall, "let's go round up the horses eh?"

"And don't forget Rachel...I think she's a keeper mate," laughed Percy.

Whilst the 4th Light Horse Regiment had dismounted at the trenches to tackle their objective on foot, many in the 12th Light Horse Regiment had pushed straight through to take the town. Limited entrances to the city had temporarily slowed them, but the front riders pushed through the narrow streets, some only wide enough for two riders abreast, as they galloped like mad men, falling beams, exploding magazines, and hidden snipers unable to stop their race.

The town, swiftly taken with its wells captured intact, owed its salvation to the shock and speed of the charge, preventing destruction by the retreating Turkish forces.

As the boys, and Rachel, rode through the narrow streets they noticed that although small, Beersheba was neatly laid out and boasted some very nice buildings with tiled roofs. But the retreating Turks had left the town in a mess with rifles and other equipment scattered everywhere, and bullocks and horses roaming freely in the streets.

By the time they rejoined their regiment, the battle on the other side of town had ended, at the expense of three dead and sixteen wounded - a small price in the grand scheme. In contrast, the charge had claimed the lives of thirty one lighthorsemen, with thirty six wounded, and at least seventy horses lost.

With the battle won, the brigade, less one regiment, assembled that night at Wadi Saba, but not before helping themselves to the abandoned Turkish stores, taking with them much needed grain for the horses, bivvie sheets, and peg posts.

As night descended, Beersheba was securely in Allenby's hands, marking a pivotal shift against the Turks in Palestine and forever changing Middle Eastern history. For the soldiers involved, it was a victory born of daring and desperation, with the most memorable aspect being the extraordinary and audacious mounted charge that had succeeded against all odds.

The camp fires crackled softly, sending embers spiralling into the clear night sky. After their exhausting day, the men gathered around, their faces illuminated by the warm glow of the flames, passing cigarettes and sharing muted conversations. The night was quiet, save for the occasional clink of tin mugs and the crackling of wood. The excitement from the battle and the charge on Beersheba lingered in their minds, but for now, there was peace.

Chugger sat beside Rachel, his eyes occasionally drifting from the flames to her. Her dark hair was now loose, framing her face in the firelight. She looked different, softer in the evening's calm, but no less formidable with her scimitar slung across her back in its new leather scabbard.

Davo, Percy, Johnno, and Boggy huddled a little further off, sharing a few jokes, whilst Alfie tucked in to another tin of bully beef.

"Bloody hell that charge today, I don't think the Turks knew what hit them," Percy muttered.

"Aye, though I reckon Chugger here had his eye on something else," Davo smirked, nodding toward Chugger and Rachel.

"Or someone..." said Percy.

Chugger ignored them for now. He glanced at Rachel, her face serene as she stared into the flames. He'd been thinking about her all evening. Ever since she'd come into their lives, something had changed. She'd found a place among them, and though they still teased him, he knew the other men respected her as much as he did.

Finally, without much thinking, he leaned closer and whispered, "I'm gonna marry you one day".

Rachel blinked, turning to look at him. Her English had been improving, but she still struggled with some words. Her eyes searched his face, confused.

Davo, who had heard Chugger's whisper, noticed and grinned.

"Looks like Chugger just popped the question! Better help her out, Alfie".

Young Alfie, who had been sitting quietly, perked up at the mention of his name. He scampered over to Rachel, as confused as she was.

"What did he say?" Rachel asked, her voice hesitant.

Alfie scratched his head, looking from Chugger to Rachel.

"Er... well, he said he will marry you one day...sawf yatazawajuk ywman ma biallughat al'iinjilizia".

"Alzawaj?" asked Rachel.

Her eyes widened. She stared at Chugger, not in disbelief, but in wonder, searching his eyes, looking for any hint of jest, but found only sincerity.

Chugger shifted, a little self conscious under the stares of his mates. He squeezed Rachel's hand, offering her a reassuring smile.

"I mean it, Rach".

The other men quietened down, sensing the importance of the moment, Percy managing a whisper in Davo's ear.

"The bloke's got more guts than I thought".

Johnno chuckled.

"Aye, well, it's about time he did something right. She's a bonza woman".

Rachel, still holding Chugger's hand, turned to Alfie once more.

"Marry... marry?"

Alfie nodded eagerly.

"Yes, that is what Mister Chugger said! He wants you to be his wife".

Rachel's expression softened, and a smile broke through her usually composed face. She'd never been treated so kindly, so respectfully. Not even her own people had shown her such care. She gripped Chugger's hand tighter, her eyes misting slightly.

"Chugger... I..., naeam...yes...yes".," she whispered in her best English, her voice full of warmth.

Chugger's face lit up, and he pulled her closer, his arm slipping around her shoulders. The rest of the blokes grinned, though they kept their distance, giving the pair their moment.

"Well, bugger me," Boggy whispered with a grin, flicking his cigarette into the fire, "looks like Chugger's done alright for himself".

Percy smiled and sighed, casting a glance to Alfie.

"Finally something good has come out of this bloody awful mess".

"Hey, haven't you got a letter to write?" said Davo.

"Yes, yes I have," replied Percy.

The night settled into a comfortable quiet and the fire crackled softly as Chugger and Rachel sat together, her head resting on his shoulder. In that moment, the war felt a world away, and under the clear night sky, they found a small pocket of peace.

The early morning sun was just beginning to rise, casting a soft glow over the desert as Chugger and Percy sat by the campfire, preparing breakfast. The air was still cool, and the scent of frying bacon filled the quiet space around them. Chugger was busy turning the bacon with the end of his bayonet, while Percy stirred a billy of tea, the flames popping gently in the background.

"You really meant it last night, didn't you?" Percy asked, glancing sideways at Chugger, "about marrying Rachel?"

Chugger didn't look up, but smiled, keeping his eyes on the sizzling bacon.

"Yeah mate, I meant it," he replied, "I can't imagine going back home without her".

Percy scratched his chin thoughtfully.

"It's a big thing you know. How do you reckon you'll manage it? I mean, the Army doesn't exactly hand out tickets to Australia for *anyone* does it, and you can't just pop her on a ship and say 'see you back in Brisbane,' mate?"

Chugger shifted uncomfortably, his expression becoming serious. He'd been thinking about it ever since the words left his mouth, but he hadn't quite worked out all the details.

"I dunno yet, but there's got to be a way. I'm not leaving her behind. I love her you know...*and* she saved my bloody life. No one's ever done that before...well, except you and the other blokes of course, but you know what I mean. Anyway, I've got all that money we won so can pay for her passage back home myself".

Percy handed Chugger a mug, then laughed to himself, though there was no malice in it, just the kind of bemused sympathy that only a mate could give.

"You're keen, I'll give you that. But, mate...what'll happen when you get her to Queensland? It's not exactly like Bundaberg is full of Arab women running about with swords is it?"

Chugger smirked at that, leaning back on his hands and taking a sip of tea.

"She'll manage, Percy. If she can handle this bloody desert and all the mess that comes with it, she'll be fine in Queensland. She's tougher than most blokes I know, and my sister will love her soon enough, like the boys here. She's got a good head on her shoulders. We'll sort it".

"True enough," Percy agreed, nodding, "she's part of the regiment now. I don't think anyone would argue that".

Chugger smiled, his face softening as he thought of Rachel.

"She's something special, Perce. No one's ever treated her proper, not even her family. So I'm going to make sure that she is treated like a queen".

Percy grinned, shaking his head.

"You're a bloody stubborn mule, mate, but if anyone can sort something mad like this, it's you".

Chugger smirked, jabbing his bayonet into the bacon.

"I'll take that as a compliment shall I?"

The two men sat in silence; the only sounds the pop and splutter of the fire and the distant stir of horses.

10

For you but not for me

The first two attacks on Passchendaele had failed due to the wet weather. On the 26th of October the Canadians were given the honour of making the third attempt. They were successful and, thanks to them, the Third Battle of Ypres finally came to an end.

On the 2nd of November the 9th Battalion relieved the Canadians in the front line on Passchendaele Ridge. The 12th Battalion were their neighbours on their right flank, whilst Battalion Headquarters was situated at Tyne Cot, a barn located fifty yards west of the crossing where the Broodseinde to Passchendaele Road crossed the railway.

As the Aussies trudged up to relieve the Canadians, the mud clung to their boots like a curse. The Canadians, looking just as filthy, were already making their way back, worn but grinning.

One of the Canadians gave a mock salute to the Aussies.

"Good luck, boys! You'll need a canoe to get through this muck".

Clancy, now covered head to toe in grime from the trek, spat into the mud.

"You lot leave any dry spots, or is it all like this?"

"Buddy...dry spots? Haven't seen one since July," one of the Canadians grinned through his mud streaked face, "better watch out for Fritz though, he's been having a go with the mortars just up the way. Likes to drop 'em in your lap, so be careful".

"Be careful? This is a *war* mate," replied Clancy.

Stowie smirked.

"We'll send him back a souvenir if he tries. Maybe a boot up his ass".

As they passed each other, one of the Canadians tossed over a cigarette to Ten Bob.

"Try not to get too comfy, eh? We've left the place nice and bloody for you".

Ten Bob caught it with a frown.

"Oh great...cheers mate".

A railway line ran through a cutting on the front line. 'D' Company occupied a line from it, extending left whilst 'C' Company occupied a line to the right. Regular patrols were sent out as the exact position of the enemy was unknown.

The following morning, with the sun barely hinting at the horizon, 'B' Company stood watch along their front, eyes straining through the early morning haze. Without warning, the distant artillery shattered the calm as 'D' Company's trenches were battered and mauled by a heavy German bombardment. The earth shook violently beneath the shells, throwing men off their feet, and the air was choked with smoke and dirt. The boys barely had time to catch their breath before the enemy came on in force, leapfrogging in groups, one wave crouching low, rifles blazing, while the next sprinted forward, splashing through the mud, then taking shelter behind fallen bodies and in shell craters to repeat the process again.

"Here they come!" yelled one of the Aussies, his voice shrill with anticipation.

Rifle butts were pressed into shoulders, as the trench filled with the harsh crack of gunfire. The Aussies fired fast and steady, the bolts of their rifles slamming backwards and forwards as they pumped round after round into the advancing Germans. The first line went down hard, bullets tearing into chests and legs, men dropping with gurgling cries, their rifles slipping from limp hands.

The Germans were pushing hard, though. Another group dashed forward, some firing as they ran. Mud flew up with every step, and the Aussie trenches were thudding with enemy bullets slapping into sandbags and snapping the air over their heads.

"Keep at it!" shouted one of the sergeants, his voice barely cutting through the noise.

On the German side, it was hell. They'd expected the Aussies to be softened up by the earlier shelling, but they were holding strong, and every few steps, one of the Germans would jerk and go down, clutching at a wound, blood spurting into the churned up dirt.

"Vorwärts!" yelled a German officer, pushing his men on, but, hardened by years of grisly sights, he barely flinched when one of his men beside him was struck by a bullet to the throat, dropping, hands at his neck, blood pouring between his fingers.

An Aussie soldier shouted as a bullet tore through his arm, but he didn't stop firing. The eerie fog caused by the cordite and gunpowder, made it difficult to see, but the Germans were still coming. A couple of them dived into a shell hole, popping up to take pot shots at the trench, while the next wave surged forward, some clutching at their rifles, others dragging wounded mates.

Another Aussie, firing from the edge of the trench, dropped two Germans with clean shots before a bullet whipped past his ear, embedding itself into the sandbags to his rear. He instinctively ducked down, his heart pounding, as another volley rang out. The enemy was getting closer, too close.

The Germans, by now, however, were starting to lose momentum. Bodies were piling up in the mud, some still twitching, others very much dead. Their leapfrogging advance was slowing, men hesitating as the Aussies' machine gun like rifle fire cut them down. One German tried to run forward, but a shot hit him square in the chest, knocking him flat on his back, blood soaking his tunic. His fellow soldiers kept moving, but the weight of the fire was too much, their once steady charge now reduced to a crawl.

Finally, the Germans broke. The few who were still on their feet, turning and scrambling back toward their lines, dragging whoever they could, leaving their dead and many wounded behind. The Aussies, breathless and soaked in sweat, held the line, rifles still aimed at the retreating enemy, ready in case they tried again. But for now, it was over, their trench held firm, the Germans had been thrown back.

But the Germans weren't finished.

Just before first light, out of the swamp to their front, a swamp that was thought to be impassable, came the devil himself. The bog had been dismissed as a natural barrier, but the Germans proved it otherwise, launching another sudden, savage rush on 'D' Company. The men, still recovering from the earlier barrage and infantry assault, scrambled to defend their trench yet again, but this time they were overwhelmed, driven from their hard won positions in a matter of minutes.

'A' Company charged in to reclaim the lost ground, but the mud, confusion, and continuous machine gun fire forced them back. Even Sergeant Porter's bombing party failed to turn the tide, the lads choking on cordite and smoke as they lobbed Mills bombs into the abyss.

'C' and 'D' Companies found themselves more or less trapped in shell holes to the rear of the front line, the rain of shells and bullets making every movement a gamble with death. Then came the Intelligence Officer, Lieutenant Butler, with a plan for a section of rifle grenadiers and Lewis Gunners to support another attempt. It was daring, but it just might work, and, of course, Clancy and the boys put their hands up for the task.

As dawn crept in, the rifle grenadiers let loose, opening fire on the enemy from behind 'C' Company's position, their explosives bursting among the German ranks like penny bangers on bonfire night, whilst Lewis Gunners took up position in 'C' Company's front line and a shell hole two hundred yards from the enemy's left flank, pouring round after round into the enemy soldiers. The deafening rattle of the Lewis Guns echoed across the battlefield, tearing through the Germans with brutal efficiency. One by one the enemy was completely silenced.

Meanwhile Tomo and the CSM had dropped into 'D' Company's shell holes and issued orders to the occupants.

On the signal of a Very Light which flared into the sky, the grenadiers ceased fire.

"Now!" Tomo shouted.

On the order, the trapped Aussies scrambled from their craters, bayonets gleaming in the grey light, racing forward in a ragged line, boots sinking into the mire as they assaulted the German held position. The Lewis Guns, having done their deadly work of enfilading the Germans, fell silent just as the first of the attackers reached the parapet.

With a collection of savage war cries, the Aussies hurled themselves over the parapet and into the German held trench, bayonets stabbing viciously in all directions. The first German, a boy no older than nineteen, barely had time to raise his rifle before Clancy drove his bayonet through the man's gut, the blade sinking deep. He twisted the weapon, feeling the resistance of bone and gristle, and yanked it free with a wet, sucking sound. The lad crumpled, clutching at his spilling entrails, his mouth opening and closing like a fish gasping for air; the look on his face betraying the terror as he grasped for the final moments of his life.

Nearby, Pip swung his rifle like a club, the butt crashing into a German's skull with a sickening crack, blood spraying as the man's head split open, as he dropped, twitching, into the mud. Another enemy lunged at Roo with a bayonet, but Roo sidestepped as Pip stuck out his leg to trip the German, whilst Roo caught the man in the throat with a swift upward thrust. The blade slid through skin and muscle, severing the jugular, and blood gushed in thick, bright red spurts, painting the trench walls as the German staggered back, choking on his own blood, his eyes bulging like a cane toad.

Steel met flesh with a sickening crunch, and many of the Germans, caught off guard, offered little resistance as the Australians stormed through, stabbing and shooting with a fury born of anger and revenge.

Archie had his bayonet buried in a man's chest, the steel blade grinding against ribs as he struggled to free it. When the German thrashed, Archie kicked him off, leaving the body flopping like a fish out of water. Tomo had been running like a mad man through the trench using his revolver like there was no tomorrow, but he had forgotten one of the first rules of battle...count your rounds. As he aimed his pistol at a huge German, the soldier flinched as he saw the barrel turn and the hammer of the weapon fall. Then...nothing...just a lifeless click of metal on metal. The German soldier saw his chance as he thrust his bayonet towards the Australian officer, but Tomo's reactions were faster as he kicked the rifle away and, his hands red with gore, grabbed the German by the collar and smashed him into the trench wall before plunging a knife into the man's eye. A scream tore from the German's throat, but it was short lived as Tomo twisted the blade, the eyeball bursting in a spray of blood and fluid, as the man's legs buckled and his lifeless body slumped to the ground.

Pip, who had witnessed the scene nodded his approval then tossed his officer a German rifle.

"Here sir, you might be needing this".

The trench was a nightmare of violence, men screaming, bleeding and dying in the mud and gore. Guts spilled from ruptured bellies, whilst blood spattered the trench walls, pooling in the mud, men slipping in the entrails of the fallen, while rifles cracked skulls like eggs. But, in the midst of it all, the Aussies fought like demons, stabbing and clubbing their way through the trench, the Germans either dead or fleeing in blind panic. The air stank of iron, gunpowder, and death, and when it was over, only the groans of the dying remained, echoing through the slaughterhouse that was the trench.

The position was captured in minutes, and all for only two wounded Diggers.

The 4th of November started like any other day on Passchendaele Ridge, except for the ominous stillness that hung in the air. The men had barely finished their breakfast when the first shells screamed overhead, ripping through the sky and crashing into the earth like angry fists.

"Here we go again," muttered one of the soldiers, crouching down as the ground shook beneath him.

Roo had only just got his billy to the boil.

"Bloody hell Fritz!" he muttered.

"Yeah, great timing as usual eh?" Clancy nodded.

But the barrage didn't let up as shell after shell pounded the trench line, sending showers of mud and shrapnel into the air. The Aussies crouched low in their makeshift dugouts, helmets pulled tight over their heads, flinching at every deafening explosion. The air was heavy with the smell of smoke and churned up dirt, every breath tasting like dust.

"We're bloody sitting ducks here," one of the men called out, pressing himself against the earthen wall of the trench. He then peered up at the lip of the trench, but the risk of sticking his head out was too great. Shell fragments were buzzing overhead like angry wasps, and anyone caught in the open wouldn't last long.

"Keep your bloody heads down!" Clancy shouted, his voice almost drowned out by the next round of shelling.

Still, they had to keep watch. Eyes strained through the haze, looking for any sign of movement from the German lines. The constant barrage was meant to soften them up, but the Hun might be lurking in the smoke, waiting for the right moment to strike. A few brave souls risked peeks over the parapet, scouring the shell blasted landscape.

The trench was barely holding together under the bombardment, rattling and shifting with each hit. Sandbags exploded into clouds of dirt, and chunks of the parapet crumbled away. One soldier was unlucky enough to have a shell land too close, sending him sprawling into the mud, clutching his leg where shrapnel had torn through. Blood soaked into his trousers as his mates dragged him to a safer spot, calling frantically for a stretcher bearer.

Others frantically hugged the walls of the shallow dugouts carved into the sides of the trench, though these offered little comfort as the constant concussion from the blasts left their ears ringing.

Occasionally, someone would mutter, "Christ, when will it bloody stop?" but there was no answer.

Some tried to make light of it, sharing quick jokes between the rounds.

"Could be worse," one soldier said, lighting a cigarette with shaky hands, "we could be in Aussie with the missus".

"Or the missus could be here," added Pip.

A few giggles escaped, though the laughter was more out of nerves than anything else.

Every now and then, the men would stick their heads up just long enough to spot the flashes from the German guns in the distance, tracking the shells as they came screaming in, the ground seeming to heave and jump under the persistent bombardment. To many it felt like the entire ridge might just collapse in on itself.

But, throughout it all, the ANZACs held their positions, rifles at the ready, battered but unbroken; keeping a watch, knowing the Germans could come at any moment.

Relief, in the form of the 2nd Battalion, came on the 5th with a move to Esplanade Sap at Ypres.

"Well that was a *cracker* of a decision lads, especially on the 5th of November," Pip laughed as they marched, expecting some form of response.

Archie turned to Pip, his eyebrows raised.

"*Any* move to a safer area is a good decision mate".

"No...don't you get it?" asked Pip, slightly nonplussed, "cracker...like fire cracker...don't you lads do Bonfire Night?"

"No they...we don't," said Captain Ponsonby, overhearing Pip's comment.

"Oh, don't yous fellas do *anything* with fireworks and explosions like?" said Pip.

"Yeah mate, we come and fight wars for *you* British," growled Clancy.

"Aha, but I'm an Aussie now don't forget," retorted Pip.

"Yeah...we'll see," replied Clancy, "we'll see".

The 3rd Brigade were now support brigade and, as a result, the next few days were spent re-organising and scrubbing the mud from clothing, equipment and bodies. This was followed on the 13th of November with their longest march to date; twenty three miles to Ledinghem, a small village with an ancient church and the ruins of an old chateau. To aid the men on this long hike their packs were transported in lorries.

"Can't *we* get on and *wear* our packs?" asked Ten Bob.

"Come on mate, how long have you been in this man's army?" laughed Clancy, "that would be the obvious and sensible thing to do wouldn't it?"

Despite their exhaustion, not one man fell out of the march.

Five days were spent at Ledinghem which included another visit from General Birdwood who had come to present Lieutenant Sargent with a Military Cross for taking the attack in at Polygon Wood.

Two days later the brigade was marched to the Samer area for a rest. They were billeted in five villages; Campamare, Herimez, Sequieres, Dalle and Grandal.

Despite the allies success at Beersheba the Ottoman Empire was still a force to be reckoned with. The Turkish garrison retreated to the defences around Tel el Sheria and Tel el Khuweilfeh, about ten miles north of Beersheba, quickly setting up new defences. They were reinforced by the 19th Division from Gaza and though they had lost Beersheba, their defensive line, stretching to the Mediterranean coast, remained strong, particularly around Hareira, Sheria, and Gaza.

EEF mounted units now controlled the crucial road from Beersheba to Jerusalem, and to counter this, three Ottoman infantry battalions were sent to protect the key metalled road to Hebron and Jerusalem from a potential EEF advance.

On the 2nd of November the mounted troops were sweeping around the Gaza line advancing towards the enemy. Their progress, however, was slowed by the brutal, harsh stone desert landscape and a desperate shortage of water. The Turks, entrenched at Khuweilfeu, however, had an abundance of water; in fact the only available water source in the area, and they guarded it fiercely. As part of the brigade, the 2nd Light Horse was about to change the equilibrium, and moved out at midnight with the intent on attacking the water rich enemy force.

The advance guard was the 1st Light Horse Regiment, with orders to attack at 0730 hours. 'C' Squadron, under Captain Evans, was dispatched to occupy a commanding and rocky outcrop called Ras-el-Nagb, whilst 'A' Squadron was sent to support the 1st Light Horse who were situated on the right.

'C' Squadron had dismounted and spread out across the rough terrain. Just after midday, a sudden commotion swept through their ranks as enemy infantry and lancers appeared on the horizon, advancing rapidly. The sight of the lancers, their long spears flashing threateningly in the sun, sent a wave of unease through the soldiers.

"Lancers! I hate these blokes," one of the men grumbled, echoing the sentiment felt by many.

The order to take cover was given, and the soldiers dropped to the ground, lying prone behind whatever cover they could find - rocks, sparse bushes, and small depressions in the earth. The anxiety was rife as they readied their rifles, eyes fixed on the approaching enemy, the ground trembling beneath their thundering hooves.

The lancers charged, their horses crashing across the open ground, kicking up clouds of dust. The ANZACs held their fire, waiting for the perfect moment. As the lancers closed in, the command rang out, and a volley of rifle fire erupted from the prone soldiers, bullets whizzing through the air, finding their marks among the charging enemy.

Some of the lancers were unseated, blood splattering the dust as men tumbled from their saddles, spears clattering beside them, lifeless bodies sprawled in the dirt. Horses reared and screamed, thrown into disorder by the onslaught of gunfire, shrieking as they were hit, some crashing to the ground, crushing their riders beneath them. But, despite their losses, the remaining lancers pushed on, lances lowered, trying to break through the defensive line.

But the ANZACs held firm, the unstopping barrage of rounds from 'C' Squadron proving too much, streams of disciplined, concentrated gunfire ripping through the air, drop-

286 - TONY SQUIRE

ping horsemen in their tracks, forcing the lancers to retreat, regroup, and attempt to charge again. Time after time, they were driven back, unable to breach the staunch line of defenders, their front ranks collapsing in a mess of blood and shattered bone, horses screaming in agony, riders clinging to their mounts, their eyes wild, as they fought to stay upright in the mayhem. Some were thrown, their bodies twisted grotesquely in the dust, limbs torn and broken, as the horses galloped on in blind terror, the desert floor turning dark with blood.

The Turkish infantry which followed the lancers tried to advance under the cover of their mounted comrades, but they too were met with fierce resistance, the soldiers of 'C' Squadron, lying low and laying down accurate fire, holding their ground, not giving an inch. A young soldier to the left of Johnno took a bullet to the neck, blood squirting from the wound as he collapsed, choking and gurgling. His mates dragged him behind cover, but they could do nothing as the life drained from him.

Smoke and dust choked the battlefield, mingling with the sharp cracks of rifles and the cries of men and horses. The battle raged on, as 'C' Squadron held their ground, each Turkish wave smashed back by precision fire, leaving the earth littered with broken bodies, men clutching at their wounds, horses lying dead or thrashing wildly in their final moments. Finally, the lancers and infantry, battered and demoralised, withdrew, leaving the battlefield littered with the fallen. The Lighthorsemen had prevailed.

Relief came from the 5th Mounted Brigade at 1600 hours, and 'C' Squadron was able to rejoin the regiment for its combined attack with the 1st Light Horse at 1700 hours. However, it was soon established that the enemy numbers were far greater than expected. The attack was, therefore, cancelled and the 1st and 2nd Light Horse Regiments withdrew to Beersheba for water, being relieved by the 5th Yeomanry Brigade, who held until the arrival of a brigade of infantry and sufficient artillery to dislodge the Turks.

The 1st Light Horse had sustained heavy casualties, whilst the 2nd had lost one man killed and seven wounded.

On the 6th of November Khuweilfeh was still in enemy hands, so it was decided to by-pass it as the garrison at Gaza was a more important objective. No doubt, being cut off, Khuweilfeu would no longer be a viable position for the Turks...or so it was assumed.

Later that day, at 1645 hours, the 2nd Light Horse Regiment, acting as advance guard for the Brigade, set off along a rough track to march the twelve miles to Khirbet-Um-El-Bakr, near Sheria.

As the column moved through the rugged countryside Percy took the opportunity to ride to the rear to check on Alfie, but, as it turned out, he had no reason to worry, as Alfie was trotting along quite merrily on his donkey, accompanied by Rachel, the two of them so engrossed in conversation that they did not even notice that Percy was now riding alongside them. Rachel, of course, was dressed in her uniform with her sword slung over her shoulder, whilst she now had a new weapon in her arsenal, a Lee Enfield rifle which was holstered in a leather rifle 'bucket' attached to the front of her saddle. Over her left shoulder was a leather bandolier which, judging by its droop was full of ammunition.

"I won't even *ask* you where you got *that* lot from," said Percy, breaking into their conversation.

Rachel smiled awkwardly, but it was obvious that she had collected these items from the battlefield. Percy didn't mind. He had seen the damage she could do with a sword, so God help anyone who rode into her rifle sights.

"I hope you two have got plenty of water with you," Percy enquired.

"Oh yes Mister Percy, I have two canteens and this goat skin bag," replied Alfie, gently patting the water bag, "and Rachel has the same".

On arrival at midnight the Brigade joined up with the Division, relieving the Dorset Yeomanry at an outpost line.

"No rest again boys," Boggy moaned as he rubbed his backside.

"How's your sore bum?" asked Percy.

"Sore," replied Boggy, a frown appearing on his face, "want to kiss it better?"

"Huh...I'd rather kiss a sheep's smelly arse...or maybe not," laughed Percy.

Stags were organised. There would be little sleep for the men that night.

The 60th Yeomanry had been busy during the night, having stormed and taken Tel-el-Sheria. As the Brigade pushed forward at dawn they engaged in a gun battle with enemy cavalry and later were subjected to incoming enemy artillery shells. But this was all part of the desert campaign and seemed natural to the troops. The light horse units had been advancing rapidly and, despite delays at Wadi Sheria, where the wells were so widely dispersed that only eight horses could drink at a time, they managed to advance at the trot on the town of Amiedat, sweeping through the streets, taking three hundred prisoners and seizing a huge stockpile of ammunition that could have fed the enemy's war machine for weeks. But victory wasn't without its frustrations. There *was* a downside in that an enemy artillery battery which had been pounding the ANZACs all morning had managed to slip away, escaping into the desert.

The advancing infantry, lagging behind, were relieved and thankful for the speed of the mounted troops, for they had allowed them to move forward unimpeded.

The regiment dispatched a patrol from Amiedat towards Jemmama, but their advance was abruptly halted by a well entrenched enemy force of about three hundred soldiers near Tel-Aba-Dilakh. Despite this setback, the strategic momentum shifted when Gaza finally fell on the 7th of November, with the retreating enemy attempting to break out and escape through any gaps in the allied lines. To counter this, the 2nd Light Horse Regiment received urgent orders to secure the vulnerable area between the 2nd and 3rd Brigades around Jemmama, ensuring no enemy forces slipped through. Time was short, and every man knew what was at stake. There could be no gaps, no escape for the Turks this time. The regiment spurred their horses forward, determined to close the net.

Both brigades now occupied defensive positions, ready to repel any enemy attempts to break through. The order to attack

Jemmama, a location of strategic importance due to its abundant water supply came at 1300 hours. The 2nd Light Horse sprang into action, quickly mounting up, gripping reins and rifles as they prepared to advance on the town. Dust kicked up in clouds beneath their horses' hooves as they moved forward, forming long, extended lines across the dry landscape. The sun hung high the sky, casting long shadows over the desert as they closed the distance to the enemy. Jemmama was defended by a well entrenched Turkish force, dug in among the rocks and scattered buildings. The light horsemen knew they would be riding straight into heavy fire, but there was no room for hesitation and at the signal, the charge began.

Troopers burst forward, their horses galloping across the arid terrain, hooves pounding like the hammers of a thousand blacksmiths. Turkish rifles cracked from hidden positions in the town, bullets streaking past, some finding their target. A soldier went down, his horse collapsing beneath him, while others urged their mounts onward, gripping their rifles tightly.

As the line closed in, the lighthorsemen dismounted, their rifles firing back at the dug in enemy. They moved swiftly, finding cover behind rocks and low walls, exchanging fire with the Turks. Dust and smoke from rifle muzzles hung in the air, the deafening sound of rifle shots echoing in the hot afternoon. A Turkish machine gun opened up from a rooftop, throwing a wall of rounds towards the advancing Australians, forcing them to drop low and crawl forward.

Percy, yelling to be heard over the gunfire, led a small group on a flanking move around the side of the town. They crept through a narrow alley, moving from building to building, before storming the machine gun position in a brief but bloody hand to hand fight. The Turks fought back fiercely, but the Australians' bayonets were quicker, and deadlier, and the machine gun fell silent.

With the flanking team taking out the key positions, the rest of the regiment streamed into the town, and the enemy, shaken by the aggressive, lightning advance, began to break. By approximately 1630 hours, they had successfully captured the town, the remaining defenders were either captured or had fled, leaving the Australians in control of Jemmama.

The regiment, bloodied but victorious, quickly secured the wells, ensuring that the precious water would now sustain *their* own forces, then, as the sun began to set, they set up a bivouac within Jemmama, the men and horses finally able to rest after hours of intense fighting; now using the town's resources to their advantage.

That night, a much needed supply of rations arrived; welcome gifts for the soldiers who had been running dangerously low on food, this timely arrival of provisions boosting their morale and ensuring they were prepared for the next phase of operations.

On the 9th of November the brigade moved to El Mejdel, an ancient city near Ascalon. A battery of the Inverness Royal Horse Artillery was attached to the brigade and the lighthorsemen were notably impressed with their shooting accuracy as they rode past a long column of wrecked and burning enemy wagons.

'C' Squadron remained at El-Mejdel; Major Stodart having been appointed Military Governor. As usual though, there was no time for a rest as there was still a threat from the rear from Khuweilfeu, where the enemy garrison still held firm.

Meanwhile, the brigade occupied Esdud, a strategically positioned town about eight miles north of Mejdel. Esdud was a small, ancient settlement with a history dating back to biblical times, offering a sobering contrast to the modern war being waged around it. The occupation of Esdud was crucial for maintaining the pressure on the retreating enemy and ensuring a continuous Allied presence in the region.

However, logistical challenges arose as the brigade's supply train, laden with essential rations and equipment, lagged behind due to the complex and unpredictable nature of the campaign. In the interim, the brigade had no choice but to procure rations from the local inhabitants, this situation requiring careful negotiation and diplomacy to secure the necessary provisions without alienating the local population, who were already strained by the ongoing conflict, and their secret hatred of the infidel soldiers.

The brigade's movements had been significantly delayed days earlier at Khuweilfeu, a region where rough terrain and stiff enemy resistance had stalled their advance. This delay proved costly, as it prevented the brigade from capitalising on opportunities to inflict substantial damage on the retreating enemy forces who were not entirely broken, and were managing to maintain a formidable rear guard to cover their withdrawal.

As the brigade pushed north, they encountered sporadic skirmishes with this rear guard. These encounters were often brief but extremely intense, characterised by quick exchanges of gunfire and tactical manoeuvres. The Turkish rear guard, composed of experienced soldiers, utilised the terrain to their advantage, setting up ambushes and using hit and run tactics to slow the Allied advance and protect the main body of their retreating forces.

Every mile gained came at a price and every delay could alter the course of the campaign, with the strategic importance of Esdud and the surrounding areas becoming increasingly evident as the brigade continued their advance. The capture and occupation of such key locations disrupted the enemy's retreat, strained their resources, and brought the Allies closer to their ultimate objective: the complete rout of the Turkish forces and the liberation of Palestine.

'C' Squadron rejoined the regiment on the 11th, the regiment then being sent to recce Wadi Sakerier and Tel-el-Murre in search of ample water. The mission was a success and the brigade was able to water before attacking Burka, alongside the 52nd Division, later being pulled out at dusk, having been relieved by the 8th Mounted Brigade.

The squadron made camp at Harririyeh, where live sheep were issued as rations. Looking at the filthy animals, heavy with their wool, Boggy was not impressed.

"You think they'd have sheared the buggers first!" he exclaimed.

The boys sat quiet, and uncomfortable in their thoughts, looking left and right with hopeful glances.

It was Percy who broke the silence.

"So...who wants to do the deed?" he asked.

"The deed?" replied Johnno.

"You know..." said Percy as he ran his fingers from one side of his neck to the other.

Chugger interrupted.

"Well *you* boys are the farmers".

"Yeah, but we took our animals to market and the butcher to be killed, although sometimes Dad would do it," replied Percy.

"Bloody hell!" exclaimed Chugger, as he cocked his rifle and aimed it at the unsuspecting sheep. But even *he* paused and hesitated.

BANG!

The sheep wobbled, and then toppled over, dead, blood pouring from a hole in its skull.

The mates all turned their heads at the same time to see Rachel standing there with a satisfied grin on her face, smoke wafting from the muzzle of her rifle. Alfie could see the humour of the situation and laughed loudly, his laughter infecting all of those in earshot.

Chugger cleared his throat.

"There you go fellas. Job done," he said, "it looks well when a defenceless woman has to drop a sheep for you".

"Defenceless? Yeah right," laughed Boggy.

The irony of the situation was not apparent to the men who easily killed the enemy in brutal ways, but could not bring themselves to slaughter an unarmed sheep.

On the 13th of November, the regiment advanced to Yebna, an ancient biblical village of Philistine origin situated on the coastal plain, about four miles east of the Mediterranean Sea. Yebna, with its deep historical roots, had seen countless armies and empires pass through its lands over the ages, but now it was their turn. As the regiment moved in, they took up an outpost line on the left flank of the 52nd Division, stretching from the city all the way to the sea. This strategic positioning aimed to fortify the EEF presence along the coast, crucial for controlling the supply routes and supporting naval operations.

The enemy, still licking their wounds from recent defeats, were in a state of self preservation and seemed more concerned with holding on to what they had than launching attacks. This led to an unusually quiet night, for a change, with the troops taking advantage of this calm to rest, maintain their equipment, and prepare for the inevitable.

However, the tranquility was short lived, with heavy enemy shelling holding them up at Zernuka on their journey to Ras Deiran the following day.

The country that the troops were now entering had a different feel now. It was noticeably more civilised, with actual roads that they could easily move along. This improvement in infrastructure was a small but significant relief, aiding their logistical efforts and reducing the physical strain on both men and horses.

Inevitably though, danger still lurked, with the New Zealand Mounted Rifle Brigade on their left engaging the enemy at Nebi Kunda, Wadi Hanein and Richon-Le-Zion during the night. While the improved infrastructure offered some logistical advantages for the EEF, it also meant that the enemy too could more effectively mobilise and fortify their positions.

At 0800 hours the 2nd Light Horse Regiment moved through the 1st and 3rd Light Horse regiments, and, without orders 'C' Squadron became the first British Empire troops to enter the old crusader town of Ramleh. This city, founded in the early 8th Century was strategically located at the crossroads of the Via Maris, connecting Cairo with Damascus, and the road linking the Mediterranean port of Jaffa with Jerusalem, and was quite a prize indeed for any conquering army.

As the lighthorsemen rode past the timeworn buildings, the narrow streets echoed with the clatter of hooves. Curious Arab inhabitants emerged from their homes, watching the spectacle with reserved interest. Their expressions were a mix of wariness and subdued curiosity, a far cry from the enthusiastic welcome the troops might have hoped for.

Among the onlookers, hawkers sprang into action, keen to seize the opportunity. They approached the soldiers, eager to sell trinkets, food, and other goods.

"Good prices! Very good prices!" they called out, holding up their wares. The air filled with the scents of spices and the sound of haggling.

Some of the Australians, however, were not amused. Having been swindled too many times before, they were tired of the relentless merchants.

Percy, his face hardening, muttered to Chugger.

"Bloody vultures, just out to fleece us again".

Chugger nodded as he scanned the crowd with a mix of suspicion and fatigue, kicking away one man who had clasped hold of his bridle.

"Too right Perce...look at 'em...I wouldn't trust 'em as far as I could throw 'em," he replied, gripping his reins tighter whilst slapping at anyone who came near.

Despite the less than warm reception, the regiment pushed forward, their mission clear. They were the victors, and the ancient city of Ramleh, with its storied past and strategic importance, was now under their control.

Simultaneously 'B' Squadron had pushed beyond the town to the railway line north of Ludd, another ancient town which had existed for over twelve thousand years, steeped in history and mentioned in the Bible as Lod. Their reception too was muted.

Thankfully the enemy was not up for a fight and two officers and twenty seven other ranks eagerly surrendered, along with their much welcome haul of grain, ammunition *and* aircraft.

As the lighthorsemen secured the area, Percy and Davo wandered over to the captured aeroplanes, their eyes bright with amazement and disappointment.

"Crikey, Davo, would you look at these contraptions. We've seen them in the sky, and they are scary buggers, but up close, they look flimsy things".

Davo nodded in agreement.

"I know what you mean. It's hard to believe these things can actually fly and drop hell on us, they look like they are held together by paper and glue," he replied.

"Yep, well they do don't they?" added Chugger, whilst running his hand and fingers along the fuselage, "but you've got to admire the blokes who fly them; that takes some guts".

The men stood around the aircraft. To them the idea of soaring above the battlefield, seeing everything from above, was a thrilling yet foreign concept, even if they had only experienced these machines as agents of destruction. The mood quickly shifted back to business, however, spurred on by the order to mount up and form ranks.

With a final glance at the captured aircraft, the soldiers mounted their horses and 'B' and 'C' Squadrons headed out to man the outpost line north and north east of Ludd.

On the 16th of November, the regiment set up camp at Safiriyeu, a location chosen for its strategic significance and relative safety. The following day, 'B' Squadron embarked on a reconnaissance mission and made an exceptional discovery at the Jewish settlement of Mulebbis in the form of six oil engines, which were valuable for both mechanised transport and powering various equipment, *and* forty wells, a critical resource in the arid environment. Additionally, they located a source of drinkable water at Wadi-Nahr-el-Auja, which significantly bolstered their supplies and provided much needed hydration for both men and horses.

This find was a morale booster for the regiment, however, this success was short lived. The next day, a strong enemy force launched a counteroffensive, driving the patrols out of Mulebbis and seizing control of Bald Hill and the settlement with overwhelming numbers.

The country in which they found themselves in now was favourable for either enemy attacks or stands, the rolling hills, valleys, and scattered settlements providing numerous vantage points and cover. The strategic significance of Bald Hill and Mulebbis was obvious to all, offering control over the surrounding area. Holding these positions would provide the enemy with a tactical advantage, enabling them to observe and disrupt Allied movements.

On the 18th of November the whole regiment, unsupported, occupied a defensive outpost line at Yasur, encompassing Ibn Ibrak, Sakia and Kafr Ana. The New Zealand Mounted Rifle Brigade were occupying the regiment's right at Jaffa, an ancient port city sitting atop a naturally elevated outcrop on the Mediterranean coastline. Some of the 2nd Light Horse were sent there on the 20th to collect a large parcel of mail, the arrival of which always went down well..

"Mum and Archie say we have a new chum in the form of a pommy called Pip. He's coming to live on the station after the war," announced Percy.

"Not *another* pom!" Chugger quipped.

"Watch it, feelings could be hurt you know," said Boggy.

"Pip? What sort of name is that?" asked Johnno.

"It's Philip, just Pip for short," replied Percy.

"Sounds like something out of an apple!" added Davo.

The mood suddenly changed when Percy announced that Taff and Mac were dead.

"Bloody artillery again," said Percy, his mood changing for the better when he told them how Stowie had found a flame thrower and scorched a few Huns with it, "oh, and there are a few medals here and there but apart from that all are doing well".

Percy folded his letter and placed it back in the envelope.

"I'd better let them know about Rachel and our little mate here too," he said casting a quick glance towards Alfie.

"I thought you'd already written about, you know who," replied Chugger.

"I have," said Percy, "just to Mum and Dad though".

Due to the overstretched supply lines the brigade was pulled back on the 21st for a short period. The number of troops in the front line was reduced in order that they could be suitably sustained, whilst the construction of the railway line through Gaza and beyond was being pushed as fast as humanly possible.

Six days later the regiment was on the move again to Haririyeh then to Yebna via Ramleh and eventually being attached to the 162nd Infantry Brigade, part of the 54th Division, at Ludd.

The regiment was to ensure that they knew every inch of this sector in order that they could reinforce it at a moment's notice or attack the enemy if the opportunity seized itself.

The 5th of December saw yet another conscription vote on all fronts, and again the troops, who needed the help, were in favour, but the people back home were not.

The result reached the troops a few days later.

As the desert the sun blazed down, the men sat under the shade of their tents, wiping the sweat from their brows and swatting at the ever present flies.

Chugger, chewing on a bit of dry biscuit, shook his head.

"I reckon they think we're still out here on a bloody holiday".

Percy smirked as he smeared gun oil along the working parts of his rifle.

"Yeah, mate. Maybe they think we're just sunbathing by the pyramids".

Davo, leaning back against his saddle, was unusually down hearted about the whole affair as he spat on the ground.

"Bastards!"

Chugger snorted as Rachel lovingly handed him a mug full of tea, his snort changing to a smile as he gazed into her eyes.

"I'd like to see them come out here and try *their* hand in this oven".

Percy nodded, the expression on his face quite serious.

"They don't see what we see. They don't see the blokes falling off their horses from heatstroke or the way we bury our mates after a scrap. We're just gonna be left shorthanded again, so we'd better get used to it".

"I think you all very brave," said Rachel in her broken English, bringing a warmth to the gathering.

But despite this the group fell into silence, frustration hanging heavy in the air. They knew reinforcements were desper-

302 ~ TONY SQUIRE

ately needed, but the people back home didn't seem to share their urgency.

In France there was no sunshine; just freezing temperatures as the rain drizzled steadily, turning the already muddy trenches into a soggy mess. The men, soaked and cold, huddled together as word of the vote reached them.

"They don't know what we're dealing with out here, do they?" said Roo.

"I don't think they care. We're just a few lines in the papers to them. They're probably too busy with their tea and scones to worry about us lot sitting in the mud," said Clancy.

"Maybe we should send them a souvenir," said Ten Bob pointing at a pair of rats scuttling through the trench, "like one of these rats...you know...let them know what luxury looks like".

Clancy chuckled.

"I know, let's send them a postcard. 'Wish you were here! Knee deep in mud, dodging bullets, and sharing a trench with rats the size of bloody dogs'. That'd change their minds real quick".

Roo shook his head.

"I doubt it. That would just give them another reason not to come".

For the 9th Battalion their rest came to an abrupt end on the 13th of December, with a two day journey via Wavrons, Wizernes and De Kennebeke to the reserve line at Wulverghem in the Messines sector.

Seven days later they were back in the front line near Gapaard Farm, with the 10th Battalion on their right. Accommodation was sparse with Battalion Headquarters located in a pill box in Hun's Walk. The next nine days were quiet, giving the troops ample time in which to construct shelters, improve their defences and, above all, to keep warm. This quiet period helped make the lead up to Christmas a merry one for a change, even despite the Battalion having to provide working parties in the forward area for the rest of December, in order to improve dugouts and defences even further.

Here too the mail finally caught up with the battalion with letters from home *and* the desert.

"The boys are rich!" exclaimed Roo as he read his letter from Percy.

"Rich? What do you mean?" asked Clancy.

"Over two thousand pounds each…won it on a bet apparently," replied Roo.

"Jammy gits!" said Pip as Archie handed him a parcel.

"Who's this from? I don't know anyone," said Pip, shrugging his shoulders.

"I reckon you're on the Christmas Cake list mate," said Clancy.

"Christmas Cake?" asked Pip as he examined the package and read the senders address, "Doriray Station…it's from Roo and Archie's family".

It was indeed a whole fruit cake, to add to the individual ones sent to Archie, Roo and Clancy. But with it came a letter not only offering Pip a job on the Station, but also a home. Pip grinned from ear to ear as he looked Clancy in the eye.

"Looks like me and you are gonna be roommates sergeant major".

Jerusalem was captured by the 60th Division on the 9th of December after the 20th Corps and part of the Australian Division had manoeuvred the Turks out of it. The enemy front line was altered significantly as a result, the Turkish right being at Tabsor, the centre in the hills and his left curving south east to the northern end of the Dead Sea, including Jericho and the entire Jordan Valley.

After rejoining their brigade on the 12th, the 2nd Light Horse Regiment took over part of the front from the battle worn 4th Scottish Fusiliers near Hill 265, five days later. The weather had turned sour, with constant rain making the ground a quagmire. 'A' Squadron was detached and held in reserve with the 1st Light Horse, ready to be called into action. The brigade's position now stretched from Hill 265 to Birket-el-Jamas, the regiment now dismounted while the their horses were sent back to Ayun Kara for safety.

On the 21st of December, under the gloomy skies, the regiment came under sudden shell fire, enduring the pounding until the 3rd Light Horse arrived to relieve them at 1730 hours. A momentary calm followed, but it was short lived, the ground shaking as a fierce bombardment hit Bald Hill, claiming the life of Trooper Davies.

Meanwhile, the 52nd Division had been pushing hard, driving the enemy's right flank back five miles and securing Jaffa from the threat of shellfire. The fight was far from over, but this small win brought a brief, much needed respite.

By the 23rd of December, the operation had ceased, and the 2nd Light Horse Regiment was withdrawn to Ayun Kara, just in time for Christmas. It was a strange setting for the boys, celebrating in the quiet expanse of the desert. The familiar warmth of a Queensland summer was replaced by the dry, scorching winter heat of the Middle East. There were no shady gum trees or ocean breezes, but they made do with what they had.

Rachel, raised in the traditions of Islam, knew that her faith discouraged Christian symbols and celebrations, but she saw no harm in this day of festivity. To her, it seemed more an occasion of joy and friendship than anything sacred. The customs were different, unfamiliar, and in some ways, more relaxed than the strict, sometimes outdated, ways of her own upbringing, and she watched with quiet curiosity as the men, hardened by battle, exchanged smiles, jokes, and simple gifts in the spirit of the day.

For Alfie, this Christmas was unlike the lonely ones he'd known in the past. He now had friends to share it with, a soldier family that had taken him in. The gifts were modest—bits of extra rations, a carved trinket, or a box of Turkish Delight - but each one was appreciated.

The arrival of the Christmas mail was an extra source of joy. Parcels from home had been waiting for them, packed with the usual fruit cake and goodies - small, familiar comforts from Queensland. Even more welcome were the Christmas Billies sent by the Regimental Comforts Fund in Brisbane and the AIF Comforts Fund, filled with treats and essentials. Many of the boys took time to write letters of thanks to both organisations, deeply grateful for the thoughtfulness.

Rachel and Alfie had never tasted fruit cake before, so when slices were passed around, they were curious. Rachel took a small bite, unsure of the dense, sweet cake with its odd mix of fruit and spices, while Alfie didn't hesitate, just diving right in. To the soldiers the reactions were priceless, Alfie gave an approving nod, chewing like there was no tomorrow, while Rachel wrinkled her nose at first, then smiled as the flavours engulfed her taste buds. The others laughed good naturedly, watching the pair experience something so ordinary to them, yet so novel to their new companions.

Chugger, grinning shyly, presented Rachel with a special gift. One of the regimental blacksmiths had fashioned a necklace for her, a fine chain threaded through a Rising Sun cap badge. It wasn't traditional or elaborate, but Rachel smiled as she accepted it, understanding the care and thought behind the gesture. She'd never worn anything quite like it before, yet it held a meaning beyond its appearance. Chugger's awkward grin widened when she gently placed the necklace around her neck.

As the small Christmas gathering continued, Percy stood up with a huge smile on his face and walked over to Alfie.

"We've got something for you, mate," he said, pulling a small leather pouch from his pocket.

It wasn't anything fancy - just a rough, handmade pouch stitched together from scrap leather, but it had been crafted with care. The leather, worn smooth, was sturdy enough to last through the toughest conditions. It smelled faintly of horse tack, a scent that reminded Alfie of camp life and the friendship he had found among this small group of soldiers.

"We thought you could use this for your boot black kit - and whatever other bits you've got to carry," Percy said.

Alfie took the pouch, his fingers tracing the neat stitching. Inside, there was just enough space for his brushes, polish, and rag - along with the few personal treasures he carried with him, like the dog eared photographs of his parents and the little trinkets he had picked up along the way.

"Thank you Mister Percy. Thank you all of you," Alfie said, his voice barely above a whisper, "but I have no gift for you".

"How about a free shoe shine and we'll call it quits mate," Boggy suggested.

"Done," replied Alfie, a satisfied smile appearing on his face.

It wasn't often that he received presents, and never something this practical, this thoughtful, but he knew the boys had put time and effort into making sure it was just right for him.

"We don't want you losing your stuff mate," Chugger said with a wink, "so this should help you out".

Alfie grinned, already imagining how much easier it would be to carry his boot black kit and his personal things together. He slipped the pouch into his jacket pocket, feeling its reassuring weight. To him it wasn't just a pouch; it was a sign of belonging.

The morning of the 26th arrived with a biting wind and leaden skies. The regiment had orders to withdraw to Esdud, a gruelling twenty mile march ahead of them. But at least, for now, they had their horses.

"Good job we're on horses," Chugger muttered, adjusting his hat as the rain began to fall in earnest.

The weather quickly turned from bad to worse, the downpour transforming the roadless black plains into vast, sucking swamps. Mud clung to everything, horses' hooves, the men's boots, the wheels of the supply carts, and progress slowed to a miserable crawl.

Percy glanced over at Boggy, who was struggling with his horse through the thick mud. With a grin, he couldn't help but shout, "Hey Boggy, with your name you should feel at home here!"

The others laughed despite the terrible conditions, their spirits briefly lifted by the joke. Boggy just shook his head with a wry smile.

"I never thought I'd miss dry sand this much".

The rain persisted, turning the plain into a morass of mud and water. But the men plodded on, knowing that Esdud - and some much needed rest - waited for them at the end of the march.

In December 1917 the five Australian Infantry Divisions in France came together for the first time in a single command under General Birdwood in the 1st ANZAC Corps, changing again on the 1st of January 1918 when the 1st ANZAC Corps became the Australian Corps, 2nd ANZAC and 22nd British Corps.

Having begun 1917 behind the lines at the Somme, the 9th Battalion had battled through 'The Maze', helped defeat the enemy at Bullecourt and taken part in the Passchendaele offensive. Their quiet time at Messines was a well earned respite before the battles to come in 1918.

For the 2nd Light Horse Regiment who had spent the year patrolling through Palestine, fighting at Gaza and Beersheba, there was much rumour on the furphy net about an eastward advance to seize the Jordan Valley in order to turn the Turkish left flank.

New friendships and bonds had been forged throughout the turmoil of war, offering small glimmers of hope amid the bloodshed. Pip, a British soldier, orphan and a former workhouse boy, had been rescued from the brink of unofficial execution, at the hands of a British colonel, by Ponsonby and the platoon. Now a member of the AIF in 'B' Company of the 9th Battalion, he had grown into a reliable brother in arms, his quiet bravery and cheeky sense of humour admired by his mates.

Alfie, adopted by Percy and the boys, had found a new family within the regiment, and then there was Rachel, whose presence among the men had blossomed into something far deeper. Rescued and brought into the fold, she had become more than just a friend, finding an unexpected connection with Chugger that defied the boundaries of war and culture. These new loves and friendships, forged in the heat of battle, had become lifelines for the weary soldiers, giving them reason to keep pushing forward.

Even Samuel Ford, uncle to the three Taylor boys, had not been far away from Archie and Roo during 1917, with the 7th Battalion of the South Staffordshire Regiment taking part in battles at Ancre, Messines, Langemarck, Polygon Wood, Broodseinde and Poelcapelle. Was a meeting on the cards for 1918? Only time and the three Fates knew the answer.

The men from Queensland and, indeed, Australia and New Zealand as a whole, have now been fighting two stubborn enemies for over three years. Although weary of battle and the dwindling numbers of new recruits from home, their spirits and determination to bring this war to an end are burning brightly in their bellies. Their enemies are still at large hoping to snatch glory from disaster, and the last lines of defence are always the most difficult to take. 1918 is set to be a strenuous and tumultuous year, so the Taylor boys and their mates must march one last time.

Tony Squire, originally from England, is now an Australian citizen and resides there with his wife Sheila. Following in his father's footsteps, he pursued a career as a professional soldier and dedicated a total of 21 years to his service. Throughout his life, he has held a deep passion for history, particularly military history, and from a young age, he aspired to craft a historical novel that would intertwine his characters with real life historical events. This dream has come to fruition in his latest endeavours where Tony has embarked on his long awaited journey of chronicling the remarkable tales of the ANZACs during the tumultuous period of the Great War.

More Books By This Author

The ANZAC Chronicles:

"...UNTIL YOU ARE SAFE".
"TO OUR LAST MAN".

Other Titles:

IN THE COMPANY OF OUTLAWS - MY LIFE WITH
NED KELLY AND HIS GANG.